Tales of Deadly Flora

SPREAD

Edited by R.A. Clarke

Foreword by Holly Rae Garcia

A PAGE TURN PRESS ANTHOLOGY

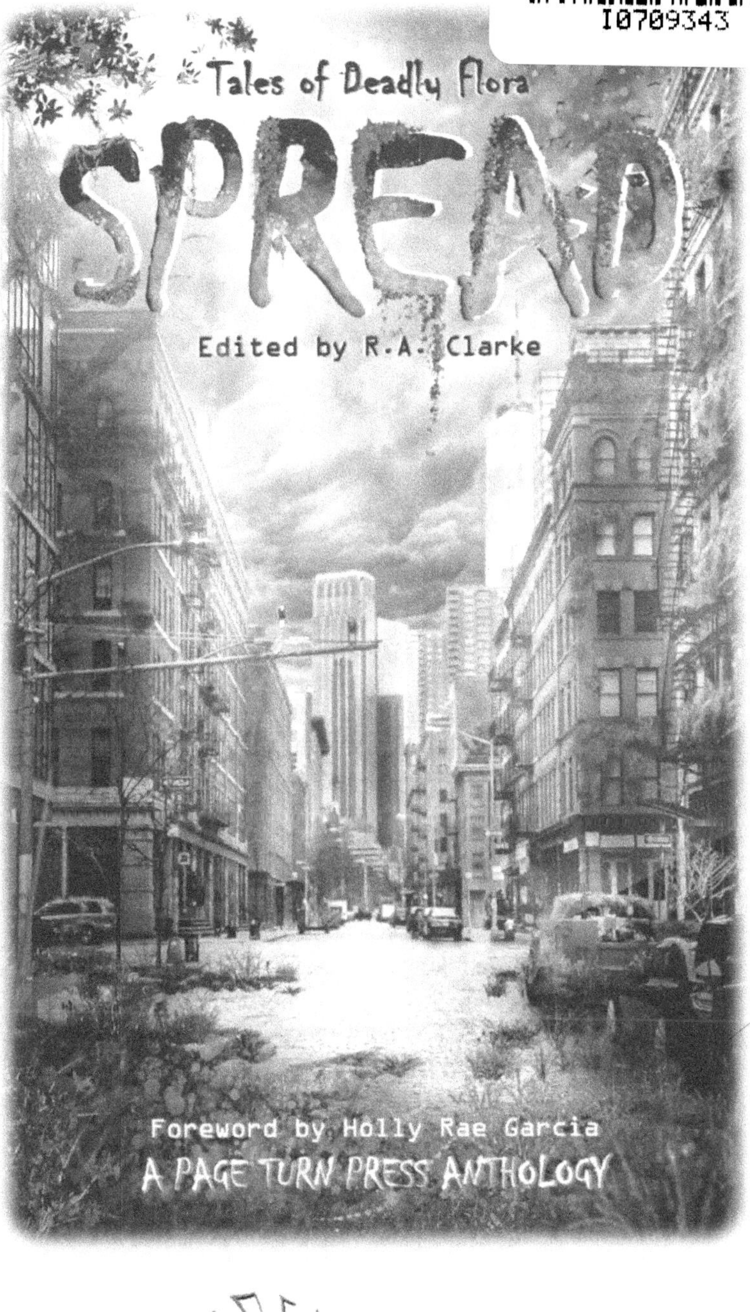

Published by Page Turn Press
9 Mellco Drive, Portage la Prairie, MB R1N 3Z5

Print ISBN: 978-1-7781821-6-7
Epub ISBN: 978-1-7781821-7-4

www.pageturnpress.com

Contents

A Note From The Editor

Given the nature of this anthology, you can expect to encounter violence and various horrific situations. However, that said, there are three stories within that deal with either sexual assault or the death of a child. Since some readers prefer not to have detailed content warnings given up front, while other individuals greatly appreciate them, we've implemented a simple system we hope will help everyone have an enjoyable reading experience.

An asterisk (*) after the story title will discreetly mark each tale containing either of the situations outlined above. This will serve as a basic heads up for anyone affected by such content. For those who aren't, simply pay it no attention and carry on.

Thanks and happy reading.
R.A. Clarke

FOREWORD
Holly Rae Garcia

It's natural to think of light when one thinks of plants; we learn about photosynthesis in grade school. It's much less instinctive to think of darkness.

In "The Colour Out of Space" by H.P. Lovecraft (1927), it was the fruit and vegetable crops and the trees surrounding the Gardner place that initially indicated trouble after the meteorite fell. First, the crops grew larger than natural, but they were bitter and later turned to ash. The trees moved of their own accord, without a hint of wind to blame. John Wyndham further explored the idea of unnatural plant life in his novel, *The Day of the Triffids* (1951). Bioengineered to produce oil, the deadly Triffids quickly outgrew the humans' ability to restrain them. Daphne du Maurier's ghostly tree in her short story "The Apple Tree" haunted readers, and Scott Smith explored how sinister vines could be in his novel *The Ruins*.

It's the unexpected, the "freaks of nature" that capture our curiosity. We take our children to the park, our dogs on a walk, or hike a nature trail, all while assuming the flora surrounding us are perfectly safe.

As a child, I was slightly obsessed with the movie *Little Shop of Horrors* (1986). I recorded all the songs on a tape recorder, and years later, you could listen to me whisper in the background, "Mom! I'm recording!" as she came to tell me dinner was ready in the middle of one of the numbers. Audrey II captivated me. That this plant Seymour adored and nurtured would completely turn on him and the woman he loved was such a fun concept. As someone who considers herself a black thumb gardener, I wouldn't blame any of my plants if they were to rise from the dead and try to eat me or take over the city. But Seymour took *care* of Audrey II. That shows it doesn't always matter what you do or how good your intentions are, nature will prevail. Fittingly, *Little Shop of Horrors* is also briefly mentioned in this anthology via the wonderful third story, "Plant Friends" by Jen Mierisch.

Another movie that I personally love was M. Night Shyamalan's 2008 critically panned, *The Happening*. The plants just wanted to live and thrive in a world determined to snuff them out. As Jeff Goldblum's character in *Jurassic Park* so eloquently states, "Life, uh, finds a way."

Of course, we can't talk about insidious flora without mentioning the 1956 movie *Invasion of the Body Snatchers*. Spores falling from space, growing into seed pods that produce replicas of humans? Yes, please.

Whether it's through aliens, corporate greed, supernatural, or defensive means, botanical terrors have long fascinated us. As such, the speculative tales in this anthology will have you eyeing the ivy on your desk at work, or maybe uprooting that tree in the backyard.

All the stories were awesome, but if I had to pick favourites, they would begin with Alyssa Beatty's "Black Thumb". She starts things off with a bang and sets the tone for the rest of the stories to follow, exploring an alien world and the grieving process with beautiful prose. *"The ice-shard leaves of the towering trees had a nasty habit of detaching and plunging to the ground, right through the skull of an unsuspecting settler below. Then the trunk sent out winding tendrils that drank the blood up with a truly unsettling slurping sound. On the other hand, the little purple-leaved plants near the beach sang when you stroked them, a lilting melody that Ciara, Lexa's boss, swore was an Irish lullaby."*

Katie Ess is next with her tense story, "Seedling." I loved the dual point-of-view here and the imaginative "screaming cacti" and dandelion invaders.

Two of my favorites wrap up this anthology, the first being "The Bubble" by R.A. Clarke. Clarke drops you into her world so deftly, capturing your attention from the very beginning. And finally, there is Alex Grehy's "Tears of Green" which holds the number one spot on my list. Told through memos, news articles, and first-hand accounts, Grehy expertly conveys the tale of genetically modified plants used as weapons of war that (of course) get out of control. You know it's good when you're left wanting more.

From plants that hug you, to islands that need time to heal and ghostly apparitions springing from the moss and mold, there isn't a story in the bunch that won't grab you and refuse to let go.

So beware, reader, as you turn the page and dive into these stories. But first, put your house plants in the garage and close your doors and windows tightly to keep all spores from entering your home. As for me, I'm going to water my plants and tenderly whisper how much I love them, to avoid being eaten in the plant-pocalypse.

Holly Rae Garcia
www.HollyRaeGarcia.com

BLACK THUMB

ALYSSA BEATTY

Lexa hated the rain on Cabos. It was tinged red and had a coppery smell like old blood; the slightly oily feel of it made her skin crawl. She missed the petrichor scent of Earth, the tap-tap-tap of droplets hitting green leaves outside her bedroom window. This rain sort of...glooped.

All things considered, Lexa felt she'd adjusted fairly well to life on the planet. The five-hundred-foot trees with ice-like shards instead of leaves, the metallic tinkling of the waves when they hit the shore, the crimson haze of the sun: she took them all in stride. It was just the damn blood rain that pushed her subconscious "this is not home" button. Gary would say it was her inability to let go of the past that was the issue. But she didn't want to think about what Gary would say.

She let herself into her pod. All the settlers were encouraged to call them apartments, but the curved walls and built-in furniture in the same bleak white screamed *pod*.

The prospect of an empty evening, watching the light fade into the vermillion night, made Lexa's chest tighten in anxiety. She patted herself between her breasts as if her heart was a frightened dog she was trying to soothe. She wandered through the living space, turning on every light.

The last years on Earth had been dim. The relentless smoke clogging the atmosphere turned every day into a monotony of grey. Gary and Lexa hoarded their meagre supplies of energy, lighting a single lamp in the apartment for a few hours at a time. Even after six months here, the glare of so many lights still felt profligate and wanton, so she did it every night.

She was just sitting down to her dinner of processed protein chunks that she could almost fool her brain into recognizing as food when she noticed the plant.

Lexa's dirty secret: for a botanist, she had a shockingly black thumb. She could identify and classify like nobody's business but give her an actual houseplant, and she'd kill it within a month, despite knowing its preferred soil pH level, sunlight, and watering requirements. So, it was a bit of a surprise to see a mutated version of Nepenthes Distillatoria, a pitcher plant, sitting in the arc of her windowsill, with a red bow on it.

She tiptoed toward it. The flora on this planet was more aggressive than the plants on Earth. The ice-shard leaves of the towering trees had a nasty habit of detaching and plunging to the ground, right through the skull of an unsuspecting settler below. Then the trunk sent out winding tendrils that drank the blood up with a truly unsettling slurping sound. On the other hand, the little purple-leaved plants near the beach sang when you stroked them, a lilting melody that Ciara, Lexa's boss, swore was an Irish lullaby.

The plant sat placidly in its pot. It didn't hiss or try to bite. Smaller pitchers surrounded a large central one, all facing it like children sitting around a teacher at story time.

Their lids were delicate blue, a rare colour in this red-tinged world. Lexa bent to the largest pitcher to smell the phytotelmata, the reserve of nectar resting in the bottom of the trap. It smelled like real rain on real soil. She heard the tapping of raindrops on green leaves. She bent closer, then stepped back.

"Nice try," she told the plant.

The lid snapped down over the pitcher. A little petulantly, Lexa thought.

She fingered the bow on the pot. The thought skittered across her mind, briefly, that maybe this was some sort of peace offering from Gary. He knew her affinity for carnivorous plants. Or at least the affinity she used to have. On this planet, where every other plant harboured a murderous urge, the bloom was off the rose for her and Dionaea Muscipula. And anyway, it was unlikely Gary was in a peace offering mood.

And there it was, that pressure in her chest again, like some unseen hand squeezing the life out of her heart. She closed her eyes and breathed. It was probably her imagination, but when she opened her eyes, she swore the little plant looked repentant.

"It's okay," she told it. "It's nothing to do with you. You're lovely, whatever you are. This is human stuff."

The stems straightened, and the pitchers opened, releasing the sweet scent of rain into the pod.

"Thanks," Lexa mumbled. Then felt like an idiot. She talked to plants all the time; they were good listeners. But this was the first time she'd thanked one.

She shut off the lights and curled into the bed, which was just large enough for one body. She scooted until her back met the curve of the wall. It was almost like being held.

The next morning, Lexa slumped into the office. She'd slept badly, dreaming of the ship. The brightening and dimming of the artificial lights meant to trick their circadian rhythms into forgetting they were in a metal tube, hurtling through the darkness of space. The hum of the generators. Sometimes she thought she'd never escape that relentless drone, the backdrop to Gary's voice rising in anger while her own got progressively quieter. She woke up in a foul mood; even in sleep, she couldn't get a reprieve from her failures.

She was glaring at the coffee machine—it wasn't even close to coffee, but they still called it the coffee machine—when Ciara sidled up to her.

"Did you get my present?" Ciara asked.

"The plant? Haven't I told you a million times..."

"Yes, yes. Your black thumb, you ruin everything you touch. This one's different. Trust me."

Ciara winked at Lexa, which was not out of character. But there was something about her, something lighter. Lexa had avoided meeting anyone's eyes for months, not wanting to read pity or judgment in someone else's expression after they all disembarked. The ship wasn't large; Lexa couldn't escape the feeling that everyone had seen and heard everything. It was easier for Lexa to duck every gaze. But now she really looked at Ciara.

Ciara's blue eyes sparkled. She looked ten years younger than her sixty years.

"You know I'm sober, right? That extends to weird alien plants," Lexa reminded her.

Ciara laughed. "Just give it a chance. It's not a drug. It's... something different. Something you need."

She grasped Lexa's shoulder in a surprisingly strong grip and walked away.

Lexa got through the day at work, chafing at being desk-bound. Every so often, she heard Ciara's laugh tinkle through the office. When they first arrived on the planet, Ciara had been taciturn, the curve of her mouth always tilting down. Her laugh was a rare treat; you felt like you earned it. Hearing it given away so freely made Lexa oddly unsettled.

By the end of the day, she was prickly with annoyance and ducked out without saying goodbye to anyone.

She let herself into the pod, bathed in the washed-out red of sunset. At the sound of the pod door hissing closed, the plant perked up, opening its pitchers like little hungry mouths. It occurred to Lexa that she should have asked Ciara what this thing ate. There was a curious lack of insect life on this planet. As far as they could tell, most of the plant life was self-pollinating. On Earth, several types of carnivorous plants would trap and digest small mammals; maybe there was some space newt the biologists hadn't discovered yet that she should be feeding into the maws of Ciara's gift. It didn't really matter; she knew she'd end up killing it anyway.

Lexa slipped her shoes off, leaving them in the centre of the living area, and lay down on the couch. The empty hours sprawled before her. Lexa wished she could cry, but she hadn't been able to since they got here. She'd felt hollowed out by the time they disembarked as if she'd used up a lifetime of tears on the ship. Mourning her mother, an endless cycle of guilt and anger she couldn't seem to break out of, no matter how Gary badgered her to just let it go. And then mourning her marriage when it became clear she wasn't going to.

It wasn't even that she missed Gary, per se. There had been more than a bit of relief when things finally ended. Their first years together had been idyllic; Lexa couldn't understand why people had said marriage was hard. And then her mother died, and Gary seemed to take her grief as a personal affront, accused her of wallowing in it.

"You didn't even like your mother!" he'd yelled at her once when she was curled up and sobbing on the floor. "You're just addicted to the drama of it. The attention."

Maybe she was. She hadn't spoken to her mother for years. Lexa always thought when her mother's addictions finally caught up with her, she would feel some release, freedom from the worry that always gnawed in the back of her mind.

She couldn't have predicted the anvil of grief and guilt that fell, crushingly, on her heart. She was aware every excruciating second of every day that she was alone, orphaned.

"Everyone ends up an orphan, in the end," Gary had said gently when he was still sympathetic to her. But Gary had both his parents and three siblings, all of them prone to raucous tales of Gary as a young boy, Gary as a teenager. They had all made it off Earth, too, sent to another colony. Gary might not see them again for years, but they were out there, sharing his memories, holding his childhood in their hands. With no one to anchor Lexa to her own past, she felt unmoored. She held onto the grief tightly, and when it was clear she wasn't able to let go, Gary left too. And now she really was alone.

Lexa patted her chest, trying to ease the tightness in her heart.

The smell of rain filled the pod. Lexa conjured up a wan smile.

"That's a neat trick."

The central tulip-shaped pitcher of the plant bent briefly, then stretched as if reaching for Lexa.

Lexa sighed. "I don't have food for you. I'm a vegetarian."

The plant reached farther and released a pulse of soft blue

light. Lexa sat up on the couch. This was new. She should grab her field book, take notes. The blue light wove across the room, searching. It touched Lexa's breastbone, just above her heart. The pressure in her chest eased.

"Thanks," Lexa breathed.

The blue light hovered for a moment in front of her, then formed into a sharp blade that stabbed forward. Lexa watched in horror as the light carved a clean, bloodless line through her skin. There was no pain, but it was disconcerting as hell. The light peeled the flesh back, like delicate petals unfurling, and probed through muscle and tissue toward her heart.

Lexa swatted at the light. When her palm touched it, she was overwhelmed with the absence of grief, of loneliness. Nothing rushed in to fill the emptiness; it was just a peaceful void.

The light probed deeper, and Lexa felt tendrils wrap around her heart.

She stood, her breath coming in gasps.

"No! You don't get to eat my heart. Bad plant!"

The light whipped back to the plant, which closed its lid with a snap.

Lexa stared at it. Sometimes she really hated this planet.

She opened the window and set the plant outside, pulling the curtains closed over it.

The next day Lexa stormed into Ciara's office.

"What the actual hell, Ciara? You gave me a killer plant? There's easier ways to fire me, you know."

Ciara smiled peacefully at Lexa. "Did you try it?"

"Did I let the evil alien plant eat my heart? I'm standing here yelling at you, so I think that answers your question."

Ciara laughed. She turned her seat toward the windowsill, where a blue pitcher plant, identical to the one currently sequestered outside Lexa's pod window, stretched its leaves to the sun. Ciara stroked it gently. The plant preened like a cat, reaching for Ciara when she turned away.

"It doesn't eat it. It just takes it for a while. Keeps it safe."

Lexa opened her mouth, but no words came out.

"I've seen how you struggle, Lexa. How much pain you're in. Let it take your heart. You'll feel so much better. Trust me."

She smiled, and the peaceful set of her lips suddenly struck Lexa as supremely creepy.

"That's not how hearts work. One, you can't survive without a heart. And two, you don't carry emotions in your organs. You're a biologist, Ciara. You know this."

Ciara shrugged. "All I know is, I've never felt this happy. All my worries, missing home, mourning my daughter...it's all gone."

Lexa never knew that Ciara had lost a child.

Ciara leaned across the desk, extending her hand. "I don't know how it works. I don't care. Just try it once. For me."

Lexa looked at Ciara's open hand. She turned on her heel and left, slamming the door behind her.

That night, Lexa sat at the molded white plastic table in her pod and stewed. She was a champion stewer; she once spent an entire evening replaying the slight tightening of Gary's mouth when she said she didn't feel up to going to the mess hall and working herself up into a froth of hurt and fury. That was early on in the voyage, when the cracks first started appearing.

Lexa glanced at the plant, still sitting on her windowsill. All the blue pitchers, the large central one and the little ones surrounding it, turned toward her slowly. Lexa pushed away the idea that the plant was looking at her.

It must release a hallucinogen of some type, she thought. *Mixed with some sort of serotonin-oxytocin cocktail that provokes positive feelings.*

That made her feel better—knowing the sight of her skin peeling painlessly back, exposing her beating heart, and that lovely empty feeling that washed over her were just the plant's chemicals messing with her mind.

She turned off the lights and curled herself into bed. She drifted off and dreamed of gentle tendrils of blue light caressing the window and the soft sound of rain on green leaves.

The next day at work, Lexa successfully avoided Ciara by logging field notes, something she usually put off in favour of actually being out in the field. She had weeks of backlog.

As she was leaving for the day, she saw a flash of blue from the corner of her eye. One of her coworkers gently stroked the leaves of his own plant. What was his name? John? Jim? Lexa hadn't made an effort to get to know anyone here, preferring to be alone in the field where she could cradle her grief in private. He turned to her and smiled peacefully. It was a perfectly normal smile, but it sent a shiver down Lexa's spine. Shaking her head, she turned and left.

Of course, it was raining again. Lexa thought longingly of Earth, of weather reports on her phone, knowing when to take an umbrella. It was strange, the way the most innocuous detail from the past could come at her out of left field and knock her down into a pit of loss. She'd be going about her day feeling, if not happy, then at least *fine*. And then she'd be hit with a faded-photo memory of her mother's scent: patchouli and stale wine. Or the feel of Gary's palm rubbing slow circles on her back as she cried.

And, of course, because this day could still get worse, there he was, striding toward her. Lexa hadn't seen him since they disembarked from the ship. Gary had wanted to talk, to get "closure," but Lexa had steadfastly refused. She'd been done with talking. Done with thinking about it, trying to parse out what was her fault and what was his.

Gary saw her and lifted his hand in a half-wave as if realizing partway through that the gesture wasn't really appropriate. There was no avoiding him now.

"Hey!" Gary's voice was filled with patently false bonhomie, and the wave of contempt it made her feel for him made Lexa relax a bit.

"Gary. How are you?"

"Pretty good! This planet is amazing, isn't it? Every day something new. How are you doing? Enjoying the work?"

It had been Gary's steadfast belief that all Lexa needed to come back to life was to bury herself in work. He refused to understand that it wasn't like that for her, that she couldn't just shut her pain away in a room and focus on something else.

She shrugged. "I've been going through a hard time. Still, I guess."

She watched Gary's face settle into that hard rage that had become so familiar during the last months of the voyage.

"Still wallowing, I see. There's something really wrong with you, Lexa. It's been three years. You've just got to get on with things."

"I don't want to do this again, Gary."

"No. Of course you don't. It has to be all about you, all the time. Poor wounded Lexa, all alone. You know how you always worried you'd turn out like her? Well, newsflash, Lexa, you always were. Both a couple of selfish, heartless bitches."

It shouldn't have hurt, but the barb found its mark. Lexa opened her mouth to give some weak retort, but Gary had already turned and stomped away. Some part of Lexa's brain idly noted that his bald patch had grown. The rest of her was humming with pain, with an undercurrent of amazement that he still knew exactly how to hurt her. She stood in the street, drenched with rain, trembling, and wishing she could cry.

Lexa arrived back at her pod with no memory of how she got there. Her palm left a sticky red print next to the light switch. She dumped her ruined clothes in a pile on the floor and stood under the shower long after the hot water ran out, eyes closed, hand over her heart, patting gently.

She emerged, clean and cold, into a pod flooded with the scent of rain. She turned to the window and saw a tendril retreat hastily from a tiny crack above the windowsill. Lexa clearly recalled shutting the window forcefully when she put the plant outside, remembered the *thunk* of plastic meeting plastic, such an unsatisfying expression of anger.

Great. The plant that wanted to drug her and give her visions of it eating her heart could open windows now. Lexa stifled a hysterical giggle that wanted to turn into a sob. She fell onto the couch and put her head in her hands. The smell of rain intensified, and despite herself, she breathed it in, letting it soothe her.

She would murder someone for a glass of wine right now. Even wine from a box, tasting faintly of the plastic bag it was packed in. Lexa had stopped drinking years before the collapse of the global ecosystem made the point moot. A waste, thinking back on it. She should have guzzled wine and whiskey and tequila like water while she still could. So what if she turned out like her mother? Apparently, she had, anyway.

She looked at the plant, whose leaves tapped gently against the window.

"Heartless bitch. I would be if you had your way, right?"

It bent its leaves toward her.

She sighed, considering the plant. Ciara was letting it spray its hallucinogenic chemicals all over her, and she seemed no worse for it. In fact, she seemed lighter, happier than Lexa had ever seen her. Jim, too. Maybe the plant was this world's version of psilocybin. Okay to use in small doses, good for relieving depression and anxiety. Lexa was well aware she was making excuses to herself for what she knew she was going to do anyway.

She opened the window and lifted the plant inside. She sat expectantly on the edge of the couch.

"Okay. Do whatever it is you do."

The plant sent out tendrils of blue light. They hovered above Lexa's breastbone. She had the ridiculous impression the plant was asking permission.

"Go ahead. I won't yell at you."

The light formed a blade, which parted Lexa's flesh. It reached in and wrapped around her heart. She felt that calm emptiness, a relief after the bitter cocktail of emotions left over from her encounter with Gary.

The light emerged, cradling Lexa's heart. Lexa thought it looked strangely pristine. Not only was it not dripping blood all over her white floor, it wasn't dark and mangled the way she'd somehow expected it to look.

Of course, this is all a hallucination, Lexa thought. *It hasn't really removed my actual physical heart. So maybe this is my subconscious telling me I'm not as damaged as I think or something.*

The light withdrew to the windowsill and gently lowered her heart into the base of the pitcher. The lid closed softly, sealing Lexa's heart inside.

Lexa woke up smiling. She usually had to claw her way up from sleep, shedding the weight of the bad dreams. Today she felt unfettered. If she had dreams, she didn't remember them.

She couldn't resist lifting the pitcher lid and looking inside. There it was: her heart. It pulsed once at her as if to say, *see, I'm safe.*

At some point during the night, Lexa had been flooded with certainty that this wasn't a hallucination, that the plant really had removed her heart and would keep it safe for her. While a part of her brain grumbled that that's just what a hallucination *would* say, it was easier, in the end, to let that certainty take over instead of worrying about the side effects of whatever drug the plant had pumped into her.

Because the thing was, Lexa felt *good*. She couldn't recall ever feeling this good, even in the early days of her marriage to Gary, when she felt like she'd finally found the one person who truly knew her and loved her. She even whistled, tunelessly, as she made her way to work.

At the office, Lexa noticed several more blue plants on desks. Her eyes met Jim's. They smiled at each other, a secret, knowing smile. Lexa felt like she was part of some select club now. It felt good. Everything felt good, without her troublesome heart making problems.

Ciara's hand closed over her shoulder. Lexa smiled up at her.

"See? Say my favourite words to hear."

"You were right."

"There they are. It's wonderful, isn't it?"

"It is. Thank you."

Ciara grinned. "You've earned a bit of happiness, love. Enjoy it. Just remember to take your heart back every so often. It's important."

On the way home, Lexa forced herself to remember her run-in with Gary. It was like poking a numbed tooth with her tongue. She knew it had been awful, but she didn't feel the pain. She searched for the familiar grief when she thought about her mother and found nothing but an ocean of calm.

As the week went on, Lexa noticed more blue plants appearing on desks until the office was awash in them. On Friday, everyone left with their plants cradled in their arms, some murmuring to them like children.

For the first time since arriving here, Lexa didn't feel dread at the prospect of the empty days ahead.

When she arrived home, she went straight to the plant. She stroked a blue leaf fondly. It looked remarkably healthy after a week in her care. She'd tried watering it once, but the pitchers had opened wide and *screamed*, a keening wail that made Lexa's body vibrate with pain. Obviously, the chemical composition of the pod's filtered water was not to its liking.

But it recovered quickly when she put it out in the blood rain, murmuring apologies.

The pitcher opened. Lexa leaned forward, and there was her heart nestled in the bottom. It looked smaller, and pale wrinkles covered the surface. Lexa felt a spike of alarm.

"I should take that back for a bit, I think," she told the plant regretfully.

The plant lifted Lexa's heart on a tendril of light while another probed gently at her chest.

Lexa took a deep breath and closed her eyes. She felt her flesh part painlessly, then the weight, the awful crushing weight, of her heart as it found its place in her body.

Lexa crumpled to her knees, then let herself curl into a fetal position on the smooth white floor.

The pain was excruciating, radiating out through her body in waves, a flood of loneliness, guilt, anger. Lexa wondered briefly, before she lost consciousness, if she had been feeling all these things before and just got used to them or if it was worse now. And then the darkness took her.

Lexa woke to a soft finger of light tracing her jaw. She felt her heart beating, a strange imposition. The pain had faded to a manageable level, so she levered herself upright and stumbled to the shower.

She stood under the water, feeling the toxic after-effects of all those emotions flooding her body at once. Little aftershocks coursed through her. A familiar tightening in her chest as she thought of the long, lonely hours of the weekend. She patted her chest gently, trying to calm her heart, but this time she resented it.

Once she dried off, she knelt in front of the plant.

"Okay. Take it back, please."

A pulse of light, a brief squeeze as the plant took her heart, and then that blessed peace.

As the weeks went by, Lexa fell into a routine. She took her heart back for an hour or two every Friday after she got home from work. The pain never got better. In fact, it seemed to get worse every time. But it was worth it to have that emptiness come and fill her up again. And if her heart looked smaller each time, well, that was fine with Lexa. She found herself wishing she never had to take it back at all. Wondering, in a scientific kind of way, what would happen if she just let it die.

At the office, a strange camaraderie had developed. They all ate lunch together now and went out for dinner after work.

"I think maybe it's a bit of a miracle," Jim said one day over dinner. "Like a gift from the planet to us."

Jim had confided that he'd watched his wife of twenty years die in their living room on Earth, gasping for air. *There was no one to call,* he'd said. *The hospitals were all closed. I just had to sit there. And watch.* And then he'd smiled brightly, free from the pain of the memory. Everyone around the table had smiled back, sharing his joy.

Lexa wondered once, on a Friday when she was hunched over her toilet retching, if Jim had to relive those last moments with his wife every time he took his heart back. How did he bear it?

And then, one day, Jim wasn't in the office anymore.

Ciara asked Lexa to come with her to his pod to check up on him.

They could see the blue light as soon as they rounded the turn in the stairs. It leaked all around the door, pulsing gently.

Ciara opened the door with her master key. Lexa stepped back, blinking at the brightness.

Once her eyes adjusted, she saw the light retreating with a slightly apologetic air.

Jim lay on the floor of his pod, his desiccated body twisted like the gnarled roots of a tree. Above him, the plant's leaves filled the window.

Without a word, Ciara and Lexa backed toward the exit. Before they closed the door, Lexa cast one look back into the room. Jim's hideously wrinkled face was locked in a beatific smile.

Ciara kept her eyes on her feet as they walked back down the stairs, worrying her bottom lip with her teeth.

"Where did they come from? The plants you gave all of us?" Lexa realized she should have asked this sooner. Much sooner.

Ciara opened her mouth, then closed it with a click. "I don't remember."

"That's...not good. Do you have your heart in, or is it in the plant?"

"In the plant, of course. Although I guess I'll have to take it back permanently, now."

Ciara's voice was regretful. Lexa felt it too. In an abstract way, she was sorry that Jim had died. But mostly, she was annoyed that she would have to carry her heart around all the time, feel all those feelings, without ever getting a break. She resented Jim, for a moment, before remembering she was supposed to be sad.

"Maybe he just overused it. Maybe if we monitor each other, like a buddy system, we can keep using them," Ciara said hopefully.

"Yes!" Relief flooded Lexa. "It's like, um, medicine, right? It's only dangerous if you don't use it correctly. If we make sure we all take our hearts back on time, we'll be fine."

There was a tiny voice in the back of Lexa's brain, grumbling something about rationalization and addiction. She blocked it out.

After that, Ciara made sure everyone logged their plant usage with her. Lexa found it a bit intrusive; they were all adults, after all. But it worked. No one else disappeared from the office.

Until Wendy. And Adam. And Nathan. All gone in the same week. All wrapped in blue light, laid out beneath their flourishing plants like an offering. They couldn't even retrieve the bodies; the plants violently defended their prizes, lashing out with blades of light and suddenly sharp leaves.

Ciara had grimaced at each new discovery. And though there were worried glances between the remaining employees, no one brought up the idea that maybe they should stop using the plants altogether. Lexa was sure they were all thinking it, though.

Lexa stumbled back to her pod on Friday. She knew she had to take her heart back that night. The image of all those bodies should have been enough to dispel the reluctance she always felt. But she also knew she would feel it all: the horror, the loss.

She stalled when she got home, eating her dinner with conscientiously methodical chews, taking a long hot shower to wash the week away. But finally, she knew she couldn't put it off anymore. She sat on the edge of the couch.

"Okay. Give it back, please." Lexa closed her eyes, waiting, steeling herself against the wave of pain she knew was coming.

Nothing happened. She opened her eyes. The plant sat on her windowsill, the pitchers turned away from her.

Lexa got up and turned it to face her. She tapped the central pitcher with her forefinger.

"I need it back. Just for a while." The pitcher stayed closed, and the plant shifted away from her touch. *Shit.* "Please?"

She tried to pry the pitcher open, gently at first, then with more force, cursing under her breath. She watched in horror as the flesh of the plant grew over the pitcher, sealing it completely.

"You asshole. Seriously?"

She sat down on the floor with a thump. Even with her emotions blissfully blunted, she could feel panic welling up. Way back in her hindbrain, she could hear someone screaming, and it sounded like her.

Lexa took deep breaths. The voice in her head was wailing about how it wasn't fair that she was going to die here, shrivelled and alone, just so some stupid plant could grow big and strong on her heart. There wouldn't even be anyone left to mourn her; everyone else in the office was literally heartless. And Gary wouldn't care, beyond being annoyed he never got his precious closure.

Lexa was aware that these thoughts were selfish and childish and not even remotely helpful. *Enough with the tantrum,* she told herself. *You have a Ph.D. Figure it out.*

She went through all the ways she had personally killed plants in her life. Too much light or not enough. She could try stabbing it with one of the ice-shard leaves from the trees; they'd proved pretty deadly. She didn't want to think about what would happen to her heart when the plant died. Maybe it would die with it. Or maybe the plant would release it. But she would be damned if the one plant she didn't kill managed to kill her instead.

Overwatering was the number one killer of house plants. And the plant had certainly not liked the few drops of filtered water she'd dribbled on its soil.

She carried the plant toward the bathroom. Every leaf and pitcher turned, in unison, toward Lexa's face. How could she not have noticed how creepy that was before?

One of the smaller pitchers opened, and the room filled with the smell of rain.

"Nice try," Lexa said.

A leaf twined around her wrist, tightening painfully. Lexa winced but shouldered open the bathroom door.

"Just a nice little shower for you," she said. "Nothing to worry about."

As she placed the plant onto the shower floor, the leaf cut into her with serrated edges. Lexa bit her lip to keep from crying out as the blood began to flow. She pulled away and reached for the faucet handle.

The main pitcher opened. The blue light quivered as it held up Lexa's heart.

"Thank you. Put it back, please."

The pain was unimaginable. The grief settled on her like a thorned cloak, stabbing at her. Every hurt came crashing back in exquisite, immediate detail: every fight with Gary, all the barbed insults they lodged in each other's hearts. Her own voice screaming the last thing she said to her mother: *just do everyone a favour and drink yourself to death already.* The familiar, crushing knowledge that she was completely alone and the whispering suspicion that maybe she deserved it. And more, it went on and on. She saw Jim and Wendy and Adam and Nathan, the horror of their twisted bodies made so much worse by the realization that she *hadn't really cared*. She'd viewed their deaths at such a remove they were just inconveniences, like the series of spider plants that withered under her care and ended up in the dumpster behind her apartment.

Lexa gasped for breath, her chest on fire with pain. Blue light stroked her face gently, the pitcher open and waiting, offering to make this all go away, replace it with emptiness. Would it be so bad to die without all these emotions wreaking havoc on her? Every one of those bodies had a peaceful smile on their faces. Wasn't it a gift to be able to live in this soothing void of emotion and then die smiling?

Lexa wrenched the faucet on.

A sheet of hot water fell down onto the plant. The pitchers opened wide, screaming, a high-pitched whine just on the edge of Lexa's hearing that squeezed her heart so hard she thought she might die after all. The leaves crumpled under the water, shrivelling and curling into themselves. The pitchers drooped and then fell off one by one, releasing a last burst of green petrichor into the air.

Lexa slumped against the bathroom door, wreathed in steam, and closed her eyes, gently patting her heart, which she was stuck with now.

When she could finally move, she closed the door on the wreckage of the plant and called Ciara to tell her how to kill the damn things.

Ciara was silent on the phone, only sighing deeply once and saying, "Okay. Thanks," before hanging up. Lexa hoped she would kill her own plant and take her heart back for better or worse. But she remembered Ciara telling her about her daughter, about how the loss tore her apart, and she wasn't sure.

The next day Lexa woke from bad dreams, bleary and grumpy. Her heart was a weight in her chest.

She decided not to shower. She felt vaguely guilty about killing yet another plant. It wasn't its fault, really. It was just doing what it had evolved to do. Although Lexa did wonder how it had survived on the planet before they came, with its lack of mammalian life. Maybe it ate them all. Maybe they arrived just in time to save the species, only to destroy it, as humans always did. Or maybe Lexa was too exhausted and heart-sore, in the truest sense of the word, to be thinking about all this right now.

Out on the street, she raised her face to the bloody rain, trying to enjoy the fact that she was alive. She thought of Gary, testing the wound, and smiled grimly at the spike of pain.

In the office, she was relieved to see Ciara at her desk, looking grey and glum. And a refreshing lack of blue on the desks around her. A sullen silence hovered over the office, everyone lost in their own thoughts. It had been nice, for a while, to laugh and joke with everyone. Maybe they'd get that back someday, after they'd gotten used to having their hearts again.

Lexa hovered at Ciara's door, annoyed at her sudden shyness. It had been easy to bare her soul to Ciara, to tell her about her mother and everything that had happened with Gary, when it was just a memory and not an ongoing trauma. But now she knew everything, just as Lexa knew everything about Ciara's loss, and it made her feel exposed.

"I wanted to say...I'm sorry. About your daughter. I didn't know when we got here."

Ciara's eyes welled with tears. "Dammit." She wiped her eyes on her sleeve.

"Sorry." Lexa stepped back from the door.

"It's fine. I mean, obviously, none of this is fine. But it's fine-ish. Listen, meet me after work, okay? I want you to go somewhere with me."

"Sure."

Lexa followed Ciara through the forest of killer ice trees toward the beach. Neither of them spoke. When they were in sight of the waves, Ciara dropped to the ground. Lexa sat next to her.

"What are we doing here?" she asked.

"Feeling like shit. Together." Ciara stroked the leaves of the purple plant that grew all around them.

A lilting song filled the air, mixing with the tinkling sound of the waves. Ciara reached out and clasped Lexa's hand. Lexa squeezed it and closed her eyes, listening to the song, feeling the soft, painful weight of her heart.

SEEDLING

KATIE ESS

"Come on, Grandpa, get in the truck!" Sid and June tugged on the old man, who wasn't exactly huge but was heavier than June expected, especially when he was mostly dead weight.

"I'm not yer grandpa," he slurred before falling backward and landing hard on his butt.

Of course, he was drunk. June rolled her eyes, and Sid shrugged back at her.

"I know you're not my grandpa, but you're old enough to be. And you never told me your name. Now get in the truck. We need to go," June said, tapping her foot impatiently.

Grandpa opened his mouth to speak. Instead, a thin line of drool came out. He started to fall backward, but Sid caught him before he hit his head on the ground.

June sighed, exasperated. "That's it! He's going in the back of the truck! He's too heavy to lift into the passenger side, and I don't want him passed out on our shoulders all the way to Colorado."

Sid nodded in agreement. "You get his feet. I've already

got his arms." His nose turned up a bit. "His breath smells awful."

They lifted the man and set him in the truck bed. It was really more of a heave, but they made sure not to hit his head. *And honestly, he's lucky we're not just leaving him here.* There wasn't a good reason to take him. Except...humans don't leave other humans behind.

June started up the truck's engine—it coughed for a second before it sputtered to life. The engine didn't exactly "purr like a kitten," as her dad used to always say about his old sports car—the one he'd owned back when people cared about things like owning sleek cars. But it should get them where they needed to go.

"Do you think we've got enough gas?" Sid asked, letting a little fear creep into his voice. His eyes were big, and in that moment, he looked young and scared. He seemed like June's thirteen-year-old brother and not like the man that the world had demanded he grow into.

"It doesn't matter," she said. "We've got all the gas there is to scavenge around here." They'd spent the entire afternoon siphoning fuel out of every car they could find when they weren't hiding inside to avoid the dandelion seeds blowing overhead. Though the tank wasn't completely full, there was no more gas to be had.

June grimaced. The possibility of them getting stranded in the desert wasn't what he needed to hear right now. So, she added, "I'm sure it's enough. How big can Kansas be, anyway?"

Sid gave her an uncertain smile, and she reached over and tousled his hair. Then she put the truck in drive and took off down the pothole-studded road toward the interstate. Dusk was starting to fall, and they needed to get to Colorado by sunrise.

With the truck windows rolled up, Sid and June could barely hear the sound of the cacti screaming in the distance.

After decades of disregarding scientific warnings and delaying climate efforts, scientists announced today that the world has crossed the goal of trying to keep global warming below 1.5 degrees C. This year, global temperatures have increased by 2.2 degrees C, and with many countries still refusing to phase out coal and oil production, the UN Panel on Climate Change says the world seems on track to warm even faster now that we have crossed this barrier. The resultant increase in wildfires and severe storms have threatened countless lives, leading to famine in many areas of the world as some farmlands flood while others are affected by severe drought. Immigrants from Sudan...

Neil flipped off the radio and turned his attention back to his research. Only now, when the changes were nearly irreversible, did people seem to really take the threats of climate change seriously. He'd devoted his life to stopping the impending disaster before it got too bad, to no avail. But now that it had become a crisis, he was finally able to get the funding he needed for his research project. *Silver linings*, he thought to himself, shrugging.

His partner, Bill, entered the lab by kicking the door open so that it slammed dramatically into the wall. This was his traditional way of entering, and Neil had grown so accustomed to it that he didn't even flinch.

"I brought saaaaandwiches," Bill singsonged, doing a dramatic twirl and holding out one brown paper takeout bag.

"Sweet," Neil said. "I think we're ready to go."

"Today's the day we change the world," Bill said. "But only after a wholesome turkey club with avocado on whole wheat."

"Tell me that's not what you got me, too."

"Who do you think I am?" Bill looked mock-offended. "Of course, I got you meatball marinara with mozzarella."

Neil smiled and saluted his partner, who took a bow before they both dug into their lunch. "The formula seems stable." Neil took a bite and then wiped marinara off his lip. "The tissue cultures we injected it into have been growing without any problems for a month now."

"And they're producing their own nutrition?" Bill crossed his fingers as he waited for Neil's reply.

"One hundred percent. The cells are able to provide all the sustenance they need with just the chlorophyll we injected into them."

"You realize that if this works, we'll be the biggest heroes in the world." Bill grinned and held his hands up as though hanging an invisible banner. "Neil Maurer and Bill Planck... saviours of the entire planet!"

"I'm pretty sure scientists don't get that kind of billing," Neil said, rolling his eyes. Secretly, he'd imagined this kind of reception himself, but he'd never admit it to Bill. One of them had to keep things grounded, after all.

"How could we not?" Bill said. "I mean, if we're able to get human cells to take up and produce chlorophyll, then there's no real need to eat anymore. No more newscasts about famine in Sudan, or Afghanistan, or wherever. Plus, now all humans will become little carbon scrubbers. We filter out carbon dioxide from the atmosphere, directly combating global warming—two problems solved in one!"

Neil laughed. "I know, you moron! I'm helping invent the process—you don't have to explain it to me."

"Sorry, I just get excited. We've been working on this our

whole lives—which I know is only twenty-seven years, but still—our whole lives! And now it might finally happen.”

Neil nodded and continued to chew, letting himself daydream a bit about how they might change the world if this worked.

“I've always hated the last name Planck,” Bill said out of the blue. “Do you think they'd let me change it to Nye?”

“Nye? Like...Bill Nye?”

“Yeah. It's got a nice ring, doesn't it?”

“Sure, if you want to get sued for everything you own,” Neil raised one eyebrow at him, not entirely sure if he was serious.

“I bet Bill Nye didn't trademark his name. And he seems too nice to sue someone.”

“We are not having a conversation about stealing the name of a fellow scientist right now.”

“It's not really stealing if it's an homage...” Bill put down his unfinished sandwich, wrapping it in paper for later. “I can't wait! Let's go turn some mice green.”

Neil looked longingly at his meatball sandwich as his stomach let out a growl. If he didn't get up now, Bill would just flit around the lab maniacally until he was done. He wrapped the sub back up with a sigh.

“Fine. We'll inject the mice. But then I'm finishing my lunch!”

It turned out, June reflected somewhere around 2:00 am, that Kansas could be pretty big. She'd lived most of her life in Missouri, about fifty miles away from the Kansas border. All she remembered from her geography class senior year (was it possible that it had only been a year since geography class?)

was that the Kansas desert was what stood between Missouri and Colorado. And word was, the nearest settlement to theirs was in Colorado. So that's where they needed to be.

She wiped perspiration off the back of her neck. Not that it helped much. She could feel rivulets of sweat running between her shoulder blades, soaking her shirt. Even with the windows down, she was roasting. "Damn, it's hot."

"That's why they call it the Kansas desert," Sid replied, staring out the window into the darkness beyond. He pointed to the dashboard, where a digital thermometer announced it was 105 degrees. "It's good we're travelling at night. I mean, I know we have to because that's when the cactuses sleep. But they say that during the day, it gets up to 130 degrees or more."

"I know," June said irritably. "I've heard the same stories as you. I just wanted to gripe about how hot it is."

"It wouldn't be so hot if you'd let us run the air conditioner." Sid turned to her, accusation in his voice.

"Air conditioners use gas. We need to conserve all the gas we can. I don't remember how many miles Kansas is, so I don't know how far we need to go. But I don't want to run out of gas before we get through this desert."

"I wish the gas gauge worked," Sid said.

"Yeah, me too. I think." *Maybe it would be reassuring, and maybe it wouldn't.*

From the bed of the truck, Grandpa mumbled something. He'd been moaning and mumbling for about an hour now, but he was still passed out. June and Sid could hear him through a little window behind their heads, which they had opened to try to get extra airflow. They could hear his voice, but they couldn't tell what he was saying.

"Can you believe they used to grow crops out here?" Sid asked, turning back to the window.

"Well, it didn't used to be so hot. And before the Missouri River dried up, I think it was well irrigated, too."

"Still..." Sid trailed off. But June understood his point. They couldn't see much of the land beyond the beams of the truck's headlights, but what they could see was cracked and dry—not the kind of soil for raising crops.

In the periphery of their headlights, June saw something moving. She looked nervously at Sid to see if he'd noticed, but he was turned in the other direction. She didn't know for sure that it was a cactus, but she couldn't come up with anything else that would be skittering around out here. It was too hot for wildlife and too dry for...well, for anything else. But maybe it was just her imagination. After all, she hadn't heard the screaming since the sun went down.

No matter what, the cacti will keep away from the truck. Right?

"Bill, you're being crazy! There's no need to rush the process. The chlorophyll is working—we don't need to go so fast."

Bill paced back and forth in the lab, running his hands through his long, unkempt hair. Over the past weeks, he'd become increasingly erratic and frustrated with their progress.

"But Neil, don't you see? We can do so much more! We can fix so many problems!"

"Yes, we can," Neil said, holding his hands up in a placating gesture. "But science takes time. And we can only fix them if we do this right."

Neil wasn't sure why Bill was so set on pushing ahead with this new set of tests. The injectable chlorophyll had been a huge success. They'd sent their first batches to a host of countries in the Middle East and Africa—places hit hard by climate change—and put an end to famine there. People who had been starving now could sustain themselves just by going into the sunlight. Eventually, they needed to take in protein and cholesterol for the maintenance of muscle, brain, and bone, but they could go for months without needing to eat anything. And because they weren't using the food for their basic energy needs, small amounts could sustain them. Experts had pronounced it "the end to hunger as we know it on the planet."

They'd sold out to a big pharmaceutical company, BioCorp, shortly afterward for more money than Neil could ever imagine spending in his lifetime. Instead of retiring, they both put their brains to work on improving their initial idea. Because, they decided together, once you have everything you could possibly want, you're free to follow your passion.

"Science takes time," Bill said, eyes wild as he continued to pace. "That's what you keep telling me. But we don't have time. The human race doesn't have time. This planet doesn't have time!"

"Where is this coming from?" Neil asked. "Of course, we have time. Why wouldn't we?"

"BioCorp—you remember them, the ones that are funding our research—want results," Bill said, turning to face Neil. "They want something new—something *better*. Or they're cutting off our funding."

"So what? We've got more money than the Pope. If they cut off our cash flow, we can fund ourselves at this point— with millions left over so we can laugh at them as we rebuild."

"*I* want more, Neil."

"We both do. But our first animal tests have been problematic. You know all the issues we've had with the mice. Mutations, bad reactions to the DNA, aggression..."

"You're not hearing me," Bill said, his voice suddenly quiet and serious. Stopping his frantic pacing, he turned to look directly at Neil. "I want more. I want to go faster, and you're standing in my way. You need to leave."

Neil felt his heart skip a beat as he took in Bill's words and the intent behind them. There was a long pause before he could find words again.

"You can't tell me to leave. This is our lab. We did this together."

"But I'm the one that BioCorp selected to continue the work." He turned away from Neil as though he couldn't bear to say the rest to his face. "I've been talking with the corporate executives. I'm sorry, but you're out."

Neil thought of a thousand angry retorts and a million more logical arguments why he should stay. He imagined throwing a tantrum and breaking everything or coming back later and erasing all their data. But in the end, he sighed, turned on his heel, and walked quietly out the door.

"Be careful, Bill. Better is the enemy of good," he said over his shoulder as he left their lab for the last time.

By 3:00 am, the truck began sputtering every few miles along their route. "Come on, baby," June mumbled under her breath every time it happened. "Just a little further now. You can do it."

But just before 3:30, the truck rolled to a stop.

"Shit!" June shouted, slamming her hands against the steering wheel. "Shit, shit, shit!"

From the truck bed, Grandpa's voice came floating through the open window. It startled June—she didn't even realize he'd woken up. "Maybe you shouldn't go shouting real loud in the middle of the desert, with the cacti all around."

"Nobody asked you, Grandpa!" June snapped back, even though she knew he was right. But she was hot and frustrated, and now she was scared, too. She had no idea how far they needed to go, and it was only a few hours until dawn.

And at dawn, the plants would wake.

"Suit yourself," Grandpa drawled. "But if you're going to make a big racket, I'm heading away from you. Regardless, we'd better all start walking. It's about to get real bright and real hot."

June snuck a glance at Sid. His eyes were wide with fear, but he nodded at her resolutely. "Let's walk," he said, opening his door and hopping down onto the road.

June grabbed a pack from the bed of the truck, full of bottled water and a first aid kit. It was heavy, and she grunted as she swung it onto her back, taking a second to adjust to the weight before she started after Sid. Grandpa had already moved ahead at a clip that surprised her, considering his age and how drunk he had been a few hours earlier.

"Do you know where you're going?" she called after him.

"Thought we were going to Colorado."

"Yeah, but do you know where you're going?"

"Following the road, same as we were doing in the truck. Just slower."

She started to ask him if he knew how much further it was but decided she didn't want to know and closed her mouth. She fell in line, more because she didn't know what else to do than because she really wanted his company.

They trudged in the dark for what felt like hours, though without the clock in the truck anymore, June wasn't sure. It was still hot, and at this brisk pace, her back and head dripped with sweat. Her long brown hair was pulled back in a tight ponytail, and its swishing against her neck made a slight breeze that was comforting in the otherwise sweltering air.

Every time June looked to one side of the road or the other, shapes moved in the darkness. So, she stopped looking to the side. No point focusing on something you can't control.

June would have been happy to keep walking in silence all the way to Colorado, but after a long span of nothing except the sound of shoes on pavement, Sid piped up.

"Are those cacti moving around in the distance?" he whispered.

"How should I know?" She realized her tone came out curt and tried to fix it. After all, he was her little brother and probably just as scared as she was. "I mean, I haven't seen one before, but I think it might be."

"They're definitely cacti," Grandpa said from a few paces ahead, not even turning to look at June and Sid.

"How do you know?" Sid asked, moving more to the centre of the road as though staying on the pavement would keep them away.

"The way they move," Grandpa said. "Kinda jittery, like they don't know what to do with themselves. Right now, they're slow, but as the sun comes up, they'll wake up, and then we'll be in trouble."

"What should we do?" Sid's voice was now full of fear. It was dark enough that June couldn't see his face clearly, but she thought he was directing this question at her.

"We keep going," she answered, trying to force her voice to sound confident. "If we can get out of this desert before sunrise, then we won't have to deal with the cacti at all. So, we just keep walking."

Grandpa gave a snort of a laugh. "Yeah, right. We're not making it out before the sun comes up."

"Why not?" June challenged, annoyed at his attitude but also concerned he might be right.

"Well," Grandpa said, "Kansas is about 400 miles across.

We started driving when it got dark, and the truck broke down about 3:30. Assuming you were going really fast—which you were not—it's at least ten miles to the Colorado border. And there's another fifteen miles or so of desert on the Colorado side before we get into tree country."

"Tree country?" Sid's voice managed to sound more terrified than before. He and June had both heard about the thirty-foot-tall monstrosities that looked exactly like non-hybrid trees until they decided to attack, crushing you to death with their massive branches or releasing pollen to infect you.

"How about let's not scare my brother half to death?" June scolded.

"I'm just answering the kid's questions," Grandpa said. "If you don't want him to know the truth, fine. Get him killed. Trees exist, whether you want to hear it or not."

"All right then," June said, choosing anger because it felt better than fear. "If you think we're going to die, then why are you even walking? Why not just sit down by the truck and wait?"

"I thought we might look for an abandoned car," Grandpa said. "If it pleases your majesty."

"Why would someone abandon a car in the middle of the desert?"

"Well, people used to live out here before everything changed. If we're lucky, maybe we'll find a car parked at an old farmhouse."

"But it's dark," Sid piped in. "How will we see a farmhouse?"

"With your eyes," Grandpa replied. "Look hard."

June couldn't think of a sarcastic retort, so she gave her brother a little side hug for reassurance. It was still dark enough that she couldn't see anything more than a few feet in front of her. She had no idea how they were supposed to find a farmhouse. As she looked, something moved at the side of the road, just a few feet away—much closer than she'd prefer. Probably a cactus, she thought, trying to be calm about the idea of them being so close. Grandpa was right—they had a jittery quality when they moved. There had been a person in their village with Parkinson's disease, and he had moved kind of like that.

That was before their village had been invaded by dandelions while Sid and June were out hunting. They had returned to find everyone they knew dead, the village destroyed, and terrifying, muscular plants sifting through the ruins. The dandelions were shaped like men but with strong tendrils for hands and wispy, white seeds where their hair should be. Each seed was attached to a small eyeball at its stalk that could be floated into the air and used to spy on neighbouring territories, scouting for places to expand. When dandelions invaded, they left no survivors. Sid and June had spent the day hiding from the eyes floating in the sky and scavenging gas to make their escape.

And now they were all alone, with this old drunk guy. Who knows where he had come from? But because they hadn't felt like they could leave him alone, now he was here, being generally sarcastic and scaring her brother to death.

After another long silence, Sid asked, "Are we really going to have to go through tree country?"

"We might make it through tree country if we find a car," Grandpa said. "If we walk, we won't be going through it for long."

"Dammit, Grandpa, are you trying to give the kid a heart attack?" June asked, clenching her fists.

"I'm not a kid," Sid replied.

"Of course, if we don't find a car, it won't matter because

the cacti will probably kill us long before we reach tree country," Grandpa said. "Or if not the cacti, the heat."

"Can't you be reassuring, even for a minute?"

"I'm *not* a kid!" Sid said loudly, then jumped as though he'd startled himself with the exclamation.

June looked around to see if anything was moving, but everything appeared still.

"You are a kid," June said. "You're my little brother, and I'm going to protect you."

Grandpa stopped abruptly and turned to face the two of them. It took June a minute to register the change in speed, and she almost crashed into him before she could adjust her own course.

"Look," he said. "As far as I'm concerned, you're both kids, and neither one of you knows what the hell you're doing. It's clear to me that you've never dealt with any kind of plants, and yet you've drug all of us out here in the middle of nowhere. I didn't ask you to bring me along, but here we are with no plan and very few supplies and no way to defend ourselves. Optimism won't fix this! What I need is for you two to shut up, pay attention, and follow my lead. Or we are all going to die."

Speech delivered, he turned and resumed his brisk walk. June and Sid scrambled to keep up, and June was once again startled by how fast he was for an old guy.

Internally, June fumed. How dare he frighten them like this? How dare he imply they didn't have hope?

But she also knew that he was right. They didn't have a plan other than escaping the dandelions. She had no idea how to defend herself against cacti...or trees. And that made her even angrier.

After seething for a bit, she found her voice. "Okay, Grandpa, if we're so dumb, then why don't you educate us? I suppose you've had thousands of encounters with plants since you've clearly survived to tell the tale. So, impart your wisdom to us *kids*."

"Little girl," Grandpa said, "I know more about the plants than almost anyone else on this planet. But no one wants to listen to me. I gave up imparting wisdom long ago."

"I do," Sid said quietly. "I mean, I want to listen to you."

Grandpa paused, then sighed. "Okay, fine, I'll talk to you. But only because I'm hoping it will give us a chance of getting out of here alive. I assume you know the three different types of plants that were created."

"Of course," Sid replied. "Cacti, trees, and dandelions. But I don't know why they were created."

"The why isn't particularly important," Grandpa said. "I mean, it's the usual motivations—greed, hubris, curiosity. We thought we could do better than what nature had already done."

"So, humans tried to turn themselves into plants?" Sid asked. They'd always glossed over this part in school, and Sid had been very curious about it. So had June, to be honest.

"Not exactly," Grandpa said. "They just tried to pick and choose aspects of plants that they liked and add them to their bodies. For example, cacti are very drought resistant—and with the difficulty we have finding fresh water, people thought maybe it would be good if their bodies didn't need so much water. Dandelions are resistant to trauma, and they regenerate fast after injury. Trees are strong, and they live a long time. Somehow, we thought that if we added those traits to our DNA, we'd only get what we wanted and not anything extra."

"Why did they think that?" Sid said, scoffing.

"Hubris, like I said before," Grandpa snapped. "Do you want me to talk, or are you going to keep interrupting?"

"Sorry," Sid said and fell silent.

"Well, as you just pointed out in your very interrupt-y way, humans got what they wanted, but they got a whole lot more, too. The human-cacti hybrids are very drought resistant, but they also grew needles—everywhere."

"Ugh." Sid shivered. Then, seeming to realize he'd interrupted again, he said, "Sorry. Please go on."

Grandpa cleared his throat. "Dandelions are trauma-resistant, but they also become extremely aggressive—driven to kill everyone around them that isn't a dandelion as well. Trees are strong, but they lose their will and stop moving—until they're threatened, and then they can attack with extreme force. And they view all humans as a threat. Which is probably fair since we spent a lot of time in the past cutting them down."

Grandpa sighed and shot a glance to either side. June followed his gaze and noticed that it was becoming lighter out. She could see things a little more clearly in the pre-dawn.

And where before she could only see a few cacti skittering in the darkness, now she could see them scattered across the horizon. Thousands of cactuses that would soon awaken as the sun rose. June's stomach knotted uncomfortably, and she felt her heart begin to pound. Grandpa was right—there was no way they could survive if all these plants attacked.

When all these plants attacked.

Grandpa picked up his pace again. June found herself struggling to keep up without breaking into a jog. Sid definitely had to jog to match their stride. But he didn't complain. June imagined he also felt the urgency of the situation mounting.

"That's enough of a history lesson," Grandpa said. "Here's the practical things you need to know about cacti. They're aggressive, but they don't think logically. Needles in one's brain will make one act a bit crazy, after all. And the needles in their head are their weak point."

He picked up a large stick at the side of the road and handed it back to Sid without breaking his stride. June saw one on the other side and picked it up, much less gracefully. She wasn't sure why, but she figured Grandpa had a reason, and she was just happy to have a plan.

Grandpa saw a highway sign that had been broken in half. He picked up the end with the sign and slung it over his shoulder. "When they wake up, they'll start screaming again. It's really distracting, so you'll have to work to stay focused. Keep away from them, and no matter what, don't let them stick you. The needles transmit DNA, and if they prick your skin—"

"We'll turn into cacti ourselves. We know," June said, panting a little from the jog.

"No interrupting!" Grandpa snapped. "You'll turn into some kind of plant—maybe a cactus, maybe a dandelion, maybe a tree. The DNA they transmit has the potential to turn you into any of the three, depending on how it combines with your own genetic code. But no matter what, it will be quick and painful.

"If one of them gets close, hit them with your stick. Aim for the needles coming out of the head—not the head or the body. Those needles are directly attached to their brains, and a good blow will do catastrophic damage."

"How do you know all this?" June asked.

"Irrelevant!" Grandpa snapped. "I'm alive because I know this stuff, and I'd prefer to stay that way." He pointed toward the outline of a farmhouse in the distance. "And that's—hopefully—going to be the thing that saves us."

"That? That house has got to be a mile away!" June could see the first outlines of the sun coming over the horizon.

"Then we'd better hurry," Grandpa said. He veered off the road toward the house and broke into a run. June and Sid followed, as all around them, the cacti began to stir.

Tonight's top story. There have been disturbing accusations against BioCorp and their newest formula, designed to be an improvement on injectable chlorophyll. The formula, which incorporated plant DNA to make humans more drought-resistant, seemed to be the best solution to our current freshwater crisis after the complete loss of Lake Mead and the near collapse of the Mississippi, Colorado, and Missouri rivers. Experts touted the new formula, dubbed Seedling, as the solution to our global climate crisis. However, disturbing reports of mutations in people receiving Seedling have surfaced, and the initial group of test subjects has been quarantined at BioCorp for monitoring. BioCorp officials assure us their medical professionals have stabilized the subjects and are working on a way to improve their formula. As you may remember, Bill Planck and Neil Maurer, the inventors of injectable chlorophyll, parted ways during the development of Seedling. BioCorp announced that Dr. Maurer had been let go over a series of careless mistakes during testing, and his work was widely discredited by his partner...

Neil snapped off the television and stumbled to the kitchen to get another beer. "My work was not discredited," he shouted at the television, though there was no one to hear it. "That was a smear job!"

Popping the cap off the beer, he wound his way through his living room, cluttered with pizza boxes and delivery containers. He fell back onto his couch, chugged the bottle, and then sat in silence. His thoughts travelled down a familiar path of anger and resentment that only alcohol seemed able to short-circuit.

The pain of his split with Bill had been difficult, but Neil had been determined to set up his own corporation and continue the work they'd been doing.

When Bill found out, he went crazy. Along with BioCorp, he started a campaign in the media and the scientific community to discredit Neil's work. Neil wasn't worried at first—he trusted his fellow scientists to see the truth, to understand the risks that BioCorp was taking by moving things along too quickly. But Bill made it look like Neil had been sloppy and careless with experiments until he became the laughingstock of the scientific world—and the public in general.

As Neil started to feel drowsy, letting the beer work its numbing magic, his phone rang. Without looking at the caller ID, he answered.

"Hello?"

"Neil. It's...it's Bill."

Instantly, Neil was wide awake, though still not remotely sober. "What the fuck do you want? What are you calling me for?"

"I've got a problem, Neil. A big problem."

"Yeah, me too. You know what my problem is? My lab partner, and best friend, destroyed my career. But then, you know that, don't you?"

"I know. And trust me, you're the last person I wanted to call. I don't deserve your help, and I shouldn't ask for it. But Seedling—it's a disaster. Bad things are happening here, and we can't figure out how to fix them. If I don't find a solution, I think they're going to fire me and replace me with another scientist who will distribute the formula as-is."

"None of this sounds like it's my problem."

"Neil, you're the only person who knows this formula as

well as I do. If you don't help me, terrible things are going to happen. I *need* your expertise. Please come—if not to help me, then to help the human race."

Neil thought for a moment. What if he could fix the formula? Maybe he was being given a second chance to realize his dream of making things better for humanity. Then he thought about the way humanity had ridiculed him, driven him out of his profession, ruined his life.

Those dreams were gone. Humanity could make things better for itself.

"Fuck you, Bill," he said and hung up the phone.

As the first sunbeams popped over the horizon, a cactus rose up right next to June, startling her so badly she tripped and almost fell. She staggered but managed to find her balance and keep pace with the others.

June had been looking out over the desert as the sky turned from black to dark blue to grey. Thousands of cacti lay, or sat, on the ground, fidgeting uncomfortably in the darkness. But now that the sun was fully out, they began to rise, and she could see them better. Her heart started to pound, and it wasn't entirely from all the running.

The one closest to her was about six feet tall. His shape was vaguely human—arms, legs, head, torso—but aside from the shape, there wasn't much human about him. His skin was green and pulpy, like the flesh of a cactus. He had a tremor at rest, but when he moved, it turned jerky, like a badly animated cartoon.

Small needles protruded from his arms, legs, hands, and fingers, while bigger needles the size of pencils stuck out at all angles from his torso and back. In some places, where they protruded from the skin, they dripped a red sap-like substance the colour of blood.

But the worst part was his head. He had scraggly, sparse hair that hung in clumps, with bald patches all over his scalp. In each bald patch protruded a spike as big as June's thumb, with a needle-sharp tip. The spikes seemed to burst through his skull as though they came from deep in his brain and dripped red fluid that oozed into his hair and down his neck. One eye looked around wildly as though trying to focus on a bug zooming around his head. But the other eye had been replaced by a huge spike—the biggest one of all—that stuck raggedly out of the socket, exposing the meat of the cheek where it had eroded the flesh.

Each cactus around them was similar, only varying in the size and position of the needles. But the biggest spikes, in every single one of them, came straight out of their skulls. Many of the cacti clawed at these spikes as though trying to pull them free.

They stood gradually, their eyes darting about as though they were trying to get their bearings. The cactus nearest June abruptly turned his head, his eye focusing on her intently.

"Get ready," Grandpa said, moving his broken sign into position the way a batter would prepare for a fast pitch.

"For what?" Sid asked, panic in his voice as he held his stick at the ready.

And then it screamed, an unhinged shriek of pain and lunacy.

The cactus nearest Sid wailed next, followed by the one next to Grandpa. Then, one at a time, the rest of the cacti started screaming as they locked their vision on the three of them. The creatures started shuffling toward them, their steps jerky and off-balance.

"For that!" Grandpa shouted. The cactus nearest him had gotten close, and he swung his sign, hitting it in the spike on top of its skull. The spike stayed intact as it took the impact of the blow, but the cactus's skull shattered around it, exploding in a spray of blood, brain, and bone.

One approached Sid from the side. He swung his stick, hitting it squarely in the legs. June had hoped it would throw the cactus off balance, but it barely slowed the creature down. June hit hers in the face with her stick. It brushed off the impact effortlessly.

"The spikes!" Grandpa shouted. "Remember, hit the spikes on their head. It's their weak point!"

"Oh yeah," Sid shouted, taking a second swing at the cactus. This time, he hit the spike, and the cactus dropped to the ground immediately as its skull exploded. June followed suit, fending off the one she'd hit in the head before, then a second one that had approached in the meantime.

"Woo-hoo!" Sid took out two more, and he jumped over their unmoving bodies as they all continued toward the barn.

The trio made good progress, but there was still about a quarter mile to go, and there were a *lot* of cacti heading their way. And the sun, still low in the sky, was already ramping up the temperature. June felt her breath rasping in and out as sweat poured down her back. Her muscles burned from the exertion, but she managed a second burst of speed, trying to will her way closer to the farmhouse. She could now see a large barn nearby, as well.

"Head toward the barn!" Grandpa shouted. "People used to store old cars in their barns—maybe we'll get lucky."

The three of them dodged and swung wildly, fending off cactus after cactus. Their screaming was disorienting—it made it hard to tell exactly where the closest ones were since the sound came from everywhere, constantly. Every time June thought she was clear, another one jerked its way in front of her or grabbed at her from the side. One caught a needle on her shirt, tearing a ragged hole before she could take it down.

June and Sid had instinctively moved back-to-back, and they sidled up to Grandpa, forming a circle so they could protect each other. Grandpa was at the front, and June watched him take out cactus after cactus. Their progress slowed from a run to a crawl as they were now surrounded by screaming plants. But they continued to push forward toward the barn.

One cactus got the idea of kicking at Sid, who instinctively stuck his foot out to block. Fortunately, the needles on the lower part of the cactus didn't make it through his shoe, but Sid did lose his balance. He fell backward into Grandpa and June, knocking Grandpa forward. A smaller cactus darted into the space he'd left, separating Grandpa from the other two. It swung its arm toward June's head. She saw the blow coming but was defending herself from another cactus directly in front of her and didn't have time to respond.

Just before the barbed limb made contact with her face, Grandpa whirled around with his sign. He hit the cactus's arm so hard that he knocked it off, the arm flying within millimetres of her face, spraying her with red fluid. A second hit destroyed the cactus's head, allowing Grandpa to get back in position.

"Thanks!" June said.

"I don't want to lose my rear defense," Grandpa said gruffly.

"I think that's Grandpa for *you're welcome*," Sid said.

"It's Grandpa for *we're almost at the barn*," he replied, less gruffly this time. He swung at another cactus as June and Sid took out two of their own. "Here's what we're going to do. We're going to turn slowly so the two of you are facing the barn door. Then, you open the door while I keep these things back. Once we're all safe inside, we'll look around."

They swivelled slowly, each lashing out with their sticks to keep the cacti at bay, until June and Sid were in position. Enough of the cacti had fallen that the others were having to climb over bodies to attack. This slowed the cacti down enough that June thought they'd be able to make it in the door.

"Sid," she said. "You set down your stick and move forward. I'll keep these guys fended off while you get the door open."

Sid did as she asked, and she moved into position, striking at the cacti from both sides to protect her brother. She had hoped that watching their compatriots being attacked would encourage them to back off, but they didn't even seem to register it. They were fixated on the humans. June wondered why but didn't have much time to ponder it as she swung at her attackers, determined to keep her brother safe.

The door had a long wooden bar set into two brackets. As Sid lifted up the bar, the doors swung open toward him as though they had been waiting anxiously for the three of them to visit.

June and Sid ducked inside and held the doors as cacti pressed against them, trying to get around. Grandpa backed in, fending off cactus after cactus as he worked his way into the barn. As soon as he was clear of the doors, June and Sid let the pressure of the cactus horde push the doors shut, and they all retreated into the safe space. When there was only a small opening in the door now, about the size of a person. Grandpa lowered his sign and breathed a sigh of relief.

But the lapse in his guard was premature. One of the cacti lunged through the door, swiping his hands wildly as he tried to grab them. Grandpa threw up his hand to block, taking a needle right into the palm of his left hand. He recoiled, digging the needle out of his flesh as quickly as possible, while June jumped in and bashed the cactus. It dropped to the ground, and the three of them kicked its body backward so they could finish closing the door. The pressure of the other cacti pushing forward held it shut, which was fortunate since they'd dropped the bar used to latch the door on the other side.

June looked around to make sure there was nothing in the barn waiting to attack them. When she saw it was clear, she ran to Grandpa. "Did it get you?"

He held up his hand in response. There was a gash in the middle of his palm, narrow but definitely there. Already, the edges of the wound had started to turn green. Small needles grew out of the ragged flesh.

"Shit, it's cactus. I will *not* turn into one of those things." Grandpa looked at her resolutely. "Let's see if there's a car in here. Then, I'll create a distraction while you two drive away."

"There's one here," Sid shouted, lifting a cloth cover over an old farm truck. Dust flew into the air, the particles hanging in beams of sun that filtered from a loft window at the top of the barn. June ran to the truck and breathed a sigh of relief. The keys were in the ignition.

Grandpa hopped in the truck and turned the key. The vehicle sputtered, and June felt her heart sputter with it before the engine kicked over.

"All right," he said, climbing back out of the truck. "You two get in. I'll push the doors open, and you should be able to drive over or past them."

"I'm not letting you sacrifice yourself for us," June said.

"Yeah," Sid chimed in, tears in his eyes. "Humans don't leave other humans behind."

"Well, you don't have to worry because I'm not going to

be human for very much longer. Anyway, I had my chance to save humanity a long time ago, and I didn't take it. Maybe this is my chance to redeem myself."

"I've got a better idea," June said. She pulled off her backpack, removing the water bottles in favour of the first aid kit at the bottom of the bag. "Maybe you can redeem yourself by getting us to that settlement in Colorado."

She pulled out a tourniquet from the first aid kit and wrapped it just above his wrist, tight. The whole hand was now covered in needles, and most of the palm was green and woody. *Damn, this stuff works fast.*

"That's not going to stop it from spreading," Grandpa said. "Just get out of here while I'm still alert enough to help you."

"I know the tourniquet won't stop it, but this might." She pulled out a switchblade from the kit. The blade was about 3 inches long and sharp enough to get the job done quickly.

Grandpa's eyes widened for a minute as he realized her intent. He took a deep breath and nodded. "Just don't make me watch."

"Look at Sid then. I need to do this now."

June poured alcohol over the knife and then cut the hand off as cleanly and quickly as she could. With the screaming of the cacti outside, she barely even noticed his screams as she worked. And she knew she had to tune them out, or she wouldn't be able to get the job done.

She bandaged the wound, trying to keep things clean, and wrapped it tight, like she'd been taught in first aid class. But her hands were trembling badly, and Grandpa was shaking too. In the end, Sid helped hold Grandpa steady so she could finish.

"Sorry," she said as she taped the bandage awkwardly. "I know this could be better."

"Better is the enemy of good, kid. Let's get out of here. It's getting hot, and we need to move before those plants find a way in."

June nodded, but before she could stand up to move, Grandpa put his remaining hand on her shaky one. "I know I've been rough on you kids. But you did great. Thanks—for saving me."

June gave him a weak smile. "You're welcome, old man. Hopefully, it works."

"Neil," he said. "You can call me Neil."

The three of them piled into the truck, Grandpa in the middle, June and Sid on either side. June put the truck in gear and drove it through the barn door, splintering wood and splattering cacti as she peeled out toward the road, then toward the horizon and Colorado beyond.

With the windows rolled up and the air conditioner on, they couldn't hear the screaming of the cacti at all.

Plant Friends

Jen Mierisch

The after-hours keypad beeped as Dr. Bo Howland let himself into the lab. The hallway lights were dimmed for nighttime, but he'd have known the way even while sleepwalking.

Bo made his way to the back of the building and out to the greenhouse. He had moved Number 102 back there a week before. She liked it out there.

He'd called 102 "she" entirely by accident. It had slipped out one day during a meeting. Bo had quickly corrected himself. "*It*, I mean," he'd said with a nervous chuckle. Thankfully, the meeting was only with Barrett, who was used to his old friend's eccentricities, who knew how much these experiments meant to Bo. But in his mind, Bo had kept using *she* whenever he thought of his lovely 102, his most promising hybrid yet.

He had placed 102 on a special platform at the back. She had thrived gloriously, her thick leaves fanning out from her fleshy green trunk like feathers on a peacock's tail. His bona fide California girl.

Bo's large eyes shone in the moonlight as he gazed at his creation. Its skin, like that of its aloe ancestor, was smooth, green, and covered in white freckles that were, frankly, adorable. He had bred out the leaves' serrated edges, of course. Sharp spines would never do.

Bo reached out and touched 102's longest leaf. Gently he caressed it, running his fingers along its length from tip to root.

The leaf responded to Bo's touch by curling itself around him. It looped around his bony forearm, snaked past his elbow, and wound softly around his slim bicep.

"Yes," Bo whispered. "Yes, my dear." He stopped stroking it. When his fingers pulled free, the leaf stopped winding and rested where it was.

It seemed to Bo that 102 was learning. That it had gotten accustomed to his specific touches and responded with just the right amount of movement. This was extremely promising, but still too early to draw conclusions. He'd have to gather some hard data to make sure he wasn't biased by his own pride and affection.

With his free hand, Bo groped in his pocket for his phone and dialed Barrett Clouse. Though it was well after midnight, Barrett picked up after the first ring.

"Barry," said Bo, his voice shaking slightly with emotion, "we've done it. We've got it. This is the one."

April Arsenault frowned at her phone and blew out a frustrated breath, causing her lips to make a noise like a lawnmower that wouldn't start. A strand of her dark hair fluttered upward in the resulting breeze and resettled across her nose. Annoyed, she brushed it aside and tucked it behind her ear.

The numbers for her Friday night were not looking good.

April had texted six friends. One hadn't responded, two were out of town, another wasn't feeling well, and one was out with business colleagues.

The sixth was April's last hope. *Call you in five*, she had texted back.

The phone rang. The name Devora Barahona lit the screen.

"Hi, honey!" Devora's voice could fill a cell connection as easily as it filled a room. "I would love to go out. But it's my fourth date with Scott tonight! He's coming over in like half an hour."

"Oh," said April. "Where are you going?"

"Dave and Busters." April heard the click of objects against a countertop. She pictured Devora in front of her bathroom mirror, applying her signature scarlet lipstick and snapping barrettes into her dyed-red hair. "We felt like some junk food and stupid games. Maybe I'll make him win me one of those giant balls from the claw machine."

April wrapped her throw blanket tightly around her shoulders. "You're so lucky," she said, "having a boyfriend now. I want someone to snuggle on my couch with."

"Girl. You need a dog."

"My landlord would definitely hate that," said April.

"You should call what's-his-name. That barista from the bookstore."

"His name is Thanh," said April, feeling a buzz in her gut as she pictured Thanh's face, his shaggy dark hair, his lanky frame. "And no, I can't, because he barely knows I exist."

"Time for some more lattes!" said Devora. "So. What *are* you gonna do tonight?"

"I don't know. Nobody's around." April yawned, grabbed

the remote, and flipped on the TV. "There's a horror movie marathon on AMC, but I've seen them all."

"Which one's on now?"

"Little Shop of Horrors." April muted the TV volume. "Is that even horror?"

"I love that one! It's cute." Devora sang, "'Somewhere that's greeeen'! Hey, that reminds me. Did you see that one influencer on YouTube this morning? The wellness woman. Lynnette what's-her-name."

"Who?"

"Omigod," said Devora. "She had the craziest guests on today. You've got to watch this with me. Open YouTube and search for 'All Well and Good.'"

Together they counted down and pressed play.

The All Well and Good studio was a bright, sunny room with cream-coloured walls and two burnt-orange couches at right angles to each other. Light streamed in from a skylight, and plants were everywhere: rising tall from floor pots, spilling from hanging baskets, sprouting out of colourful pots on side tables. A freckle-faced woman sat on one of the couches, her brown curly hair spilling like a waterfall over her floor-length cotton dress and denim jacket.

"Hello, and welcome to another episode of All Well and Good!" the woman said. "Where we feed our bodies, minds, and souls! I'm your host, Lynnette Moncada, and I cannot wait to introduce today's guests. But first, because I know you're gonna ask me in the comments, yes, this dress is a vintage 1970s Gunne Sax, and I picked it up at Crossroads Trading in Santa Monica. Thrifting is good for the environment and your wallet, people!" Lynnette stood and gave a twirl. The cream-and-brown prairie dress flared, revealing fringed leather boots.

"Hippie," said Devora into April's ear.

"Shush," said April. "Also, I kinda like that dress."

"Hippie."

"Now, folks," said Lynnette. "We've got something truly special in store for you today. If you watch my show, you've probably been called a tree hugger at least once in your life. Well, my guests have invented a plant that can hug you back!"

Lynnette gestured to someone off-camera. Two men walked into the frame, carrying a potted plant between them. The white pot was stenciled on the side with the number 102. Rising from it, a fleshy green trunk, about four feet tall, brimmed with thick, aloe-like leaves.

"Please welcome Dr. Bo Howland and Barrett Clouse. And their extraordinary plant!" Lynnette clapped, and canned sound effects added a crowd's worth of applause. She gestured toward one of the orange couches and seated herself on the other.

The men placed the plant between the two couches and sat across from Lynnette. The skinny man with the large grey eyes and messy dirty-blond hair, dressed in a blue collared shirt tucked into khaki pants, sat nearest the plant. The other man, who had short dark hair gelled to within an inch of its life, wore a linen button-down whose short sleeves revealed tanned, swollen biceps. His broad shoulders occupied a sizable chunk of the couch's width.

"Thank you both for coming," said Lynnette. "It's wonderful to meet you."

"The pleasure is ours, Lynnette," replied Biceps. "Thanks for having us. I'm Barrett Clouse, and this is my old friend, Bo Howland, the genius behind Plant Friends."

"Plant Friends!" repeated Lynnette. "Please, tell us about yourselves, how you started the company, and how you came up with this product."

"Barrett and I first met in high school," said Bo.

"Let me guess. Science club?"

"Anime club," said Bo. "But we were biology lab partners."

"Guess we're still lab partners," said Barrett with a chuckle. "We met up again after college. By then, I was an entrepreneur looking for my next venture, and Bo was getting his PhD in plant physiology."

Bo cleared his throat. "I've always been interested in plants that have certain—abilities. My area of specialization was seismonastic flora. These are plants from multiple species that produce a sensory, nondirectional response to mechanical stimuli—"

"What Bo means," Barrett cut in, "is that certain plants respond to physical touch."

"Of course," said Lynnette. "Like Venus flytraps, right?"

"Yes," said Bo.

"So then, we—well, Bo—found a way to cross-breed different touch-sensitive plants to interact with human touch in friendly ways," Barrett continued.

"Fascinating," said Lynnette. She was leaning forward over her crossed legs, stealing glances at the tall plant between herself and Bo. "Tell me what goal you hope to achieve with this product?"

"People are lonely," said Bo. "It's reached epidemic levels. We live far from our families, or we're estranged, or we're too occupied with our jobs and our phones." His gaze was distant, dreamy. "Many modern people have forgotten nature. We spend our days enclosed in concrete buildings and metal cars. Living more in harmony with the natural world can only benefit us."

"Absolutely," said Lynnette. "That's what this show is all about."

"Pets are great, of course," Bo went on, "but some of us are allergic to cats and dogs, and many apartments don't allow animals. We wanted to create a plant that could be a companion."

"A Plant Friend."

"Exactly."

"How long did this take to develop?"

Barrett looked at his friend. "A year and a half, right?"

"Yes," said Bo, "and many experiments until finally, we got our perfect hybrid, Number 102." He beamed at the plant. "The mother of all the plants that came after."

"This is quite something," said Lynnette. "But I'm dying to know, and I'm sure our viewers are, too. Can I try it out? This Plant Friend that you've brought here today?"

"Of course."

"What do I do? Just touch a leaf?"

"Yes. Run your fingers along it lightly."

Lynnette pushed up the bell sleeve of her dress, reached out her hand, and touched one of the plant's long leaves with her fingertips. It curled around her palm, resting its tip gently on her wrist, where the veins pulsed.

"Oh!" said Lynnette. "It tickles!" Her face was a picture of wonder. "It's so soft."

"The more you run your fingers along it," said Bo, "the more it will curl around you."

"So, it's like a vine."

"About fifteen percent." Bo smiled faintly. "When you want it to stop curling, take your fingers away."

"Okay." Lynnette touched the leaf gently again. She laughed. "It's holding my hand!"

"It does that."

"How do I make it let go?"

"Touch the tip," said Bo, "like this." He firmly tapped the leaf's pointed tip with the open palm of his hand. The leaf uncoiled and shrank away from Lynnette's arm.

"Incredible," said Lynnette, eyes wide. "So, what if I wanted, like, a full hug? Or a friendly pat on the back?"

"Just move the leaf where you want it," said Bo. "Lift it into place before you run your fingers along it."

Lynnette reached for another leaf. Her acrylic fingernail stabbed its side, leaving a momentary indentation in the fleshy skin. "Oh, sorry, sweetie!" Lynnette exclaimed, then laughed at herself. "Did I just call a plant 'sweetie'?"

"It's their special charm," said Barrett, winking.

Lynnette lifted the leaf carefully, placed it onto her shoulder, and stroked its length. The leaf extended itself across her back, wound around her opposite shoulder, and curled itself against her arm.

"Wow," said Lynnette. "It really feels like someone has their arm around me."

Bo and Barrett smiled back at Lynnette's delighted face.

"Okay, sweetie, that's enough for now." Lynnette tapped the leaf's tip, watched it shrink away, and shook her head.

"Frankly, Dr. Howland, Mr. Clouse, this is amazing," said Lynnette. "I'm not a botanist, but even I can see that this is truly unique, what you've done here. Unprecedented. Am I right?"

"Yes," said Bo.

"Nothing like this exists on the market today," said Barrett.

"If I may ask," said Lynnette, "why isn't this on CNN?" Her laugh was friendly, wry. "Not that I'm not thrilled to have you on my show! But I'm just a health and wellness influencer. You're legit scientists doing groundbreaking work. Why are we just hearing about this?"

"Because they wouldn't believe it," said Bo, his voice a near-whisper.

"What was that, Dr. Howland?"

"We contacted a few networks," Barrett said. "They declined to do a segment on our innovation. You must understand, Ms. Moncada. We're two no-name science geeks running a tiny startup in California. We're a bit too—how to put it?—*fringe* for the mainstream media."

"I have a feeling that's going to change," said Lynnette. "I wish you every success with Plant Friends. I'm delighted that you've shared this with us today."

Lynnette turned to the camera. "Dr. Bo Howland and Barrett Clouse, everyone! And of course, Plant Friend Number 102!" She applauded again, her shiny nails flashing, and the nonexistent crowd cheered with her.

"We're almost finished with today's episode of All Well and Good," she continued. "Don't forget to like and subscribe for more Wellness Wisdom That Can Change Your Life! But I have one more question for our remarkable guests. When will Plant Friends be for sale?"

"We've engaged three independent growers," said Barrett, "and we expect to have product on the market in about two months."

"We'll look forward to it!" said Lynnette. The show's outro music swelled.

"Two months. Ha!" said Devora into April's ear.

April jumped. She had become so absorbed in the program that she'd forgotten she was on the phone. "What do you mean, *ha*?"

"Two months and one day," said Devora, "until people start using those plants for porn."

"Devora! That's disgusting."

"Tell me I'm wrong." Devora giggled wickedly. "You can't, can you?"

April sighed.

Through the phone came the muffled buzz of an apartment doorbell. "There's my date," Devora said. "I hope you find something good to watch! Maybe Nat Geo?"

April groaned. "I've had enough nature for one night. Have fun."

She hung up, set the phone aside, and looked down at her arms. Her left forefinger slowly traced a winding route around her right forearm. The hairs stood erect as they responded to the touch.

"Sorry I'm late," said Bo, lowering his skinny behind into an office chair. "Traffic."

"Not a problem," said Barrett, who was standing restlessly, as if he'd been pacing. He'd been very specific about meeting Bo in the lab's smallest conference room, the dungeon-like room off the centre hallway, the one that had no windows.

"So, what's the big news?" asked Bo. Beneath the table, his clasped hands fidgeted. "It's too early for our first-quarter sales report, isn't it?"

Barrett crossed to the door and closed it firmly.

"Bo," he said, "we've had an incident."

Bo's large eyes regarded Barrett with no indication of understanding. "What do you mean? Some problem at the growers?"

"No."

"A customer complaint?"

"It's a bit worse than that," said Barrett. He sat next to Bo and rubbed his temples. "The LAPD contacted me at 9:30 this morning."

"What? Why?"

"Are you familiar with State Senator Hoyt Kirkwood?"

"No."

"He represents the 44th district," said Barrett. "Blond guy, average height, thick neck, skin that's seen one too many suntans. Ring any bells?"

"Not really."

"He was one of the first in line at our grand opening two months ago," said Barrett. "Talked a big game about how he was getting a Plant Friend for his wife. To keep her company while he was off in Sacramento."

"Oh yeah, I remember him, I think."

"Well, this morning, he turned up dead."

"What!"

"And guess what was sitting right next to him?"

Bo swallowed. "I'm guessing it wasn't his wife?"

"It was not."

"Dear God," said Bo. "Don't tell me..."

"Whatever you're thinking," said Barrett, "it's worse."

Bo closed his eyes and dropped his face into his hands.

"We'll find out more in an hour when we go down to the station," said Barrett.

Bo looked up sharply. "Are they going to arrest us?" His voice had climbed an octave.

"I don't think so," said Barrett. "They would've come here for that. And our liability waiver is pretty watertight. Still, we'd better play it safe. Tell them only the minimum."

"We can't get arrested, Barrett!"

"They just want to talk to us."

"If we get arrested," said Bo, near tears, "who will take care of the plants?"

April paused at the bookstore's entrance, checking her reflection in the glass display windows. She smoothed her dark hair, tucked it behind her ears, changed her mind, and pulled it loose again to frame her face. She took a deep breath and pushed the door open.

She already knew Thanh was working that morning, having peeked through the window. But it was still a thrill to see him close up. April joined the café line and tried not to stare. His forearms flexed below the short sleeves of his white, collared shirt while he tamped down espresso and frothed milk. Thanh appeared to be training a new barista, a chubby young Black man who looked no more than seventeen.

Six minutes later, Thanh set a paper cup on the pickup counter. "Grande oat milk latte with a shot of hazelnut," he said, "for April."

April stepped forward, reached for the drink, and smiled. "Thanks," she said.

"No problem," he said, making eye contact.

April's heart skipped a beat. "You remembered my hazelnut, right?" she said, still smiling.

"I always remember," he said, lifting his chin just a bit, narrowing his eyes just a smidge.

"Do you?"

"Always."

"You're good," she said.

"I'm excellent."

"So am I," she said, "now that I've got my caffeinated beverage, made by my excellent barista."

"Glad to hear it." Was that a smile tugging at one corner of Thanh's mouth? April felt her cheeks flush and tried not to think about how it was the longest he'd ever looked at her.

A violent hissing sound and a thick cloud of steam seethed out of one of the large countertop espresso machines. Thanh turned and raced over to where the poor new guy was desperately poking at the machine as if trying to find an undo button. "Sorry, bud," Thanh was saying. "I forgot to tell you that steam wand's busted..."

April sighed and glanced at the wall clock. Her train was leaving in ten minutes. With a last look at Thanh and his panicked trainee, she walked out of the store and crossed the street to the station.

On the train, April climbed the narrow stairs to the upper deck and took a seat. She sipped her latte, which contained exactly the right amount of hazelnut syrup, and opened her phone.

For weeks, she'd had the same tab open on her web browser, to the same page, with the same item in the cart.

The product photos were sharp and bright, depicting the Plant Friend's deep-green trunk and thick, aloe-like leaves. The price was high, but not so terrible, April told herself, when you thought about how much it cost to adopt and take care of a dog. Never mind moving to a building that allowed dogs.

Her finger hovered, hesitated one last time, and clicked the green button: SCHEDULE PICKUP.

The squat, steely-eyed brunette extended a hand. "Detective Jeanine Shanahan," she said, gripping Barrett's and Bo's hands in turn. "Thank you for coming." Her greying hair was pulled back as if it were being forcibly taken into custody. Though she looked fortyish, the skin around her eyes was completely smooth, like she'd forgotten how to smile sometime in the late nineties.

She led them down a beige hallway into a small room with

a single table. Fluorescent lights shuddered to life like a vampire waking at dusk.

Shanahan did not invite the men to sit, but she plunked herself down so authoritatively that they meekly followed suit. She flipped open a laptop and tapped at the keyboard.

"Gentlemen," she said, "these photos are not pretty. I'm showing them to you in the interest of this investigation, so that you can see what we're dealing with and be prepared to answer questions."

Bo and Barrett glanced at each other.

Shanahan turned the laptop to face them.

Bo gasped, pulled back, and covered his mouth with his hands.

The man in the photo might have had sun-kissed California skin once. His blond buzz cut now contrasted obscenely with his purplish-blue face. He was naked, lying on his back on an unmade bed. A pornographic magazine lay open next to him, and a half-empty bottle of gin sat uncapped on the nightstand. One of the man's hands was between his legs. His other hand, as well as his neck, was wrapped tightly in the green, white-freckled leaves of the Plant Friend rising from the pot next to the bed.

"Erotic asphyxiation," said Shanahan, in the tone of voice a waitress might use to rattle off side dishes. "Not uncommon. Kills 500 people a year in the United States alone. Loss of consciousness leads to a loss of control over the mechanism used to achieve the asphyxia."

Bo cringed.

"Here's a close-up of the neck," said Shanahan, clicking open a new photo.

Barrett stared, eyes wide. Bo turned his head as if he'd been slapped. "No," he said. "No, no, no." His eyes were squeezed shut, his hands clasped over his nose and mouth as if in prayer.

"The ICD-10 code on this death," said Shanahan, "was T71.19. Asphyxiation due to mechanical threat to breathing. However, we're having trouble coming up with a subclassification. See, there's one for when it's accidental, one for intentional self-harm, and one for assault." She narrowed her eyes. "Any comments on that, gentlemen?"

Bo opened his eyes, saw that Shanahan had turned the laptop away, and let out a breath.

"Well, obviously, it's accidental," said Barrett. "Or maybe self-harm. But it can't be assault. A plant can't assault someone."

"No?" said Shanahan. "A beetle caught by a Venus flytrap might beg to differ."

"Plant Friends are not carnivorous," Bo broke in. "They were bred to be gentle, loving companions."

"Loving?" said Shanahan with a smirk.

Bo fidgeted. "Okay, maybe that was a bad way to say it, given the, um, circumstances. But nobody should be using a Plant Friend in this way. It's horrible. It's beastly—"

"I'm not sure what information you're after, Detective," Barrett interjected, "but the plant's expected behaviour is to curl its leaves when touched in specific ways. So, in this unfortunate case, it was working as designed, so to speak."

"Working as designed," Shanahan said.

"Correct. We instruct all customers in its use when they purchase a Plant Friend. That's why we don't ship. We place high importance on in-person training on how to handle the plants' unusual abilities."

"And no one at your organization foresaw harm from improper use?"

"The plant has a release mechanism," said Barrett,

"although obviously Senator Kirkwood, er, wasn't able to use it. But it's all covered by our liability waiver."

"I'd like a copy of that."

"No problem," said Barrett. "I'll have our lawyer send it over."

"See that you do." Shanahan produced a business card from the pocket of her khaki pants. "Today."

"Detective," murmured Bo, "are the police giving a statement to the press about this—accident?"

"Not at this time," said Shanahan, "but it's not up to us whether the press hears about this."

"Who is it up to?"

Shanahan arched an eyebrow at Bo. "The widow."

As soon as the car doors closed, Bo's emotions boiled over.

"This is horrible," he shouted. "How dare someone use our babies for their filthy fetishes! They're supposed to be pets. Not prostitutes!"

"Kirkwood might not be the last," muttered Barrett.

"Do the investors know?"

"I'll give them a heads-up," sighed Barrett, "right after I call our lawyer."

"Barry, what are we going to do if this gets out in the press?" Bo's hands wrung.

"Believe me," said Barrett, "I'm as concerned as you are. I've got a lot of capital tied up in this." He rubbed his temples. "But I think we should lay low for now. Not make a statement."

"Really? Why?"

"You know what they say," said Barrett. "There's no such thing as bad publicity."

"Barry, if anything is the exception to that rule, it's a man dying by erotic asphyxiation with our product wrapped around his neck!"

"Frankly, Bo," said Barrett, "with what it's gonna cost to beef up our liability insurance, we could use a few hundred extra customers."

April tossed her coat onto a chair, flopped onto her couch, and sighed out the stress of three interminable meetings, two train commutes, and one micromanaging boss. She kicked off her high heels, extended one bare toe, and rubbed the lowest leaf of her Plant Friend, whose pot sat next to the couch.

The leaf wound itself around April's foot and gently squeezed. "Ahhh," sighed April, sinking into the cushions. "That's the stuff." She wiggled her toe against the leaf, and it squeezed again, massaging the soreness away.

She sat forward a bit and nudged an upper leaf with her elbow. It extended itself across her upper back and kneaded her shoulders. Grip and release, grip and release. "You're the best, Boo," April told it.

The people who sold April the plant had mentioned that it would adapt itself to her and might begin to anticipate her requests. A natural element of its design, they'd said. The mechanism, of course, was a trade secret, but the people in the online Plant Friend forums theorized that it had to do with plant estrogens.

April picked up a leaf and kissed it. "Boo," she said, "you were worth every penny."

She tucked her throw blanket around her legs and flipped on Disney Plus. A nice cartoon would be a way to forget the day.

The beginning of *Up* was cute and funny. Then came the

montage of Carl and Ellie's life together, ending in poignant loss and never-realized dreams. April watched, devastated, tears dripping onto her dress. A leaf snaked its way around her shoulders in a comforting embrace.

April's cell phone rang. Eyes glued to the TV, she fumbled with the device, saw an unknown number on the display, and rejected the call.

A minute later, the phone pinged with a text message.

Hey. I think you left something at the café this morning.

April sat bolt upright, seized the phone, and stared.

That morning, she had ordered her usual hazelnut latte, plus a breakfast sandwich, then lingered at a table in the bookstore's café. When Thanh left the counter with a spray bottle and a rag, April had stood to leave. Beneath her empty plate, she'd tucked her business card, on the back of which she'd written her cell phone number.

She paused the movie, found the number in her call history, and smashed the callback button.

He answered after the first ring. "Well, hello there, Hazelnut Latte."

"Hi."

"Can I call you Hazel?"

The plant stood at attention as April leaped from the couch and paced the living room, talking animatedly. Its leaves seemed to rise a bit taller, invigorated by the kinetic energy of her motion and laughter.

When April hung up the call, she immediately dialed again. "Devora! Guess who just called me!"

Still talking, April walked into the kitchen, disappearing around the doorframe. The plant's leaves drooped a bit, like the jowls of a bloodhound.

Bo rubbed potting soil off his hands and trotted into the small office in their rented laboratory space. He sat across from Barrett, slumped against the chair, and wiped his brow. "I planted twenty more seedlings this afternoon," he said. "If we don't find another grower soon, I'm going to need an intern!"

"Don't relax yet," said Barrett, who was shifting his attention between a laptop computer and papers scattered across the table. "Our second-quarter sales look to be triple what we saw in Q1."

Bo groaned happily. He picked up a printed graph. "I still can't believe this spike."

"That was the day Kirkwood's widow went on cable news," said Barrett.

"All publicity is good publicity!" said Bo. "So. What's the latest?"

"Arizona residents now comprise ten percent of our buyers," said Barrett. "And if we get many more customers driving up from Mexico, we'll need to offer our training in Spanish."

"Great," said Bo. "What else?"

Barrett opened a video on his laptop. "Apparently," he said, "we've caught the attention of Senator Nemeth, that fundamentalist from Idaho."

The pudgy white man standing behind the microphone had a face like a peeled potato. "Fellow Idahoans," he said, in a voice like expired sour cream, "do not be fooled by pretty ads. These so-called Plant Friends are abominations. The Bible is very clear on this matter. I'd call your attention to Matthew 15:13. 'Every plant that my heavenly Father has not planted will be rooted up.' Only God can create new plants, and Genesis states that plants shall be used for food, not companionship." He spat the last word like he'd found a worm in his apple. "Therefore, I've introduced Senate Bill 138 to ban the sale or possession of Plant Friends in our great state."

"But Senator," came the voice of an off-screen reporter. "'Only God can create new plants'? What does that mean for Monsanto's regional headquarters in Twin Falls?"

"That's all we have time for today," said Nemeth, slithering backward into a nest of handlers.

"Typical." Bo chuckled. "Should we be worried, though?"

Barrett snorted. "One whack job isn't going to keep me up at night." He opened another video. "The local ABC station did a segment on us today."

"It seems everyone is talking about Plant Friends," said the news anchor, a woman with short brown hair. "Sales are reportedly through the roof for this botanical phenomenon. But who's buying them? Probably your own friends and neighbours. ABC's Jim Bowman has the story."

"The whole family loves her," said an obese blond woman in a magenta tracksuit, sitting in an armchair next to her Plant Friend. "The kids play with her all the time, teaching her tricks and stuff. The dog didn't like her at first. But he got used to her once she started giving him belly rubs. She's become another member of our family."

"She?" asked Bowman. "Do these plants have genders?"

The woman shrugged. "She just seemed like a *she* to me. We call her Anthea." She turned to the plant, smiled, and rubbed a leaf. "Don't we, honey?" The leaf stroked the woman's hair, like a mother might do to a child.

The film cut to a thin, elderly Black man standing next to his Plant Friend and beaming. "My grandkids call her my girlfriend," he said, stroking her leaves, which twined themselves around his midsection, just above his belt.

"Did your grandkids put the wig on her, too?" asked Bowman. The plant's thick central trunk was topped with long, wavy, synthetic red hair.

"No, that was my idea!" The man chuckled. "I named her Poison Ivy! After my favourite DC Comics villain. She's not just beautiful, you know. Ivy's very smart. I have osteoarthritis, and every morning she rubs my legs and hands for me. I don't even ask her anymore. She just knows exactly what I need."

"A friend, indeed," said Bowman, turning to face the camera. "Back to you, Claire."

Barrett stopped the video. "The r/PlantFriend subreddit now has over 36,000 members. And we just passed 100,000 Instagram posts with the #PlantFriend hashtag."

Bo smiled. "I was so stressed after the whole Senator Kirkwood debacle," he said. "What a relief to have so much good news!" A second later, he frowned. "Barrett," he said, pointing, "what's that?"

The web browser was still open to the ABC News site, which had just refreshed. The video now at the top was headlined FIREBOMB ATTACK AT PLANT NURSERY.

Barrett gulped and pressed play.

An aerial shot showed a building surrounded by greenhouses. Two of the greenhouses were on fire, flames licking the interior, smoke surging upward, a grey smear across blue sky.

"Oh my God," said Bo. "Is that—"

"Synthesis," said Barrett. "The startup grower that produces 60% of our product."

"We have an update on this developing story," said the newscaster, a Hispanic woman in a blue dress and matching eye shadow. "Police took a suspect into custody about half a mile from Synthesis Growers. Our team captured this video of the arrest."

The video was jerky, as if the camera operator was running or jostling for position with other news crews. It showed a woman with greying blond hair, struggling and shouting, her body pressed against a red Ford sedan as police officers cuffed her hands behind her back.

"Did you see that, Sam Calabrese?" the woman hollered. "That's what I think of you and your disgusting perversions! A little preview of what it's gonna be like to BURN IN HELL!"

She looked around wildly, then faced the camera. "You. Come over here with that camera. I want everyone to hear about how MY HUSBAND, SAM CALABRESE, left me for his PLANT FRIEND!"

"Fuck," muttered Barrett.

"It was just a house plant, he said." The woman resisted three officers' efforts to shift her toward the open back door of a police car. "Just massages, he said. Then he was on the couch next to it every night, oh, whoops, honey, guess I fell asleep watching TV again, he said. Then it was in our bedroom. And that's where I caught them red-handed!"

The officers pushed on the woman's head and shoved her into the squad car.

"HE NAMED IT PETUNIA!" the woman screamed, angry tears streaking her flushed face as the door slammed.

"Police say the suspect is Britta Calabrese, age 46, of Lancaster, in North Los Angeles County," said the newscaster. "Prosecutors are expected to pursue charges of malicious arson..."

"Turn it off," interrupted Bo. "Those poor babies. I can't watch them burn."

The plant perked up, displaying its leaves proudly, as April entered her apartment.

A second person entered after April. The plant twitched slightly, as if surprised.

"So," said April, "this is my place!"

"Cozy," said Thanh. "I like all the plants. What's that big one next to the couch?"

"A Plant Friend."

"Really? I've heard of those."

"It's pretty cool." April shrugged. "So, you still up for watching *World War Z*?"

"Definitely."

"You're not gonna get scared, are you?" She winked.

"If I do, will you hold me 'til I feel better?"

April laughed and headed for the kitchen. "I'll get us popcorn and drinks."

"I'll help you." Thanh followed her in.

As zombies ran amok through the streets of Philadelphia, Thanh and April scooted closer together on the sofa. When Brad Pitt and his family fled in a stolen car, April and Thanh's fingers interlaced. April looked up at her date and smiled, acutely aware of the warmth of his fingers, of how close their faces were. "Hi, Boo," she said.

The plant's leaves trembled like a disturbed hornet's nest about to spill forth its stinging contents.

A few minutes later, the movie watchers were no longer watching, due to the fact that their lips had locked and their eyes had closed.

As they leaned together against the arm of the couch, a

strand of Thanh's hair brushed against the plant's longest leaf. It wound itself tightly through the hair on top of his head.

"Ow!" shouted Thanh. "What the—"

"Omigod," said April. "Hang on, I'll release it—"

Thanh tried unsuccessfully to pull the leaf free of his hair. His hand knocked a second leaf, which sealed itself around his wrist like a handcuff.

"Oh, no!" April scrambled to her feet. The leaf around Thanh's wrist was wrapped so completely that its tip wasn't visible. She reached for the leaf that held his hair, but his flailing arms blocked her access. His foot lashed out, knocking yet another leaf, which wrapped itself around his ankle.

"Hold still," April pleaded. "So I can make it release."

"What?" Thanh's hand was turning an alarming shade of red. With his free hand, he seized and yanked the leaf that had wrapped his wrist. The leaf snapped clean off the trunk, oozing a gelatinous liquid from the wound. The amputated leaf released Thanh's wrist, fell, and bounced underneath the couch. Another leaf snaked itself around Thanh's other wrist.

"No!" April managed to whack the tip of the leaf that held Thanh's hair. Though she was well practiced at the release mechanism by now, she had to hit it several times before it let go. A fourth leaf snaked itself around Thanh's other foot.

Thanh watched, wide-eyed, as April fought to release the leaves that had seized him. Like the first, the other leaves obeyed only after several blows, as if grudgingly. "What is wrong with you?" April shouted at the plant.

Finally freed, Thanh leaped away from the couch, rubbing his wrists. He eyed the Plant Friend suspiciously. "That thing grabbed me," he said.

"It was an accident," said April. "It didn't mean to. When you rub it, it—"

"I know how they work," Thanh said. "Or at least how they're supposed to work. Two of those leaves, I never touched at all."

April gulped. "I'm so sorry, Thanh. I don't know why—"

"I'm out of here," he said, grabbing his jacket.

"No, don't go!" April hurried after him, but the apartment door closed in her face.

She whirled and stormed back across the room. "Bad Plant Friend! You ruined my date!"

A leaf extended, trying to wrap itself comfortingly around April's shoulders. She shoved it away, stalked off to her bedroom, and shut the door.

The broken leaf wept pinkish ooze onto the wall-to-wall carpet.

Bo was heading for the greenhouse, but when he saw the look on Barrett's face, he walked into the office and set the potted seedling on the table. "Another call?"

Barrett hung up the phone. "Ninth one this week," he said, rubbing his temples. "The usual. Kill yourselves, you fucking perverts, I hope they gang-rape you in prison, yadda yadda."

"But why are they suddenly calling us?"

"I keep forgetting this is your first gig outside academia." Barrett sighed. "It's an organized campaign by chicken-shit assholes with nothing better to do."

"What do they want?"

"To intimidate us," said Barrett. "Normally, I'd say fuck 'em. But our third investor dropped us today."

"That's bad, right?"

"Very bad."

"I suppose they heard about the accident," said Bo. "I do feel bad for that woman and the fingers she lost. But it's a clear violation of the agreement to go to sleep with the Plant Friend still wrapped around—"

"One more like that, and it won't matter, Bo." Barrett shook four ibuprofen from a jar and swallowed them dry. "Our insurer will drop us like a drunk off a cliff."

"Barry," said Bo. "I hate to tell you this..."

Barrett closed his eyes and sighed.

"There's a porn star using a Plant Friend in her, uh, act."

Barrett dropped his head onto his folded arms.

"I wasn't going to mention it," said Bo. "But she's been the most popular creator on OnlyFans for two weeks running."

Barrett stood up and grabbed his car key off the desk. "Come on. We need to get to the bank. They want to have a chat with us about our loan. I hope to God they haven't heard about the, ahem, movies."

As they left the lab and turned toward the parking lot, there it was, in big, red, spray-painted letters on the side of the building.

PLANT FUCKERS

"Ready to go?"

"Just grabbing my purse," April replied.

She looked at her bedroom mirror, tucked her hair behind her ears, shook it loose again, and took a deep breath. They were going out to lunch, and Thanh's brother and sister would be there. It wasn't quite meeting the parents, but it was enough to twist her stomach into knots.

"Which one of your siblings has the twins again?" April asked Thanh, who had just walked into the bedroom.

"My sister."

"And she's the oldest?"

"No, that's my brother."

"Damn." She chewed her nail, then pulled it away so as to not chip the polish.

Thanh came up behind April and rubbed her shoulders. She relaxed at his touch.

"Don't worry," he said. "They're gonna love you."

April turned, smiled, and pulled him in for a kiss.

They walked out together through the living room, past the empty spot next to the couch where the Plant Friend used to be.

The leaf that Thanh had broken off weeks before lay underneath the couch in a bed of dust, which stirred as April walked past. Though the leaf was a shrivelled husk of its former succulence, its tip twitched toward April as she and Thanh strolled, arm in arm, out the door.

After all the crazy stories in the news, April hadn't even tried to sell or return the plant. Instead, late one night, she had walked with a shovel to the park behind her apartment building, dug a hole between two coffeeberry bushes, and planted it. "I'll visit you, buddy," she said, wiping her hands on her jeans to get rid of the dirt. Its leaves had seemed to wilt as she walked away.

Bo was in the greenhouse, adding fertilizer to seedlings, when the rag-stoppered bottle broke through the window, hit the floor, and shattered into a burst of flame.

Bo yelped and backed away from the blaze. He spun toward the window in time to see a man in a black ski mask running away from the building.

He spun again at the second crash behind him. Flames from the second Molotov cocktail licked up the side of a wooden cart.

Bo sprinted across the room, seized the white pot stenciled with the number 102, and ran for the hallway. "Barry!"

Barrett poked his head out of the office. His eyes were sunken, his hair dishevelled. He looked past Bo at the flaming greenhouse, where two men in black ski masks had entered through the broken windows and were whooping triumphantly.

"Who the fuck are those guys?"

"I don't know!"

One of the men in black approached a row of mature plants. He took out a switchblade. "Hey, Glen," he called to his buddy. "I heard about this online. You open up a little glory hole, and they're real juicy inside…"

Two plants' leaves whipped forward and smacked the man's arm. The weapon clattered to the floor.

"Whoa," said the knife's owner. "Glen, did you see—"

But Glen was pointing at Bo and Barrett. "There they are!"

Barrett turned and sprinted for the front door. Bo, still clutching 102, clambered after him.

As they sped away in Barrett's car, Bo stroked the plant's leaves and murmured to it. Barrett looked in the rearview mirror at their laboratory, consumed by flame, smoke licking at the sky, and at the two black-clad men, who hopped into a pickup truck to pursue them.

Barrett yanked the steering wheel, jerking the car through alleys and cutting across neighbourhoods until finally, the assailants' truck could no longer be seen. He slowed the car and parked near a beach.

Bo and Barrett walked to a bench, sat, and slumped like

deflated balloons, staring at the setting sun and the orange sky.

"Well, Bo," said Barrett, "I guess that's it."

"Did you see 102's children?" said Bo. "Knocking the weapon out of that asshole's hand?"

"I did."

"Heroes." Bo sniffed and wiped his eyes.

"Truly."

"I'm so sorry, Barry," said Bo.

"For what?"

"All that money…"

"Well," said Barrett, "easy come, easy go."

"Do we have anything left?"

Barrett groped in his jacket pocket and retrieved a lighter and a single joint.

For a few minutes, they passed the joint back and forth in silence.

"You know, Bo," said Barrett, "we could still work together."

"We could?"

"I have an idea," said Barrett. "It's a lucrative line of business. It's legal in California. And it could use a good botanist to get it going."

"What's that?"

Barrett pointed to the joint. Bo smiled.

"What'll we call the new business?" asked Bo. He giggled. "The Roach Motel?"

"Something that says science, but also lightness and tranquility," said Barrett. "Herb-LT."

"Perfect," said Bo. "Let's text Lynnette. I bet she'll have us back on."

The two old friends shook hands.

Bo patted the earth around 102, now transplanted into his small backyard.

"You're going to live here now," he told the plant, "where no bad people can hurt you. And I'll come and see you every day." It curled a leaf around each of his hands and gently squeezed as if it understood.

The house backed onto a park, where, between two coffeeberry bushes, grew a plant very similar to 102. Its leaves waved in the breeze, and its roots outstretched, tunnelling through the soil toward Bo's backyard. And soon, underground, in the cool secret earth, the mother and daughter's roots twined together in a perennial embrace.

The Koi Pond*

Josephine Queen

There was something Thea had forgotten. Something vital. But she put it aside for the moment and stared at the painting. Vivid green leaves crowded together on the concrete strut in front of her, intricate graffiti standing at least ten metres high. There were more struts beyond this one, more paintings, each one as gorgeous as the next, but this one had captured Thea's attention. Felix leaned against her, his head tilted back to see to the top of the painting. His weight against her legs warmed her, even in the shadowed enclave beneath the highway bridge.

"Can you see the faces, Mum?" His voice echoed.

Thea shook her head. "I don't. I just see leaves. Lots and lots of leaves. But no faces, love."

"They look like the quiet screaming ladies," he said.

The quiet screaming ladies. Felix talked about them all the time. He wasn't supposed to go beyond the tall grass behind their house. Owen said there was a deep and stagnant pond back there, one that would suck a small boy down into its black depths without hesitation. But the thought of adventure was enough to make Felix risk defying his father. He'd snuck back once when Owen was on double-shift and came back pale and quiet. Later, when Thea tucked him into bed, he had told her about the big goldfish that lived in the pond and the women who gathered around it, wide mouths screaming silently at him. He'd always had a big imagination.

She looked down at her son now, his face half in the sunlight seeping through the gap between the lanes on the bridge above, half in shadow.

"You have to do your face like this." He squinted his eyes so that his smooth brown face crinkled.

Thea turned back to the graffiti and copied Felix, her own face feeling tight and dry as she narrowed her eyes. At first, all she could see were the leaves spanning the width and height of the concrete strut. They were painted an astonishing green, the sunlight drifting through from the gap above, highlighting the colours, dipping the shadows between the leaves into blackness. Ferns, she thought, or rubber plants. Huge anyway. Something about the painting made her stomach churn. Maybe it was the size of the leaves.

"Jurassic plants," Felix said as if guessing her thoughts. "Can you see the faces yet? They're in between." His cheeks were flushed from their walk from the hotel.

Thea tried again. She had a bitter taste in her mouth, and the beginnings of a headache throbbed at her temples. She narrowed her eyes further, and the world blurred out of focus. Where just a few seconds before, there had been only leaves, faces emerged from the concrete. Dead faces hiding among the leaves. Glassy eyes, wide mouths, grey skin. Thea gasped and stepped back, almost losing her footing on the sloped ground.

"You see them." Felix sounded triumphant. "See, I told you."

Thea took a step forward and raised her hand to the graffitied art, mesmerized by the eyes that seemed to look back at her, pleading with her. Her fingers grazed the surface, feeling paint and concrete, but something else too. The surface seemed to pulsate. Feverish heat radiated into her fingertips, and she pulled them back. Tears pricked at her eyes. She closed them. The faces looked familiar. When Thea opened her eyes again, the faces were gone, leaving the plants still and cold once more. She shook her head and smiled shakily down at Felix.

"So," she said. "Which one's your favourite?"

"Which...face?" He frowned.

"No, no, which painting?"

Thea glanced around at the other graffiti-covered struts, hoping the image of the dead faces would dissipate. She thought, perhaps, that it had been her imagination, an optical illusion brought on by the light-headedness she'd been feeling all morning. Thea loved this place; even the name of it inspired her—The Upside Gallery. But then, she loved Bournemouth. It was the last place she remembered being something close to happy.

The last time they were here, she'd been close to bursting with news she hadn't been quite ready to share. And it was as if Owen had been affected by her good mood. He'd been almost playful, paddling in the sea, feeding pennies into the arcade machines, downing pints and fish and chips. It was only once they were home the darkness descended on him again. Thea tried not to read too much into the contrast between Owen's sour mood after returning from Bournemouth and his buoyant mood whenever he returned from one of his solo trips. She didn't like to think too hard on things; it only invited trouble. And she had to admit she enjoyed the few days of calm that followed whenever he came home from one of those excursions. Thea didn't know where he went or what he did—she never asked—but she assumed there was another woman. Maybe other women. But if it offered her a reprieve each month, she'd take it. Coming back to Bournemouth was like a balm for her soul, a return to paradise, even if just for a weekend. She couldn't recall who'd suggested the trip, but it was just what she needed.

"I think," said Felix, that frown still troubling his forehead. "I like the fly the best."

Thea followed his gaze. Another strut, further into the shadows, showed a gigantic green-bottle, its diaphanous wings at rest, the painted wallpaper it rested on seemed to peel away from the top of the column. "Yes," she said. "It's amazing, isn't it?"

They stood looking at it for a moment. The shadows deepened, and Thea had the feeling that the faces were watching her from the leaves. "Shall we go to the beach?" She turned away from the graffiti. Felix nodded. All thoughts of flies and silent screaming faces forgotten. Together they headed back to the path.

The signpost beside the path pointed toward the beach in one direction—Thea knew that way trailed through the gardens beside coffee shops and ice cream stands—and the other direction took them to the upper gardens, a quieter walk away from the crowds of tourists. Below those two signs, there was a third one, looking as if it had been stuck on as an afterthought. "The Koi Pond" had been scrawled across a piece of cardboard in crayon...

...Before Felix sees the women screaming silently at him from beyond the weeds, Thea's standing in front of the fridge. She's forgotten why she's here; it's been happening a lot lately, so she stares

at the refrigerator door. There's a photo beneath a magnet. Sun glinting off graffiti scrawled across the concrete struts of a bridge. The Upside Gallery. They went to Bournemouth a few days after she found out she was pregnant with Felix—weeks before she told Owen. She yearns to go back there. To take her boy and show him how beautiful the world is outside their confines.

A scream pulls her from her reverie, and she rushes to the window. It's Felix. His face contorted with pain. He's running toward the house, holding one hand in the other.

"It bit me," he cries.

She sits him on the edge of the kitchen table and pries the hand he's favouring away from his body. Splinters cover his palm. He must have grabbed one of the rough wooden posts of the swing set. He protests when he sees the tweezers.

"Once upon a time," she says because she knows the power of stories. Felix's sobs dissolve into sniffles. "There was a prince who lived in a lonely castle in the middle of the enchanted woods."

"Is it me?" asks Felix.

Thea smiles. She leans close to his palm and starts extracting the splinters. She feels him flinch. "The prince desperately wanted some friends."

"It is me," he whispers.

Thea closes her eyes briefly. She wants to tell him she's sorry, but as she's learned from Owen, 'sorry' doesn't mean shit.

"He would do anything to find some friends, so one day, he took a walk into the woods to the witch's cottage."

"Witch? Is she scary?"

"Of course not." Thea pulls another splinter from Felix's hand. "She welcomed him into her bright and sunny, very unscary cottage. She made him a big mug of hot chocolate and sweet scones with butter and jam. She sat across from him and asked him, 'What can I do for you, little boy?'"

Felix laughs at her croaky voice.

"The prince told the witch he had no friends, and he was so very lonely in the castle."

Felix nods sagely. Thea's almost done pulling out the splinters. There's just one more left, but it's deep, and the skin around it is an angry red.

"'I've got just the thing,' the witch said. She gave him a small bag. 'This is magic powder. Sprinkle it on anything and it'll turn into a friend.'

'Really?' asked the prince."

"That's so cool," says Felix.

Thea nods. If only it was that easy, she thinks. "The prince wondered where he should go with his bag of magic powder. There weren't a lot of places in the forest where living things banded together, and he wanted more than just a friend or two. He decided to go to his father's fish pond..."

Felix perks up. "What kind of fish?"

"Goldfish," says Thea. "No, koi."

"Koi?"

"Like goldfish, only bigger. And they have whiskers. They're friendly, like puppies."

"Like water puppies." Felix smiles. His cheeks are streaked with the salt of his tears, but at least they've dried up.

"He sprinkled the powder onto the fish, and they jumped out of the pond. They all ran to hug the prince."

"So now he's got friends?"

"Yep. And you're all done. No more splinters."

Felix holds his hand in front of his face, so close his eyes cross. "Wow."

Shards of sunlight pierce through the slats in the blinds at the kitchen window, and dust motes drift lazily through the light. Felix waves his hand through the beams. "Mum, look. Magic powder." He giggles, and the sound goes right into Thea's heart and nestles there. She wants to gather him up and run. But where can they go?

...Thea felt Felix tugging at her hand, snapping her out of the daydream. "Mum, look. There's a koi pond, like the one you told me about in the story today. Let's go see it." He pointed at the third sign, raising his eyebrows at Thea. "Can we?"

Thea's stomach churned again, her mouth watered, and acid bubbled up from her gut. She winced at the taste in her throat and closed her eyes against the nausea. It wouldn't do for her son to see her get sick. Once the feeling passed, Thea thought about what Felix had just said and frowned. He was confused; she hadn't told him the story today. It was a distant memory, but then, why was it so clear? And she didn't remember a koi pond from when they'd come to Bournemouth before. She'd spent a lot of time alone, walking through the gardens, reflecting in The Upside Gallery. That had been before Felix.

Before the darkness fully engulfed her husband.

She swallowed, trying to rid her mouth of the bitterness. Her head thumped and pounded. She closed her eyes again and felt Felix's fingers graze her own. She opened her eyes and attempted a smile. "I thought you wanted to go to the beach," she said.

"But it's late."

Thea looked up at the sky, the clouds edged in purple and the sun drifting toward the horizon. How could that be? They'd left the hotel less than an hour ago, right after breakfast. Thea thought of the toast they'd eaten in the room. The tea Owen had made for them. It had been so bitter. Had they left after breakfast? She couldn't recall the walk from the hotel. She rubbed at her temples. And where was Owen? Thea couldn't remember the last time she'd been alone with Felix away from their house. Owen always insisted on being with them. She wasn't allowed to leave home while he was working, and Felix was consigned to the four walls of the house or the tame patch of grass at the back where his dilapidated swing set stood. But they were on vacation, so maybe things were different, and Owen's rules were not as rigid.

Thea glanced in the direction of the beach, yearning for the company of other people, of children laughing and running through the waves. Why did Felix want to see a pond? Surely the one beyond the weeds in their yard was enough to deter him? She looked at her son, smiling up at her, the gap where his missing tooth used to be, black in the darkening day.

"Sure," she acquiesced. "Let's go see the fish."

"Do you think they'll jump out and hug me?" asked Felix. "Maybe they want a friend?"

Thea put her hand on top of his head and gave him a watery smile. "Sure," she whispered.

The path wound through the gardens, following a narrow stream that trickled playfully along beside them. Thea made Felix pose beside a tree and lean against a graffitied wall as she snapped photos on her phone. But when she went to send them on to her mother—even though she knew the old woman would never respond—she saw her battery was dead. Or close to it. The screen juddered, and just before it winked out, Thea saw leaves with faint faces leering out from them. When had she taken a photo of the graffiti?

Owen always said she was forgetful; she could hear his voice in her head, "Your mind's like a fucking colander, you stupid cow." He was right. She'd been losing hold of more and more thoughts and memories recently.

The feeling that something important had slipped her mind persisted.

Thea thought of her mother. She'd know just what to give Thea to restore clear thinking. Holy basil, maybe, or turmeric. Her mother had known everything there was to know about the natural world. But they hadn't spoken in over seven years, since the day after Felix was born. And before that, the day Thea had brought Owen home to meet her for the first time.

"There's something vile and unnatural inside that man. He's not even a man. He's a demon." Her mother's brow had furrowed, and her eyes grew dark as she spoke.

Thea had stormed out and refused her mother's calls until she simply stopped trying. Then Felix was born, and Thea found she missed her mother's wisdom, her strong arms. But the old woman had told her, in no uncertain terms, either she banished Owen from her and Felix's lives or they would never see each other again. Thea had felt as if she hadn't had a choice. And now her mother was out of her life.

Felix skipped along beside Thea, occasionally stopping to examine a stone or an insect. He returned to her side every time he found something worthy enough to show her.

The sky was growing dark quickly, but she didn't want to turn back yet. This time alone with Felix was more than she could have hoped for. Of course, she spent time with him at home, but there he was, always insular, turned inward as he escaped into his imagination. Here, he was a regular seven-year-old, running ahead, stomping in the puddles left over from the previous day's rainstorm. He turned occasionally and grinned at Thea. Her head throbbed. She tried to catch hold of the thoughts swirling inside. When had they come to Bournemouth? Try as she might, she couldn't picture them in the car together. She grimaced at the pain behind her eyes.

As the path took a sharp turn to the left, Thea lost sight of Felix for a few seconds and lost her breath. She quickened her steps and sighed with relief when she saw his small form stopped in the path ahead. She came to a halt right behind him, her heart racing. A woman stood motionless a few yards in front of Felix, her back turned toward them. Something about the way the woman just stood there, unmoving, unnerved Thea, and she placed both hands on Felix's shoulders. As she did so, the woman began walking away. Thea had a sudden need to see the woman's face. She wanted to shout at her, get her to turn around. But Thea stayed silent and waited for the woman to get further ahead of them and out of sight before she urged Felix to start walking again.

"Who was that, Mum?"

"I don't know, sweetie. Just someone else walking to the pond, I suppose." But her arms had broken out in gooseflesh, even as the day seemed to heat up and the air thickened with humidity. The sky had gone from twilight purple to a strange orange. Everything was tinted the same colour, giving Thea the odd feeling they were walking through an alien landscape. Even the plants that had edged the path so sedately for much of their walk now grew wild and untended. Thea recognized poison hemlock growing amongst the other weeds. She thought to warn Felix to stay away from it, but he grasped her hand suddenly and pushed his body against her in a way he hadn't since he was a toddler.

"Mummy, who's that?"

Thea followed his pointing finger. Two figures stood side by side, their backs to Thea and Felix, looking out across the unruly vegetation. Again, she had the urge to call out, to demand to see their faces. But she didn't trust her voice to stay steady. They looked unsuited to be together. One wore a black, hooded sweatshirt, and her jeans were ripped and stained with something resembling blood. Her dark hair draped down her back, and her body listed to one side as if one leg was shorter than the other. The other woman had blond hair tied in a neat chignon. She wore a light grey sweater and white linen pants. The pants and sweater were splashed with red streaks. Her arms dangled at her sides, and something dripped slowly from her fingertips. *Drip, drip, drip.* Suddenly, Thea didn't want to see their faces anymore.

She held tightly to Felix's hand and pulled him along the path. The women didn't turn to watch them go, but Thea knew they were aware of them. Listening. Knowing. She thought to turn and go back the way they had come, but that would mean passing the women again, and she had no desire to do that.

The vegetation was becoming thicker, covering the path, hiding their way forward. They had to step over stems and leaves.

"Jurassic plants," Felix whispered. "They look like the painting, Mummy."

A susurration drifted through the air around them as if a crowd of people were whispering to one another. Thea turned, risking a glance over her shoulder. A group of women, five or six, were following them. Their heads were down, hair hung in front of their faces. They moved between orange light and black shadow, giving the impression they were images on a stuttering screen. Thea tightened her grip on Felix's hand, pulling him along faster. The whispering got louder; footsteps shushed through the weeds. Thea began to run.

"Ow, Mummy!" But Felix ran along, his short legs pumping hard to keep up.

Faces loomed from the vegetation around them, now growing over their heads. Grey faces with blank, unseeing eyes. Thea's breath came short and sharp. She heard a keening, like the whistle of a kettle, then realized it was coming from her own throat. Her foot snagged on a vine caught taut across the narrowed trail, and she fell, face forward, into the leaves…

…and she lands in marshy ground, mud splashing into her mouth. She should have waited until morning, but seeing the terror in her son's eyes when he told her, at bedtime, about the silent, screaming ladies, she had to come out and see for herself. He wasn't supposed to go out there, but the story she'd told him had pushed him to go and explore. He thought there might be fish in the pond. And if there were fish in the pond, maybe the magic powder would work, and they'd be his friends. She tells herself her son just has a big imagination. That it has nothing to do with the girls that have gone missing over the last year or so. That there's nothing unusual about her husband's trips or the ecstatic mood he's in for days after he returns. She tells herself her husband forbids her and Felix to come back here because it's dangerous. The marsh she's lying in right now can attest to that.

She reaches for her flashlight and stands up. The ground squelches as it reluctantly releases her. No need to brush herself off; this outfit is ruined now. She steps carefully forward, through the overgrowth of weeds and cattails, of ferns and hemlock. She avoids the latter as best she can, knowing how toxic it is.

An owl calls in the distance, frogs chirp and croak, and night animals scurry through the vegetation. She has to breathe through her mouth; the stench back here is foul. She comes through the last of the weeds, and the newly risen moon lights up the night. The pond stretches on toward the trees, its surface fetid and covered in scum and pond weed.

She takes one more step and gasps as her foot breaks through something that she knows instantly is not swampy ground. She shines her flashlight down and freezes in terror. She feels hot liquid rushing down her leg, and her breath burns as she gasps for air.

A face. Glassy eyes, wide mouth, grey skin. Her foot went through the torso. Shreds of black fabric cling to the rib cage.

"Oh no. No no no no no no no no..." Her voice keens through the night...

...Thea cried out. She'd fallen amongst the weeds, those alien leaves a putrid green beneath the orange sky. She reached out a hand to push herself up but screamed again at the sickening heat pulsating outward from the plants. And the faces. They were embedded in the leaves, watching her with their milky eyes, their mouths open wide like mewling babies rooting for a breast.

"Mummy." Felix was pulling her hand with both of his. "Mummy, get up, Mummy, get up, Mummy, get up." His voice was a high-pitched squeal edging close to panic. Thea found her feet and stood. The plants wavered in the stillness, brushing against her legs, her arms, her stomach. Reaching for her face. Their mouths searching, searching. That feverish heat rising all around her. Sweat dripped down her back. A soft murmuration arose in the air—off-key voices calling to her. "Look, Thea. Look. Look. He did this..."

...he did this." She knows it. She can't turn away from it anymore. Earlier, she'd made her way back to the house beneath the moon, pushing her way, sobbing, through the weeds. She'd made one more trip out to the edge of the overgrowth, a pair of kitchen gloves and shears in her jeans pockets. She's back to the house before Owen comes home. She lies in bed that night, next to her husband, and stares sleeplessly at the ceiling. Faces stare back at her from the darkness. She has a choice.

Owen finds her muddy clothes and ruined sneakers in the laundry room the next morning when he goes to get his tackle box for an after-noon on the river. He walks into the kitchen and drops them on the floor at her feet. She's browning lamb for the shepherd's pie she plans on making for Owen's dinner. Felix looks up from his bowl of cereal and frowns. Owen stays silent and reaches for the kettle. He makes tea for Thea and Felix...

"...he did this," she whispered and covered her face with her hands. She remembered the stalks on the chopping board, the crushed white flowers of hemlock dusting the countertop. She remembered Owen brushing off his hands, then handing her the mug of tea. She could still taste the bitterness in the back of her throat. But that can't be right, can it? When did they come to Bournemouth?

"Mummy?" Felix wrapped his arms around her, burying his face in her side.

"We're home," she said, marvelling at the realization. "Home." As she said the word, the moon glinted off the surface of the pond, and the weeds swayed in the night breeze. The sky, just moments before a sickly orange, looked to Thea like a velvet throw of midnight blue draped over the world. The plants were just plants, and she and Felix lay in them by the side of the water. Her head pounded, and the night tipped, making her stomach turn.

She felt Felix's arms drop from her torso and she turned to look at him. Her precious little boy. Foam dotted his chin, and his eyes stared unseeingly at the constellations above. She turned to the other side and saw the girl's body she'd discovered half submerged in the mud, the remains of her black sweatshirt soaking up fetid water from the marshy ground. Thea could feel the world drifting away.

She'd been happy in Bournemouth, so that's where her mind had taken her in her final moments. She hoped Felix found the koi pond and the friends he'd yearned for so deeply.

Thea wondered where Owen's mind would take him. She managed a smile as she thought of the shepherd's pie she'd left him in the fridge. Of the heads of hemlock she'd snipped for that extra seasoning. She hoped the silent screaming ladies would be there to guide him.

A flicker passed just beyond her sight, and she turned to

see the silhouettes of ten—no, twelve—women standing at the edge of the pond. She wished Felix could see them now, no longer bloody and broken. Young girls, smooth-skinned and bright-eyed; women with smile lines etched around their mouths and grey hair tucked behind their ears.

They held out their hands and smiled as Thea joined their number.

An Invitation To The Grovener Mountain Resort

Lisa Fox

Annie stepped through the damp rot of the deserted indoor pool at the once-thriving Grovener Mountain Resort. The lone skeleton of a lawn chair sat in the shallow end like a confused carcass awaiting company in an empty tomb. A slick layer of moss coated the surface, nature's vomit trailing into the deep end, where it gathered in a murky cesspool filled with despair, rancid water, and various microscopic life forms. Ivy vines rose through cracks in the surface of the surrounding concrete and strangled the crumbling structure of the diving board, marking it. Claiming it. Graffiti screamed from every space not occupied by flora; colourful tags the legacy of urban explorers who dared venture where the well-to-do once dangled their smooth, pale legs.

"Hello?" Annie's voice fell dead in the open space.

The chill of spring morning rain teeming through the broken floor-to-ceiling windows skittered up Annie's spine. Showers streamed through various gaping openings in the fragmented roof. Dark clouds tinged the rolling hills beyond, brushed from a palate of grey. Annie wondered at the decrepit nature of the place, the mountain oasis where her grandmother found love in the days of her youth, where she'd left her heart in the bittersweet nostalgia of what once was. Now, the resort was nothing more than a graveyard of long-forgotten memories, overgrown with moss, weeds, and ivy.

Annie shuddered as her gaze skittered across the pool. The algae quivered, too, as if mimicking her.

Grandma had told her stories of childhood summers spent at Grovener Mountain. Swimming lessons in this same indoor pool that had succumbed to nature's sprawl. Roasting marshmallows in the open fields at night. Playing shuffleboard under the stars. And that most enchanted evening on the cusp of her eighteenth birthday, when Grandpa offered her his hand in the grand ballroom, and they waltzed. Grandma had always said they were so enamored with each other, it was as if the surrounding walls faded away and the other dancers dissipated, swirling around them like clouds. All they felt was the cool satin swish of her dress whispering about their legs and their heartbeats in perfect syncopation with the band's whimsical *Moonlight Serenade*. They'd danced all night, holding each other long after the music ended.

Grandpa died when Annie was six, not long after the Grovener Mountain Resort shuttered for good. And although Grandma led Annie's mother and father to believe that Grandpa's ashes were safely at rest in the engraved bronze urn on Grandma's mantle, Annie knew the truth. Though her recollection was a child's—like faded Polaroids protected under the yellowed cellophane of an old photo album—Annie remembered the one and only time she'd ever visited the resort with Grandma and, she supposed, with Grandpa too:

Grandma wiping her eyes as she beheld the hulking, sleeping buildings and the rolling emerald hills that cradled them.

A wisp of Grandpa's finer ashes lifted by the breeze, twirling in a magnificent eddy as they drifted toward the padlocked doors of the main lobby—his spirit dancing one last time.

Offering Grandma that little plastic yellow pail filled with pulverized gravel from outside the foundation of the hotel, a secret, special job. Grandma looking left and right as she scattered Grandpa's ashes and dumped the contents of Annie's pail into the empty urn.

Lily of the valley rising and blooming through each blade of grass upon which Grandpa's ashes fell, draping its eruption over the vast lawn outside the hotel.

Grandma whispering that Annie 'must not touch' the 'special flowers' no matter how beautiful or captivating they were.

Watching the resort sigh and settle into the surrounding greenery as they drove off, leaving the most important parts of Grandma's past to be nourished by nature.

Grandma had never again spoken of that day, and until Annie wandered the resort's ruins, sometimes she thought she'd dreamed it all.

Despite her losses, Grandma had kept both Grandpa and the Grovener alive through stories she'd shared so often that they had become family folklore. As she entered her teen years, Annie had grown tired of Grandma's tales, snapping her bubblegum, and rolling her eyes with each repeated event from *back in the day*. Like most kids, she lacked the appreciation for nostalgia that only comes with age. But once Annie went away to college, she looked forward to Grandma's weekly letters—to hearing about rotary club meetings and rhododendrons and the secret recipe for her famous Rye bread. Mostly, she appreciated how Grandma always seemed to link her present with her past. How she'd note that flowers outside her house reminded her of the intoxicating fragrance of early summer at the Grovener. Grandma's insistence that her bread rivaled that of the Grovener's award-winning baker;

with just one bite, Grandma could recall the crisp feel of the resort's table linens, the ringing of the dinner bell in the evening.

Once Annie graduated and settled into a job and an apartment, she moved as close as she could to her grandmother; partly to help with doctor's appointments but mostly to be near enough to have a random cup of tea at Grandma's table whenever she wanted, allowing the comfort of years to warm her even on the coldest days. Grandma had refused to relocate to Florida with Mom and Dad (*too far from the past*, she'd said); Annie chose to stay behind, too. She spoke to her grandmother every day.

Until the day Grandma vanished.

Two months had passed since that rainy Sunday night when Annie opened her apartment door to the flashing badge of a local police officer. They'd found Grandma's gold Mercury Grand Marquis empty and idling on the side of a quiet country road over a hundred and fifty miles from her house. *Is she senile?* the cop had asked. *Confused?* But Annie had replied a vehement 'no.' At eighty years old, Grandma was sharper than most people.

Which was how Annie found herself breathing in this moist, rank air in the overgrown greenhouse the Grovener Resort had become.

Around her, a quick breeze rattled the broken windows and whistled through the barren space, momentarily brushing the hovering overgrowth away. Ivy vines growing from the dilapidated roof stretched and swayed in celebration, dancing in the cooled air. Annie stopped to listen—was that a whisper of Grandma's favourite *Moonlight Serenade* caught in the wind that rustled the plant life? A phantom sound rooted in decades of memories shared so often they'd become real in Annie's imagination, though they were never her own. Annie shook her head. It couldn't have been anything more than the whistle of air through the surrounding trees or a lone coyote howling in the woods. Anything else would be... insane.

But not any more insane than a lone young woman trespassing around an abandoned indoor pool in a condemned resort in the middle of nowhere.

Annie reached into her pocket. Retrieving the most recent postcard sent from the Grovener Mountain Resort, Annie found it directly addressed to her with her name written in perfect, old-fashioned cursive and bearing yesterday's date stamp—May 2, 1998. On the front of the card, a blonde bombshell in a shimmering satin gown was pictured descending the Grand Ballroom stairs. The woman's face was obscured by the netted veil and large flowers on the chaplet hat that covered her ringed curls but based on the attire (Annie had done her research), Annie guessed the postcard was from the early 1940s.

It was the sixty-second card Annie had found left on her doormat as if they'd been hand-delivered. The first arrived the day after Grandma's disappearance, addressed to her grandmother, *Mrs. Carrie Robbins*, with a postmark from the *Grovener Mountain Post Office* with date stamps from over three decades past. Except for the most recent card sent to Annie, the anonymous sender addressed all the others to Grandma. But somehow, they appeared at Annie's doorstep, as if the sender knew Grandma was not at home.

Grandma never mentioned receiving any recent postcards from the Grovener, despite talking about the resort almost daily and *sending* hundreds out to friends and family during her vacations over the years. Annie had spotted no cards when she'd retrieved Grandma's mail before the disappearance, and Grandma had kept the ones she had from years past as sacred treasures in the old hope chest that resided at the foot of her bed.

Every day another postcard arrived, each with a different image from the resort in its heyday: bocce ball courts and horseshoe throwing, the opulent Main House with rolling mountains in the backdrop. This indoor pool, sparkling and filled with smiling bathers. An image of the resort was sketched on the front of the first printed piece, the paper like parchment. After that, each card became more modern, the most recent featuring guests with beehive hairdos of the 1960s and trailing off with the shag look of the 1970s.

Yet, aside from Grandma's name and address, nothing else appeared on the cards. Only the single card addressed to Annie bore any message, and even then, to an outside observer, it would seem innocent, at best. Cryptic at worst.

After receiving the first ten cards, Annie approached the police. They'd still been actively searching for Grandma, yet they dismissed the mail as nothing more than an odd coincidence, given the decades-old postmarks and the lack of any ominous notes or threats. Annie had returned to them after the next fifteen arrived, when the search for her grandmother grew colder by the day. It felt to Annie that the police considered her—and Grandma's disappearance—nothing more than a nuisance. Still, the Sherriff had humoured her by researching the source of the postmark. With a thin-lipped expression that read *case closed,* he informed her there was no post office at Grovener Mountain.

Two hundred miles separated Annie's home from the resort. None of the officers had heard of it, nor did they care to investigate. They also reminded Annie that women, particularly befuddled elderly women, who wandered off into the woods alone rarely came back alive.

'You should prepare for the worst,' they'd told Annie.

Mom and Dad, too, had given up hope of finding Grandma. They explained away the postcards as "some old mailing list" Grandma must've still been on and warned Annie not to read anything into them. *This kind of thing happens all the time,'* they'd said. *'Let the police do their jobs.'*

Her parents returned home to Florida after the first week of searching, but Annie wasn't willing to give up on Grandma.

She glanced at the card in her hands. Whether from Annie's tight grip, the humidity in the poolroom, or some other force, the edges had curled around the cursive writing, that written message piquing Annie's curiosity enough to bring her to this godforsaken place:

"Relive her most precious memories at the Grovener Mountain Resort!"

"Hello?" she called again. A crow fluttered inside, settling on the diving board's rusted railing. Through the carpet of vegetation growing from the cracks in the concrete slabs, Annie tiptoed toward the bird. It was the only living thing in the space besides the ubiquitous plants. A moldy coil of anchored rope, once a divider between the shallow and deep ends of the pool, curled like a dead snake in the corner. An old rotary phone, a tarnished silver teapot, someone's stained and ripped underwear briefs, and shattered vodka bottles all littered the floor—each had its own story, told only because it existed in this space, this *mausoleum*, that time seemed to have forgotten.

The crow regarded her with its beady eyes as she approached, its slick wings pulled back, gnarled feet dancing on the railing. It cocked its head, listening.

"What am I doing here?" Annie whispered to the crow but more to herself. It was time for Annie to leave. The post-cards to Grandma certainly were odd, and the invitation in hers odder; and despite the blatant ignorance of her local police and her parents' nonchalance, there had to be someone else who could help. County police? State police? The FBI? Perhaps a psychic medium. Walking toward the opening that once held a door, Annie imagined Grandma's likely response to the latter thought—*My granddaughter sent a fortune teller to find me?*—causing Annie to laugh out loud.

A residual echo of Annie's laughter reverberated all around, a clanging echo. The sound morphed into a booming chuckle. It rattled the broken windows; it raised waves in the sludgy waters of the pool's deep end before settling into the tinkling of a child's giggle, in time with fat raindrops that fell through the non-existent ceiling. A shudder ran over Annie's body and through her mind like a parade of baby spiders. She drew in a sharp breath, bit her lip, and stood still as an oak. Annie prayed that her thrumming heartbeat was contained enough within her chest to avoid amplification in this dilapidated room; this room she needed to escape, where her fear was as palpable as the moss-covered concrete upon which she stood.

The sensation of wet, prune-like fingers tickled the back of Annie's neck. "Who's there?" she croaked, her voice barely above a whisper. She thrust the postcard in front of her like a sword, spinning and turning until she found herself wrapped in cold perspiration. It felt as if someone had thrown a damp pool towel over her. Annie slipped, landing with a dull thud, and skittered closer to the pool. The lichen was like a carpet pulled from under her. She pushed herself up, retching as her hand sunk into the muck that consumed her, a moist mouth plagued with vegetative thrush.

Her cheeks heated; her mind dizzied. Cold steam rose from the surface of the pool in a cloud, and Annie's peripheral vision succumbed to a fuzzy haze.

The crow cawed. It shuddered; its chest feathers momentarily raised like a thousand hairs of gooseflesh before smoothing down. The bird spread its wings. They stretched wide... wider... until they grazed the broken walls on either side of the poolroom.

Annie blinked hard. She gagged at the rotten tang of mold that landed on her tongue, *or was it Rye seeds?* It pushed down her throat as the steam cloud engulfed her, the fog generating an impenetrable blindness. She coughed and sputtered. Yet when she opened her eyes, the mist had disappeared as if it had never been there at all. The giant bird, too, had vanished, and a man in a black tuxedo emerged from behind the diving board. His hair was slicked-back blonde. An old-fashioned moustache curled up over his grin.

"Dearest Annette, thank you for accepting my invitation." He gestured toward the postcard that Annie still gripped tight with both hands. It crawled with moss from her fall. "Welcome to Grovener Mountain. I am Charles Grovener, the proprietor of this resort."

Grovener bowed with exaggerated drama, the sleeves of his jacket slipping away from the white gloves on his hands. Sagging, purpling skin melted around his wrists. Annie clenched her jaw, trying not to gape.

"You sent the postcard," Annie said. She swallowed back the panic that rumbled through her gut.

"I sent *all* the postcards." A split-second sneer flashed across his smile as he sized her up—something like polite disdain for a request for ketchup on quiche or white shoes after Labor Day. "It took much convincing to bring your grandmother back to us. She ignored my letters for so long. The cost of postage these days..." Shaking his head, he tsked.

"So my grandma *is* here." Annie straightened, glancing left, then right, then left again, trying to ascertain where, in these ruins, Grovener could be keeping her.

"This is the only place she's ever wanted to be." Grovener smiled. "And your Grandpa Marvin has missed her so. There's nothing sadder than a man who's forced to waltz alone."

"Grandpa is dead. We—" Annie stopped herself. She'd told no one about that day with Grandma and wasn't about to start with this odd and creepy man. If that's what he was.

"Oh, I know what you and your grandmother did. I was watching from my quarters in the main hotel. Such a dutiful grandchild with your little yellow pail and shovel."

"But nobody was there," Annie said. The resort had been abandoned. Shut down and boarded up. Her mind swam, her thoughts floundering.

"Not by my estimates, my dear." He paused and steepled his gloved hands, his lips pulled back in a thin line. His tone was genteel, and he continued. "This resort is, has always been, very much alive! Never, ever abandoned by our esteemed guests. Your dear Grandma Carrie, your Grandpa Marvin—and now, yourself—have given this resort its magic white-glove touch for well over a century!"

Charles laughed, that same booming chuckle that had rattled through her bones only moments ago. Or a lifetime ago. Annie struggled to tell.

The weeds and vines, even the pool sludge, seemed to wriggle with his laughter as if in on some secret in-joke.

"What have you done with my grandmother? Where is she?"

"Your Grandma-ma is having the most *marvellous* stay." Red flashed across Grovener's eyes as the weeds coalesced and sidled up next to him, rubbing against his pant legs, cat-like. "Carrie was always a feisty one, even as a young girl. Things were rather... dull... here without her."

Annie felt herself swooning and dug her heels into the ground for stability. Vegetation pricked at her ankles; the rogue plants appeared to be sprouting, thorny leaves growing up to her knees. The vines wrapped around her legs and pulled her down—hard. Stinging nettles bit through her jeans as she knelt in front of Charles Grovener. He, too, grew taller, like an early-evening shadow hovering over her.

"We never leave those places from which we depart." With his gloved fingers, he snapped, the sound a thunderclap. Instantaneously, the rot fell away from the room.

Summer sunlight blared through intact and shining windows. White marble gleamed around the perimeter of the pool, which held clear, crisp water. A man in a poolside chair glanced from his newspaper and winked at her. "Hi, Annie Doll," he said.

Grandpa. Only Grandpa called her 'Annie Doll.'

Children sat at the edge of the pool, kicking their feet and splashing, and a woman in a rubber bathing cap swam by, her strokes cutting through the water with perfect precision. She turned her head, and Annie glimpsed the woman's face—the high cheekbones, the dimpled nose. Blue eyes she'd recognize anywhere. It was the young woman in the ballgown on Grovener's most recent postcard.

Grandma.

Annie reached out toward this vision of Grandma and Grandpa in their youth, the paper slipping from her hand. It floated, carried by some unseen breeze, where it hovered above the water's surface.

"Your grandparents always appreciated the workmanship —the intricate details—of our resort. Why, my father and I built the place with our own hands. Daddy always said to me, *Son, this resort is my legacy. As long as it lives, so I shall, too.* In fact, before I came to greet you, I left my father in the library, sipping his brandy, pondering his next move on the chess-board. Aside from tending his gardens—and as you can see, the plant life here is abundant—chess has always been his favourite pastime."

Grovener snapped again, and the postcard fell, landing in the pool full of algae-riddled muck. He gestured toward a decomposing body that bobbed in the black sludge of the deep end. Slugs slithered from its open mouth, twisted in a death rictus. Its face sagged, its rotted skin melting and dripping, melding as one with the decay in which it floated. "Guests such as your grandmother have always been—will always provide—the lifeblood of this resort."

Annie's mouth dried to cotton. That corpse... that thing... it couldn't be.

"Grandma?" she croaked.

Ivy slithered over Annie's legs, rising from her knees to her torso. The vines wrapped around her arms until they fully tethered her to the ground. She barely noticed that she was being strangled by them. Annie's mind fixed on her grandmother, her disappearance, her final moments spent in the company of this monster.

"Yes, yes," Grovener said. "Your Grandma. Dear, beautiful Carrie, who always loved to dance the night away. I could always smell her perfume across the dance floor, Chanel Number Five, and as she swayed to the music, it was as if her heartbeat kept time with the orchestra." Grovener hummed a single bar from *Moonlight Serenade*, his song rising and growing until it morphed into a full orchestral rendition. Saxophone and brass haunted the room, and Annie began to weep. "The resort needed her. I needed her, as did her beloved Marvin, to come home."

He frowned as he glanced over the decaying space around them and then turned toward Annie, his brown eyes flickering with flashes of red. "Those men in those crisp modern suits and their yellow hardhats showed up again with their metal death machines," Grovener said. "Would you believe they had the audacity to call this beautiful place condemned? Condemned...to a most horrid death. But I won't have any of that nonsense. *We* won't, now, will we?"

The weeds and the vines and the moss shuddered, a whistle of wind flowing through them like a murmur of assent —or a call to uprising. Grovener swirled about, extending his arms as he breathed in the rancid air. "The Grovener Mountain resort is very much alive. It breathes and thinks. It weeps and rejoices with each guest. What those men aim to do, why it's nothing short of murder. And WE..." he said, gesturing toward the overgrowth. "We will stop them."

"You are a murderer. YOU!" Annie shrieked. "You killed my grandma. And Grandpa? Did you kill him, too? He died just after this place shut down! Did you take him? To feed all this?" She struggled against her plant-based captors to no avail. They only pulled her limbs taut until each muscle in her body numbed itself to ward off the pain.

Grovener wagged a gloved finger at her, tsking again "These are rather harsh allegations, my dear. You and Grandma Carrie chose to plant the soul of your beloved Grandpa Marvin in the earth, here, at Grovener Mountain. Her choice. And you were complicit." The mottled skin above his shirt collar bubbled, his neck pulsing in alternating states of smoothness and decomposition. "I am but a humble proprietor who seeks to offer our guests a pleasurable experience. To stay afloat, my resort needs new guests. Fresh blood. And you will do nicely."

He moved toward Annie and touched her face, the sharp bone beneath his glove pressing into the underside of her chin. She heaved with his touch. "Running a business such as mine requires great sacrifice. It would be tragic if the Grovener Mountain Resort were ever to die. So many memories would cease to exist." Grovener frowned, and his eyes glowed red beneath his furrowed brow.

With the swiftness of a lightning flash, he grabbed Annie's arms and ripped her from the vines binding her. Before she could take one last breath, he flung her into the deep end of the pool, her grandmother's putrefied arms rising to catch her, to embrace her in the ever-living memory of the Grovener Mountain Resort. Annie flailed and kicked. She opened her mouth to scream, and her grandmother's putrefied lips offered one last kiss, pushing fetid air and slick slugs into her mouth. Annie's body succumbed; her form rigid as she drowned and sank with her grandmother into the filth.

The water bubbled. Lily of the valley sprouted through the algae and spread over the surface of the pool, its sickly-sweet aroma of death hovering.

Grovener again steepled his gloved hands and pressed them to his lips. He flickered like an old-fashioned movie reel, in and out of existence, until he transformed into that sleek black crow.

The bird shuffled its tail feathers, its beady eyes surveyed the quieted pool, and with a final caw, it flew off through a jagged window. The weeds, vines, and moss released one final sigh before settling back into dormant sleep. Crickets chirped, cutting the silence as they stood sentinel beneath the vegetation that blanketed the room.

A lulling breeze blew through the shattered windows, touched with a whisper of children's giggles and the final resonant notes of the *Moonlight Serenade* that ceased to be.

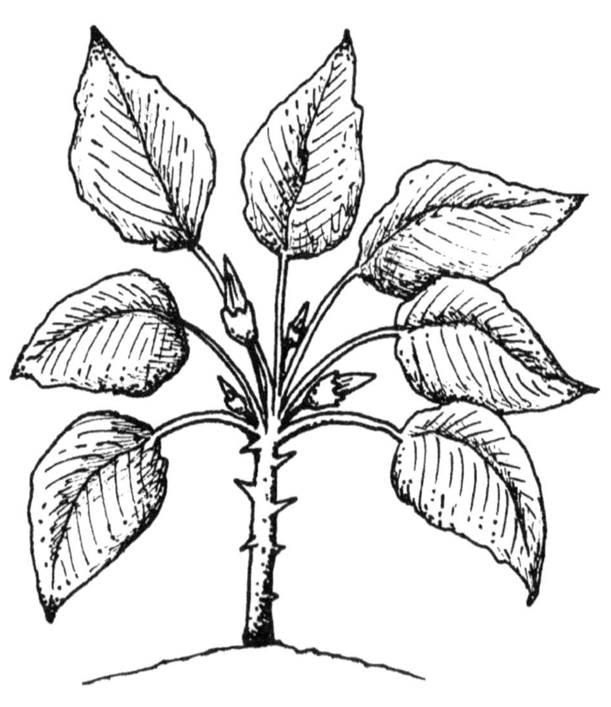

Mother

Katie Jordan

Nani used to say that the old world bred love, and the new one bred hate. "Never forget the island died twice. First, after the massacre when foreigners arrived to illegally mine for gold, copper, and diamonds." Native blood stained the olivine crystal sand. "Second, after the ecosystem perished."

Hina was five-years-old when she and her grandmother fled to the mainland—the last of their people. Nani took a job as a tailor, living in the studio apartment above the shop. She spoke broken English. Her days of tending the island crops were over, but her green thumb occasionally proved useful, nursing discarded plants back to health. "All lifeforms are connected. We must respect Mother Earth, so she can sustain us."

Hina only knew how to say hello and goodbye. She enrolled in kindergarten mid-year, unable to communicate, and came home in tears. Nani embraced Hina in her strong arms, speaking in their native tongue. "Life is hard, but it continues. Just as your life must. Promise me you'll never go back home."

Hina didn't understand. *How could I go back?* The island belonged to their people, but their people were dead. She asked, "Who owns the land now?"

Nani avoided the question.

Hina overheard whispering. People were illegally abusing the island; to mine, to live, to camp. But those trespassers perished. The government put up signs, but more people came—and more died. Eventually, Hina quit asking who owned the land.

Hina's teachers found her to be bright and inquisitive. She learned English in a few years and became engrossed in books, her vocabulary expansive.

"Tell me about the island," Hina would plead to her grand-mother. "About the three-foot-long iguanas basking under the sun and palm fronds. Tell me of the cerulean water and green sand. Describe the sweetness of the coconut flesh."

"There is no sweetness remaining. It all turned bitter."

The island wasn't the only thing affected. Nani was forever changed. Hina could see it in the curvature of Nani's frown lines and the way she stared in the direction of the ocean for hours.

And still, the island—what she thought the island might be like—infiltrated Hina's dreams. Overlapping waves tickled her toes. Scuttling crabs inched past her fingertips. The screeching of monkeys assaulted her eardrums. Coconuts thudded against the sand. Thunder cracked. Torrents of rain battered the trees. At the height of Hina's imaginings, when tranquility morphed into nightmares, perspiration drenched her sheets as she stirred. Crisp, fresh air filled her lungs and cooled her cheeks, drawing her back into her dreamscape.

Hina couldn't remember her past. Maybe her mind

blocked out the memories, or maybe she was too young. But she vividly recalled a single feeling—lying in the warm sand like the iguanas did, half exposed to the elements, half shaded. The sun radiating a delicious heat. Her lips salty. Her mind at peace.

That peace was annihilated the minute she came to the mainland. She could still feel it in her core: a longing for home.

Last week, Nani's heart gave out. The loneliness which Hina pushed deep down has become too strong to be ignored. Being the last two of their people was hard. Being the only one left is devastating.

And now Hina finally knows the why—why Nani was concerned she would return home.

Because she could.

The man in the stiff grey suit, a VP of a developing company, extends a stack of papers, pointing to the name at the top, Nani's name. "See?"

Hina stands in the apartment entryway. She pulls her long black hair over her shoulders, tugging. "What are you saying?"

"You're her only living relative."

She presses her shaky hand to her chest. "The island belongs to me?"

"All forty-two acres." He adopts a hard smile. Cold. Insincere. "But it's uninhabitable."

Hina grits her teeth. "Then why do you want it?"

"We have the resources to employ field experts. Botanists. Biologists. Ecologists. You get the picture."

"So, you think"—she inhales sharply—"the island can be sustainable again."

"Sure. If we throw enough money at it. Right now, it's too dangerous for just anyone to live there."

By 'just anyone,' he clearly means her.

The island—which its people endearingly called Mother—is the topic of many legends. When they left, Nani said Mother was dead. Others say she's alive but forever changed.

"You must take me to Mother."

The suited man crosses his arms. "Impossible."

The door creaks as Hina starts to shut it.

"I think we got off on the wrong foot. My name is Sam. I'm here to leverage a deal that helps both of us." He crinkles his brow. "If I take you to the island, will you sell?"

"Probably not."

Her refusal fuels him. He wants her to sell Mother. Because of money. Because of greed. Because of that warped 'me mentality' that annihilated her people. She will never, *never* sell Mother.

Sam stares at the yellowed walls of the studio apartment that sits over the shop below. The place reeks of soup and old coconuts, discarded in the trash that needs taken out. Honking horns and speeding cars sound from the busy street below. It feels cold here, even with all Nani's bright, hand-stitched blankets strewn over the secondhand furniture. The air tastes overpoweringly salty. Perhaps only Hina can sense it, though. The salt is from all the tears she's cried in a place she's never belonged. And now, having taken over Nani's position at the shop, the prospect of leaving is slipping further away.

In the evening, Sam calls. "How much will you sell for?"

He thinks everyone sees green, like him. "Two million?" he offers. "Three?"

She blinks. "Take me to Mother."

He finally agrees.

In the old world, the islanders cut down trees, stripped off the bark, and hollowed the trunks, crafting water vessels. But Hina doesn't depart in a handmade vessel. How could she? Her people weren't alive long enough to teach her their ways.

Sam stands on the dock, wearing board shorts and a hokey button-down shirt, the kind tourists wear. His arms spread wide as he motions toward a seventy-foot yacht, grinning ear to ear. "Welcome. Mi casa es su casa."

Including Hina, there are five passengers onboard, in addition to a crew of four. The male passengers, Associates at the developing company, wear attire nearly identical to Sam's. The woman, who is dressed more for tennis than a day on the water, introduces herself with a wave. "Hi. I'm Mary. I'm Tom's assistant."

Hina boards the boat and stands, lingering as the yacht pulls away from the dock. She doesn't join the others until the shore becomes a distant speck, lost in the vast expanse of ocean that gobbles it whole.

The ship's crew prepares for lunch, meticulously laying out each table setting; two forks, two spoons, a single knife, a bread plate, a cup, and a cloth napkin. A man barbecues chicken breasts and bigeye tuna on the open charcoal grill, then slices thin slivers of watermelon. Next, he pulls out pre-prepared side dishes from the under-counter fridge and arranges pats of butter on a plate.

A woman slides a pink napkin in front of Hina as she sits at the table. "Hello, miss. What can I get you to drink?"

"Water, please. Coconut water if you have it."

The woman retreats behind the bar, hacks off the top of a coconut with a machete, then sticks a pink straw in the opening.

Sam's lips draw up in the corners. He slouches into his

lounge chair while raising his pointer finger in the air. "I'll have the same. But make mine with a splash of El Dorado."

The woman tightly grips the rum bottle as the boat sways, pouring. Hina's stomach lurches. She stands and moves to the back of the boat, gasping for breath.

Mary approaches. "Seasick?"

Hina nods.

Mary has long black hair, like Hina, but her disposition is much cheerier. Too cheery, perhaps. Mary gently brushes the hair away from the nape of Hina's neck with one hand, gripping a cup of water with the other. "Hold still. This will help."

Hina gasps when Mary dumps the cool water onto her neck. It runs down, soaking her orange t-shirt and the waistband of her cutoff jean shorts. The seasickness dissipates, lessening until the sensation is replaced by a dull stomachache.

"Stay at the back of the boat," Mary orders. "It's the best place."

Nani used to talk like that. All-knowing. Forceful. The wind whips Hina's hair around her face, hiding the tears streaming down. Eventually, she begins to sweat. Her stomach turns. She retches over the railing as a sinking thought hits. *So much for being the last survivor of my people. I am a failure to what I am and where I came from. An outsider on the mainland and an outsider to the ocean I was born to.*

The groan of the boat's engine quiets to a purr as the pace stalls. Hina looks up. Her jaw goes slack.

She groans, wiping the remnants of vomit away from the corners of her mouth with the back of her hand. The land resembles fileted flesh. Blood—a vile imitation produced by the contrast of translucent water traversing red sand—navigates the soil's surfaces and crevices. Streams of water gush haphazardly. Red sand. Red water. Red rock.

Dense, green thickets composed of vines, thistles, bristly brush, and too-small trees trying to poke through, cover the island in sporadic mats. Hina shivers. Nani used to describe Mother as a paradise. Lush. Green. Bursting with life. The plants here are stunted and competing with one another. Far from thriving.

Mary leans against the railing. "If it were me, I'd sell. He'll pay more. Five million. Maybe ten."

Hina forces a smile. Nani used to say, 'Kindness is in the eyes. Don't be fooled.'

"Well," Mary prompts, nudging Hina with her elbow. "Is it like you remembered?"

Hina doesn't admit that she doesn't remember, that she has no intention of selling Mother, or that Sam telling her to name her price is a waste of time. It's like someone asking for a dollar amount in exchange for her soul.

Mary keeps talking as she points to various areas on the island. "Sam is going to build a luxury resort there. Huts on the water on the far side. Pools with swim-up bars adjacent to that hill. A town centre with shops and restaurants

Hina's laugh hits the breeze sharply before it's whisked away. "A town centre? Here?"

"It's going to become a port for cruise ships."

Hina cocks one eyebrow. *Not if I have anything to say about it.*

The yacht navigates in a semi-circle, revealing a pristine area next to the shoreline, which stands out in stark contrast to its blemished surroundings. It's approximately twenty-five yards long—olivine crystal sand, palm trees heavy with coconuts. A stream of water bypasses the area, snaking through the oozing, bleeding sand in back of it, then draining into the sea. Red sediment stains the water and then dissipates.

Mary chimes in as if on cue, "This part of the island wasn't good for mining."

Sam approaches, eyeing Hina. "Well, here we have it. As you can see, it's bleak. Can we go?"

She shakes her head. "What will you build here if I sell? Mary said that you want to commercialize it."

He chuckles uneasily. "No, of course not. We just want to make it accessible to more people, so they can experience the natural beauty."

Hina winces. "I'm going to get off the boat."

"I don't have time to play explorer," he mutters. He scans the land, grimacing as he lets out an exaggerated sigh, then blurts, "Ten million, but we have to leave right now."

She studies his face and the rigidity of his body. "You've never been here before, have you?"

His expression hardens. The silence confirms the truth.

Hina pulls herself over the railing and jumps overboard. She opens her eyes underwater as a school of brightly-hued fish darts away. Her arms flap at her sides, pushing up to keep herself submerged. The water is clearer than it is in her dreams. Pure. Untouched. Immaculate.

She rises to the surface. Sam is shouting from the yacht. She ignores him, swimming, then rolling up onto the shore. The sun beats down. She sighs contentedly, gazing up. The sky is bluer here than on the mainland. A perfect pale blue.

Her elbows press down as she props her chin onto her hands, breathing hard. The island is no less forgiving up close. *Mother is angry.*

Sam leans against the railing, his eyebrows furrowed.

"Hey," Hina yells, smiling. "You know you want to see it for yourself."

He paces the ship deck. "All right. Let's go check it out."

The yacht anchors, and the passengers disembark,

jumping off the side of the ship, leaving the crew onboard. Sam stands on the sand, dripping wet. He cups his hand over his eyes, shielding them from the sun's glow, as he points, shouting orders.

"Dave, check out the area to the left."

"Tom, you take the right."

Hina playfully kicks at the sand, unbothered.

Mary is the last to plunge into the ocean and swim ashore. She collects her long hair in one hand and twists, squeezing water out. "Are you sure traipsing around here is a good idea? We should wait for the experts. We should—"

"Just do your job," Sam snaps.

The island climbs, the steepest terrain straight ahead. Dave and Tom obediently cooperate with Sam's orders, fighting the foliage. The red water burbles, splashing Dave's ankles. He jumps, then wipes the moisture away with the palm of his hand, inspecting and sniffing it, then chuckling.

Tom teases, "Did the stream bite you?"

"Guess so."

Tom makes it to the top of the incline, surrounded by thin tendrils of vines. "It's a beautiful view," he shouts. "Or at least it would be if the island didn't look like death."

Dave hollers, "We'll offer parasailing!"

Tom steps back with his right foot. The vines snake, snaring like a web. He jerks his leg, which causes more vines to latch on.

Hina tilts her head to one side, reminded of the snap peas Nani used to grow. Nani arranged them around the trellis, but when Hina tried moving them again, they refused to unlatch, tugging.

Tom takes a step back with his left foot. Vines net it, refusing to relinquish their hold.

"Guys," he says. "A little help?"

Dave is a couple hundred yards away. "Seriously, man?" He points and laughs. "Put some muscle into it."

"I'm trying!"

Dave scoffs and kneels, inspecting a plant. "What is this thing?"

Hina squints at the four-foot-tall thistle. Her eyes water. She searches her mind for a memory she's sure is there, but it won't surface. A lump forms in her throat as Dave moves closer. The thistle's stem is thick, supporting a giant, spiked head, its open mouth revealing dozens of thumb-sized black seeds.

Nani used to talk about the dangers of plants and the stupidity of careless people, saying, "Thistles kill. On the island and in other places."

Dave stoops lower.

The words scratch as Hina forces them out. "No! Don't touch it!"

Dave inadvertently jumps. The spikes slap down like a Venus flytrap on steroids, trapping part of his face. The cry that emits from Dave's lips is sharp, animalistic, but it doesn't stop the predator from consuming its prey. The thistle's mouth continues closing, cutting off the flesh inside. Dave forces himself upright. Blood runs down his chin. His eye—where his eye once was—is a gaping red hole, as raw as the island's surface. His wailing escalates, the blood running into his mouth and spraying out as the shrieks become more piercing. And then, without warning, Dave's body slams into the ground. Silent.

Tom tries to move toward Dave, using brute force to try to kick his feet free from the vines jailing his feet.

"No," Hina whimpers. "Stop."

Tom fights harder, falling to the ground. Only a few tendrils snare his hands at first, but more latch on as his struggle intensifies. He puts all his strength into trying to rip his way free.

"You're making it worse!" Hina screams.

Her mind flashes black, then red. A suppressed memory returns with ferocity, ripping through her mind—the destruction of her blissful childhood.

It happened at nightfall.

A waning crescent moon hung high in the sky, stars twinkling. The embers of a fire illuminated the hut with a faint glow. Arms were wrapped around Hina's waist—her mother's arms—but the hands were limp, the skin unnaturally pale. The crown of her mother's head bled, forming a puddle underneath.

Hina shudders.

She said something before she died.

A searing pain stabs the centre of Hina's forehead. She falls to her knees, pressing her hand against the clammy skin, forcing herself to finish unearthing the memory.

There was a before.

Before her mother's last breath.

Before the bludgeoning.

Before the intruders entered.

Hina holds her breath, eyes widening.

"Lay down," her mother ordered.

Hina obeyed, thinking she would be held as she slept, and the next morning she would wake in a warm embrace, as she had all the days of her life. Her father died when she was an infant. Her mother never let her out of her sight, even for an instant. Others thought it was an irrational fear. *What will happen? The island is safe!*

But the island wasn't safe.

"Stay asleep," her mother whispered. Fear crept into her

voice. Hina's heart thundered. "No matter what happens, don't open your eyes."

"Evildoers," her mother whispered. "Taking what isn't theirs."

Footsteps pummeled against rock. Fast. Unforgiving.

She grabbed Hina and shook her, wailing, "No! Not my daughter! What have you done? You are monsters! You—"

There was a whoosh, followed by the sound of a knife slicing through flesh. Hina soon felt her mother's heart beating beside her own, the rhythms slipping further and further apart.

Hina didn't move. She opened her eyes for a moment, then closed them. Maybe if she never opened them again—maybe if she stayed still and forgot that any of this happened—she would wake up to her mother.

But when she opens her eyes, it's here and now, on the shores of the island that is no longer her home. The huts are gone. Her people annihilated. The life she once had has vanished.

"No," Hina whimpers. "Come back."

She closes her eyes again but opens them to find nothing has changed. Tom continues wrestling with the vines until he's unable to move under their tight hold. Mary covers her face, her chest bobbing with weighted sobs.

Sam moves further back on the shoreline, lips trembling. He shouts. "We need to go! Now!"

Hina crinkles her forehead as calm settles in. She ignores Sam's command as she studies her land, whispering, "Mother, why are you angry?" As the words exit, her cheeks redden. She fixes her gaze to the ground. The answer is obvious. Mother—both the island and Hina's own mother—have been violated. Stripped of their children. Ripped open and left to bleed out, then expected to provide more. What more is there? They were killed. Left to rot.

There is nothing left for them to give except wrath.

"Sam," Hina glares. "You need to help Tom."

He throws his hands in the air. "I'm not going up there."

"I'll sell it," Hina says, deadpanning him. "Ten million for the island, but you need to help him right now."

Sam folds his arms, then unfolds them and storms forward. He tries to rip the vines away from Tom, but they cling to his fingers. He twists and pulls every which way, then falls to the side near a thistle and screams. It's one loud painful shriek that stops short. His body rolls toward her, revealing a chunk missing from his throat. Blood gushes out.

Mary tries to run. Hina latches onto her arm. "You're not leaving without us. Got it?"

She thrusts Mary onto the sand.

Mary rubs her arm. "Are you crazy? They're all dead!"

"Tom isn't."

"Just leave him!"

Hina hikes up the incline and lies down beside Tom. The tendrils wrap around her gently.

"I'm not going to leave you to die," Hina whispers. "Sam deserved it. You don't."

Tom's voice muffles in the foliage.

"You need to stop fighting," she says. "Be still."

Ever so slowly, she caresses a vine. She remembers Nani's snap peas. "You can't fight them," Nani would say, laughing. "You'll lose."

"But they won't let go!"

"Be gentle. Careful. Patient." Hina remains calm as vines wrap around her hand. She leaves them, breathes, then carefully unwinds, positioning them against a thistle, careful not to lean too close. It takes several minutes to untangle each vine covering Tom. When only a few are left, he flings himself upright.

"Don't," Hina orders. "The vines don't like it."

His face reddens. "This place is going to get levelled."

"No," she says as she works to untangle another tendril. "This is my island. You will leave her alone."

"But you said you would sell it!"

"I will never, *never* sell her."

Spittle forms at the corners of his mouth. His complexion becomes a shade redder. "Are you telling me that you brought us all the way out here for nothing?"

Hina glares. "It's not yours. You can't have it just because you want it."

"Just get me out of here!" he demands.

Her fingers work diligently until he's free and able to stand. Every step, they pause, reworking the vines. They make it to the unaffected sand at dusk and swim to the boat, exhausted.

Mary is onboard, wrapped in a blanket, munching on salmon and freshly baked sourdough bread. "The authorities have been notified," she announces, not looking up.

Hina clenches her fists at her side. "What are they going to do, arrest the island?"

"If it were mine, I'd bulldoze it and turn it into high-rises."

"Bulldozing it wouldn't help."

Mary's fork clatters against her plate when she drops it, glaring. "How would you know?"

"I just do."

Hina returns to her job at the tailor shop and catches up on alterations. Every night she dreams of Mother—both her native land and the woman who laid down her life to protect her. The dreams become increasingly vivid until Hina can no longer discern reality. She wakes with weighted raindrops on her face but tells herself they're tears. Another time she bolts upright, her shirt sopping wet. She smells the salt of the ocean. But when she wakes up clutching a shell, she *knows*. She can leave the island, but the island will never, *never* leave her.

Mother calls to her.

As the tide ebbs and flows, so must Hina. She whittles down the contents of the apartment, donating and tossing items, selling furniture, and packing up the remnants, then stands in the middle of the room in anticipation of closing the door for the final time. The taste of salt is gone, but the scent of trash lingers, reeking of mildew and rot. Without Nani's colourful blankets strewn about, it's dark and unbearably cold, despite the blazing heat.

Hina accepts the rules and constraints of the world she lives in. She does the things an adult must do, sets up a postal office box, pays bills, checks accounts, and updates her address. When her affairs are in order, she makes purchases—a motorboat, a tent, many gallons of water, and miscellaneous supplies. She hauls her possessions to the shore of the mainland, loading them. The ocean lulls, rocking increasingly harder until she concedes and pushes off.

Mother is still bleeding when she arrives. Hina's heart bleeds with Mother's as she flails her body onto the sand. Somehow, she knows she will survive and will reclaim this as her home. She can feel Mother here, offering protection, and begins to lose sight of the difference between her own mother and the land.

She has decided to respect Mother's grief. Mother doesn't need to sacrifice anything else. There is a time for mothers to take care of their offspring—and a time for offspring to tend to their mothers. The time has come for Mother to rest.

Hina stoops before a vine and gingerly extends her hand, allowing a tendril to wrap around her fingertip. "It's okay to fall apart," Hina whispers. "Just make sure you come back."

Mother never gave up on her, and Hina will never give up on Mother. The life she's chosen isn't sustainable, and yet she has faith that Mother *will* sustain her. Together they will grieve. Together they will find a way for the new world to respect the old one. There is no room for hate in Hina's heart, but maybe one day, side by side with Mother, their rhythms will slip closer and closer together, and they will find a way to heal and love again.

Where The Fireflies Fall

Melissa R. Mendelson

When I moved to Minerva, I was trying to escape my old life. I thought that you were supposed to get married, have kids, and move into a community where people would accept you and your family without any kind of animosity. But I was wrong, and after a hellish year or two, I took my family and ran to the countryside, where those people would be left far behind. There was nothing here but trees, so many damn trees, and they did not bother me. Well, except maybe, at night. The trees seemed to come alive, especially under the full moon, waving and looming close, almost reaching toward the windows, and even my wife and kids seemed to shudder at their shadows. But I assured them that we were safe, we were better off here, and the trees would never harm us like those people did. But now those trees, all those trees, are gone, and I only see *them*.

I felt sick watching them tear up the land, but I thought that they would only take half. I was wrong. They took all, leaving the earth dark and brown, no sign of life, and if a shred of green dared to reach upward through the dirt, they would rip it out. And they looked at me, at my land, and I knew they would come for me next. But I refused and still refuse to leave.

The house is quiet these days, feeling a lot smaller than it is, and I don't like to spend my time inside. I'd rather sit on the porch with my dog Oscar, especially in the evenings. There was something about how the sun disappeared, a sense of peace, and it used to be beautiful watching the sun set over those trees. But now the view is nothing but those people dressed in their custom-made clothes, looking over at me as if I were nothing more to them but a piece of dirt. I shrug it off, sitting in my chair and lighting a cigarette. If they look at me, I merely wave back. *You cannot touch me here.*

The days were going by fast, and June was almost at an end. I sighed, and Oscar glanced at me. I pat him on the head, reassuring him that nothing was wrong, but I looked around. What few trees were left hugged my land, begging not to be destroyed, but there were no birds, no wildlife. They'd chased most of them away. What about the fireflies? I loved seeing them when the sky grew dark, loved chasing them around as a kid, but even they were gone.

The news listed them as extinct.

Did *they* have a hand in that? It wouldn't surprise me.

Oscar stretched out on the porch but made sure his body rested close to my feet. His tail thumped against the wood, and a fly buzzed by, brushing against his fur and my hand. The road was quiet, but they liked it that way. And where were they? Tucked inside their apartments with the shades pulled closed. Maybe because they knew that I was staring at them, and they didn't like it. But that was too damn bad.

"Stop looking at them."

My wife passed away several years ago, and after she died,

I still heard her voice. Sometimes, I could even see her, but that was a long time ago.

"Stop looking at them," she repeated. "Focus on the road."

"The road?" I asked.

I was no longer sitting on the porch with Oscar but driving along the road with her, my wife. It wasn't the truck I bought a few years ago. No, this was the minivan when the kids were young.

"You act like you've never seen deer before." She sat back in her seat and sighed.

"I've seen deer," I replied. "Just not in real life."

"Real life?" My son sat in the backseat behind my wife. "I'd rather see the deer than the people in the neighbourhood that we just left behind." He touched his face, avoiding the bruise around his right eye.

"Same," my daughter said as she sat behind me, but she didn't say anything else.

"Are we almost there? My leg's falling asleep." My son rubbed his leg. "We've been in the car for hours."

"Two hours," I corrected him. "And yes, we are nearly there."

I was excited to see the house. It was just built, but why they placed it on a small hill, I would never know.

"I feel bad," my wife said.

"Why?" I asked.

"Because they cleared all that land for one house. All those trees torn down just so we could live there. Why? What was the point of that?"

"Maybe, there wasn't enough room for two houses," I said. "I don't know, but the house is built unless you want to go back."

"We're not going back," my daughter hissed.

My wife glanced at me and then over into the backseat, but my daughter turned away.

"No," my wife said. "We're not going back." She glanced at me. "We never did anything to those people," she said in a low voice, but I'm sure the kids heard her.

"No, we didn't, but they did not like our last name. We're here."

I always hated the driveway. It was long and winding, filled with rocks and gravel. I promised myself that I would get it blacktopped, but I never did.

"Welcome to Bumblefuck," my son said.

"No, Minerva." I parked the car. "Okay. Movers were here yesterday, and they brought everything inside. So, with the exception of the bags in the trunk, we should start unboxing things. John?" My son met my gaze in the rearview mirror. "Could you please get some of the bags from the trunk?"

"Yeah, Dad." John hopped out of the car.

"I'll go help him." My wife stepped outside.

My daughter opened the door. "Me too."

"Alex?"

My daughter looked at me.

"You okay?"

"Fine, Dad." She slammed the door shut behind her.

My wife and John took the bags from the trunk and carried them into the house. I followed them but stopped. Alex was standing by the road, looking across to all those trees on the other side. "So many trees," she said.

"Yes, so many trees," I repeated.

Alex did not look at me but crossed her arms over her chest. "I've never seen that many trees before or ever. Where we lived, it was just house after house and then the town."

I placed a hand on Alex's shoulder, and she cringed. "I'd rather the trees," I said.

"No, they're scary too." She walked toward the house.

I blinked, and those trees were gone, torn out of the ground, and for what? So they could build their homes on top of each other like LEGO blocks, but they were not built from metal or plastic. They were wood, and even the fire escapes were wooden. The only plastic was the hideous yellow bikes that their kids rode around, and when they weren't doing that, they were throwing rocks at the cars that dared to pass by.

"You're looking at them again."

I sat back in my seat and looked at Oscar, who wagged his tail at me. I pat him on the head again.

"Yes, I am looking at them again because there is nothing else to look at," I said.

"I miss the trees."

I could smell her perfume. How I loved that scent.

"There were so many trees. Now, they're all gone. All of them."

"I know," I replied. "I miss them too."

I found myself back in the house, sitting at the kitchen table with a cup of coffee in my hand. I hadn't had coffee in a long time or read the local newspaper, but there it was, laid out in front of me, announcing the town had caved in to them.

"The town made an agreement with them," I said. "The town gave them what they wanted, and they have their piece of land. Let's hope they're happy with that, and they don't look to come here and take all of these trees down."

"Those people are never true to their word," my wife said, shaking her head. "They came to this town ten years after us, and they were so kind and friendly. But it was all an act. They paid off the town, secretly stealing land away that could've been used for something else, and they started to harass everyone that they couldn't get to move. Those phone calls late at night and early in the morning? That's them. I'm telling you it's them, and they will make their way over to our land."

"I hope you're wrong. I don't want to see those trees go, and the local teens love to disappear in them and get high. Our son's one of them. He was high the other night."

My wife finally laughed. "He's just blowing off some steam. Probably worried about going off to college after this year, and then it'll be our daughter's turn."

"Alex doesn't say much anymore," I said.

"I know." My wife hovered close. "She doesn't talk to me either."

"She doesn't talk to anyone. She just stares at all those trees like she's waiting for something."

"They're just trees," my wife said.

"I don't know. Sometimes, it feels like something else." I stared at her. "It feels like there's something over there in those woods. Don't you feel that?"

"They're just trees," she repeated. "And they're not going anywhere. I hope they stay there even after we're gone."

"I hope you're right," I said.

A burning sensation seared through my hand. I almost dropped the cigarette but caught it quickly before it could land on Oscar. I shook my hand, blowing on the skin, trying to cool the burn. That's what I get for daydreaming or remembering the past.

Oscar lifted his head up to look at me, but his eyes shifted over to the cigarette. "I'm sorry. I didn't mean to almost drop this on you." Oscar lowered his head, but his eyes remained on the cigarette. "I was just thinking," I said. "She was wrong. She might be gone, but I'm still here. And those trees aren't, and whatever might have been over there with them... Well, it's gone too, or they wouldn't still be living there." I snuffed the cigarette out on the porch away from Oscar. "See? No more." But Oscar turned his back on me, his tail whipping against my leg.

"Why are you still here," my wife whispered in my ear.

"Please, just leave me alone," I said. "It's not time yet, or I least I hope that it's not time yet."

"Dad."

When was the last time I spoke to John? I don't remember, but he was standing before me now, looking concerned.

"Dad, they tore down the trees. Did you see what they did? The whole land is cleared."

"I saw what they did."

"Then, it's time." Alex appeared, standing beside John. "Dad, you've stayed here long enough by yourself. It's time."

"Time for what? A nursing home? A grave?"

"Jesus, Dad, don't be like that. Just pick one of us to live with," John said. "I won't be mad if you choose Alex."

"And I won't be mad if you choose John," Alex said.

"No," I replied. "Thank you, both, but I'm not leaving my house. I'm not leaving because of them."

"Dad," John and Alex said together.

"No. I'm sorry, but the answer is no. Your mother's buried here," I said. "So, I'm not going anywhere, and that's final."

"Dad, they're going to harass you," John said. "You know that. I'm sure they've been calling already and emailing you and probably walking across your property like they already own it."

"I'm staying," I said. "That's it." I opened my eyes, and both of my kids were gone. "I'm staying," I whispered, and Oscar whined in response.

"You should have listened to them. You should have gone with them."

Why was she still here with me?

"Why are you here?" I asked.

She drew into focus, wearing that dress she was buried in. I couldn't decide what to have her wear at the funeral, but Alex picked it out, saying that it was her favourite. I didn't remember her even buying it, but now I was looking at her in that dress.

"I'm here," she said. "You should have listened to them. You could have been with our kids and grandkids right now instead of being here alone and glaring over at them. They won. Can't you see that?"

"I'm not leaving you," I said.

"I might be buried here, but my spirit is always with you." She tried to touch my hand but failed. "You need to go. You need to leave here right now."

"Why?" I asked.

"Because something terrible is about to happen." My wife disappeared.

"Jasmine?" She struggled to reappear but barely. "What's going to happen?"

"You were right," she whispered. "About something being over there with all those trees. I never saw it until... Until the day I died, but I couldn't tell you. And..."

"And?" I asked.

"And it's back. It came back."

Something buzzed past my face. I thought it was a fly and swatted at it. It brushed by again, and I saw blinking lights. No, it couldn't be. The fireflies were all dead, but there it was again. And it shot up toward the sky.

"I just saw a firefly." I smiled, but she did not. "What's wrong? It's just a firefly."

I stared up at the sky. It was filled with so many stars,

large, bright stars, and they seemed to sway across the sky. Their lights flickered on and off.

"Those stars look like fireflies," I said.

"Yes, because they are," my wife whispered.

"No, that can't be. There's so many of them. The news said that they were extinct, so where did all of them come from?"

"They've been waiting." She struggled to reappear completely and grabbed hold of my hand. "You need to go." I flinched at her tone. "Get in your truck with Oscar, and go."

"The sky...the fireflies... They're moving."

"No," my wife cried. "They're falling."

One after another, the fireflies fell from the sky, raining down over those people's homes like kamikazes, spinning and twirling, pummeling the ground. Dirt flew up into the air, and a sound that reminded me of spitballs being blown at my head during school thundered across the land.

"What the hell?" I jumped to my feet, and Oscar positioned himself in front of me, barring his teeth. "Easy, boy," I said, but neither one of us felt easy as we watched the fireflies bombard their homes, even striking the hideous yellow bikes. "Why are they doing that?" But my wife had disappeared again.

"Kelly," I heard her whisper. "Run."

"No, it's okay. I think it's okay."

Little clouds of smoke like the ones that rose up out of my cigarette hovered over the ground, but the fireflies were gone. Why did the fireflies bombard them like that? But I couldn't blame them. I was angry too, and Oscar growled as if he sensed something. Was it that presence from all those years ago? Was my wife right that it came back?

The people inside their homes hurried outside with their children beside them. They looked afraid and confused, staring at me as if this were somehow my fault, but I had nothing to do with this. And they looked up at the sky, but all those stars, all those fireflies were gone.

A little boy pulled away from his mother, and she yelled for him to come back. He didn't listen to her, giving her a look and then shooting a dirty look my way. He kicked at the ground, at one of those holes, and he knelt down toward another hole in the ground, pushing the dirt aside with his hand, but then he grabbed his finger as if something bit him. And he jumped back.

"There's something in the ground," the little boy shouted to those near him, but they paid him no attention. "Something bit me." But they still ignored him. The little boy looked over at me. "There is something in the ground," he shouted louder.

"Silence," an older man snapped at him. He looked over at me and then at the holes in the ground. "It no longer matters, and it's over, whatever it was. Let's go inside." He gestured for the others to follow him, but the little boy did not move toward him.

"There's something in the ground." The little boy was smacked across the face by the older man, and as he stumbled backward, a glowing yellow bulb pushed itself out of the ground. "See? I told you." The little boy danced around the glowing yellow bulb. "It's a large firefly."

"That's not a firefly," I said to myself.

The little boy got on his knees and knelt over the glowing yellow bulb. He reached for it with an extended finger.

"No," I screamed, and all heads turned my way except for the little boy. "Hey, don't touch that!" But the little boy ignored me. He poked the yellow bulb, and the thing shook like one of those large sudsy bubbles my kids once played with and chased in the backyard. Or maybe, it was more similar to the bubbles that would escape from the dish-washing bottle.

And the bubble popped.

"It burns," he howled and wiped at his face, trying to get the stuff off his skin.

As the older man grabbed the little boy, trying to help him, a long, green stem slithered out of the ground. The older man and boy turned toward it, watching the stem sway back and forth, and the stem pushed more of itself out of the ground. It froze mid-sway and then slowly split four ways, revealing yellow, glowing veins, each part of the stem now a blade. One blade swiped against the little boy. He turned to ash, and before the older man could run, a blade snapped across his leg. He was gone too.

More glowing yellow bulbs pushed their way up out of the dirt, and one by one, they popped. A moment later, long green stems rose up, and they too swayed back and forth as if to some unknown tune, one only they could hear, and then all those stems slowly split four ways, their blades wasting no time. All the people nearby turned to ash.

"Run," I screamed. "Run!"

I looked at Oscar, who barked wildly at what was happening over there, and I held onto his collar, keeping him by my side. I did not want him to run into that, and I quickly looked at my property. No fireflies. No glowing yellow bulbs. No long, green stems, but why?

We watched the people run. Well, they tried to run, but it didn't matter. The blades followed them, swiping at their feet, their legs, and their backs. The people turned into dust. Even the ugly yellow bikes melted from the blades as they moved over them, and I realized the blades were making their way to their homes. But no, some were already inside. Ash was painted across many windows, and a few windows shattered.

Sparks ignited along the wooden apartments, and flames ate their way across everything.

But the people were gone.

"Shit," I said. "At least we're safe. Right, Oscar? We're safe." But then I felt it. That presence. And it was close, closer than it ever came to me before. And I knew that it was looking right at me.

Oscar tried to leap toward it, but a piece of dirt nearby caught his attention. The ground was moving, and a glowing yellow bulb pushed its way up out of the ground and popped. As it did, more followed, filling the land in front of me.

"Run," I heard my wife scream.

"Oscar, come on!" I threw open the front door and pushed him into the house. "Oscar!" I knew that he was looking at it, but I could feel that presence moving away. Why would it attack me? I didn't do anything. *Yes, I did.*

"Shit," I said. "They cleared this land for one house, my house."

I didn't have much time. They would get inside, and then me and Oscar would become nothing but ash. I had to get out of there, so I grabbed what I could from downstairs. Keys to the truck. My wallet. A flashlight. Cash from the pretzel jar hidden underneath the kitchen sink and, of course, Oscar's leash. I hooked him up to his leash, pulling him toward the garage. *I hope they are not already in there.*

The front door started to smoke. Little flames licked across its surface, and a window shattered from the living room.

"Come on." I led Oscar to the garage, and we hurried inside. It was pitch black. My hand shook terribly as I fumbled for the switch on the wall. I could already imagine the blades waving in front of my face when the lights went on, but there were no blades. At least, not yet.

"Please, God. Just let us get out of here."

As I got Oscar into the truck, the ceiling cracked overhead. They were in the house, wrapping around the structure, and if I didn't move fast enough, the house would come down on us. I slammed the driver-side door shut and pushed the button for the garage door opener. It struggled to open, and there they were, blades and blades of green and yellow that rose upward to meet us.

Oscar and I looked at each other, and Oscar whined.

"Hold on, Oscar. We're getting out of here." I threw the truck into reverse and slammed my foot down on the gas pedal, peeling out of the garage, but the blades wrapped around the truck. The truck lurched back and stopped, and I could see the panic on Oscar's face. *No, we are not going to die like this.* I hit the gas harder. The truck broke free, spinning wildly around and around, then finally out onto the road. As I sped away, the house came crashing down.

"Yes," I screamed. "Yes!" I hit the steering wheel with my hand. "We made it, Oscar. We made it."

We were far enough from their development and my house. Well, what was left of their development and my house. The truck shook, struggling to push forward, and it died.

"No." I tried the ignition but nothing. "Come on." Still nothing.

It was quiet. Not a sound at all. No stars either. Everything seemed okay, so maybe, it was over. *Please, let it be over.*

I slowly exited the truck, and Oscar followed me. I looked around, pocketing the keys, but my hand rested on them. It didn't matter. The truck was dead. The house was gone. We had no choice but to walk. But where would we go?

"I hope Alex or John's family like dogs," I said, and Oscar turned his head, looking at me.

"Kelly," I heard my wife whisper. "You should have left when I told you to."

"No, we made it. We're okay."

Oscar suddenly pulled away, and I wasn't holding the leash tight enough. He hurried from me, running down the road.

"Oscar!" He didn't respond. "Oscar, come back here!"

Oscar stopped a short distance away and barked. He glanced at me, but he was barking in the wrong direction. The house and their development were behind me, and he disappeared into the grass. He barked again, but it was cut short.

"Oscar?" No response. "Oscar?"

I hurried toward where I last saw him. As I walked, the dirt on both sides of the road moved with me. With every step that I took, the dirt shook even more.

"Oscar?"

I didn't see him, and he should have been there. But he wasn't, and a long stem rose up out of the ground, reaching for me. I hurried back toward the road, and I was surrounded by rows and rows of those yellow bulbs. One by one, each popped.

"Just get to the truck." I could see it up ahead, and there were no green and yellow blades wrapped around it. At least, not yet.

I tripped and fell onto the road. A light shined across my face.

I stared into a glowing yellow bulb.

And it popped.

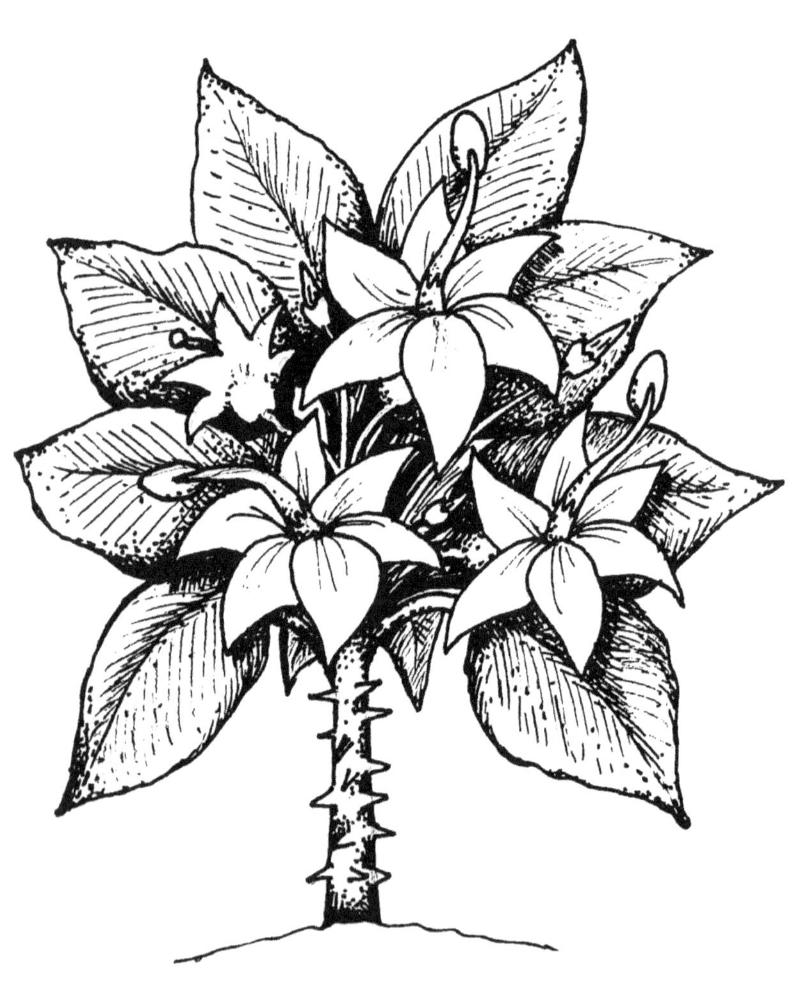

BLOOD & THORNS: A FAMILY*

ANDREA GOYAN

MOTHER'S LESSONS: NUMBER FIVE

There's a moment as you cut into a green branch, and the blade's edge severs the skin when the insides fight back. The tension between the pressure and surrender, between the force of your muscles closing the handles versus the strength of the branch's fibres. In that moment, something akin to magic happens.

Then...

Ka-Thunk.

One segment becomes two. The severed piece will wither into dust, while the other part, the one with roots, will remain—well, not whole exactly, but alive.

DAILY LIFE

There were five of us girls, and we all grew up caring for our family's three-acre manicured garden. I was the second oldest and nearly seventeen. The youngest was five. Her name was Jewel, but we all called her Sprout. The eldest, Susanna, left home four years earlier, never to be heard from or spoken of again, at least by Mother. "Wipe your sister from your memories," she'd ordered. That rule marked the first time I defied Mother, though in secret. I kept Susanna alive, stored inside my mind, along with the digital address she'd written on the back of a wildflower seed packet. Sometimes, when my little sisters couldn't sleep, I told them stories about her— Susanna, the one they'd barely known and almost forgotten. My other two in-between or middle sisters, Amy and Annie, were identical as twins could be. They also looked exactly like miniature Mothers because they came into the world by different means than the rest of us. When we wondered why no roses bore their names, Mother told us Amy and Annie were her experiment. Then, she'd let us touch the smooth skin over the missing part of her left hand's baby finger.

"Two joints. One for each of you," she said, wriggling that same shortened pinky at Amy and Annie. "No roses were needed to make you."

I never knew whether to be sad or happy for them, different as they were. But it didn't matter because I loved them just the same.

Our lives were regimented and orderly. Mother home-schooled us the same way she'd been taught by her mother.

We'd wake at dawn when Mother entered our shared room.

Clapping her hands, she'd say, "Chop-chop, children."

She'd stand to the side, hands behind her back as we donned overalls and removed our gloves and our cleaned, oiled shears from the cubbies where we stored them.

"Chop-chop," she'd say again, chuckling at the phrase's double meaning and how it referred to many of our daily chores.

We'd line up in a perfect hedge row for her to inspect our shears. Then, before we filed out for breakfast, she'd point to a plaque on the wall, and we'd chime our family motto in practiced unison.

"Keep your shears and wits razor sharp."

Most of our school days centred around the care of our spectacular property. We didn't want for learning the basic skills; Mother simply taught them to us in practical ways. Addition lessons came naturally by counting the apples on our trees or the days it took for a tomato to ripen. Fractions, division, and multiplication are all part in parcel of caring for the earth. Calculations were needed to determine the square footage of different planted areas, and more were necessary to measure out proper amounts of fertilizer. We learned the familiar and Latin names of all the flora in our garden and the different animals who entered our domain.

We memorized generations of family proverbs as other children learned bible passages.

MOTHER"S LESSONS: NUMBER THREE

The Proverbs:

"Why? There are no answers. Prune. Water. Weed. And feed." - Great-Great

"Aerate the soil, and breathe. Oxygen and carbon dioxide, the yin and yang of all our lives." -Auntie Madge

"Home is what you choose to make it. Feed your land as you feed your children, and neither will ever hunger." - Mother

My girls, you are all special. You are a part of this place, this land, these plants, this family. From the start of our legacy when Great-Great first tilled to now.

HOMESTEAD

We knew no better. We knew no different. Mother guided, and we followed.

Spring of the year I'd turn seventeen, the year everything changed, began like all others. I turned the soil, amending it with worm castings ensuring Grandmother Oak a bumper crop of acorns and Auntie Lilac blossoms in her favourite shade of purple. Amy, Annie, and Sprout flitted around me like butterflies. They pulled weeds and trimmed what Mother called the *wild hairs,* the leaves and branches of plants that strayed beyond their perfectly manicured shapes. My younger siblings were still too little to till and dig, just as I was too young to prune the family's prize roses. No one but Mother handled those, and if we dared to ask why, she'd answer with one word.

Thorns.

Young as they were, my sisters wielded their shears as they moved through our land like tumbleweeds in a tornado. Blurs of disorderly chaos as they played and worked, eager to show Mother their developing abilities.

"Look, Mother!" Annie held the errant branch of a pine tree over her head. The needles had grown over Aunt Lilac, stealing bits of her sun, so Annie lopped it back to its trunk. The tree needed *proper training,* as Mother called it. The thickest part of the limb was bigger than Annie's wrist. "I am ready for battle with the thorny ones."

We laughed, and Mother said, "You, my precious, will never touch the roses."

Annie pouted and threw down her prize. "I want to!"

Mother patted Annie's head and pointed to the trimming. "A job unfinished is a what?"

Annie remained silent until Amy pinched her arm.

Together they said, "A blight that takes root and destroys everything."

Annie took the branch by its needles and ran with Amy chasing toward our chipper, where I'd mulch it later.

MOTHER'S LESSONS NUMBER TWO

The roses are a part of our family. One is planted with every new child and named after that daughter. The rose garden lies at the centre of our land because those plants represent the heart of our land. If a rose carries your name, the day will come for you to prune them. But your gardening skills don't determine when you'll be ready. That is defined by your body's maturation.

Caring for the roses is a rite of passage.

NECESSARY THINGS

Amy and Annie had no roses bearing their names. We were all a little fuzzy about why that was, but we knew it had to do with the way they'd come into the world. And Mother made it clear they'd never prune the roses. Their fates were different than mine or Jewel's, and I knew the day would come when we'd each use our sharpened shears to tend to the thorny ones. This caused some sibling jealousy because Mother glorified the event and told us how special the ruby-red flowers were. After all, pruning ranked as Lesson Number Two. I couldn't blame the in-between sisters for wanting to partake, but Mother laid down the laws; we simply followed them.

As for my part, I worried about the prospect.

My seventeenth birthday loomed—and loomed was the

correct word because I knew Susanna had been seventeen when she'd left. And I knew the roses were the reason why.

But looming or not, destiny had a way of catching up to me.

Rose pruning came after the boy.

TEMPORARY FREEDOM

On my birthday, Mother gifted me a new pair of shears and informed me the time had come for me to bring a boy home.

My skin prickled like the tendrils of climbing vines crawled over me.

"What if no one likes me?"

"Trust me, Zoe, you are ripe for picking," she'd said. "Like the perfect blush on a peach."

She dressed me for my part and schooled me in the important, practical things. How far to unbutton my blouse. How to bend over just so in front of my target. How to toss my hair over my shoulder and glance in his direction. When she handed me the keys to the old Chevy, Mother said. "Remember your grandmother's cautionary words, *'Cast not your seeds into the wind lest they propagate in your neighbour's yard.'* The boy must be brought home for your passage."

She slammed the truck's door shut and rapped on the roof three times for luck. And, yes. I knew how to drive; you learn those things on a farm. And, no. I didn't have a license.

So just like that, I was off to community college. Mother picked out my classes, but I didn't care. For the first time in my life, I tasted freedom. Freedom to leave the farm in my rearview mirror, freedom from toiling in our garden, freedom away from Mother's constant lessons and regimens. And my nerves disappeared because I fit right in with others my age.

Of course, I commuted daily and had a sunset curfew. Mother had learned her lesson about giving a child too much freedom. She wasn't doing that again, no siree.

"Though I don't need to worry. You've always listened to your mother like a good girl."

I met the boy I wanted on the first day. He sat near me in my Vegetative and Reproductive Morphology of Plants class. His name was... I don't remember—

Mother told me to forget, but he was the most beautiful specimen in the class. Six feet tall, wavy brown hair and eyes the colour of jade, the plant, not the gemstone. Getting his attention was as easy as Mother said it would be.

By the end of the first week, we were meeting for lunch every day.

He dreamed of having a cannabis farm, and I... well, I wanted to bring him home to meet Mother and see whether he met her approval. I admit, I lied to him a bit so he'd come willingly. I said my family's garden was legendary. That part was true if we're allowed to write our own legends. I didn't exactly say we grew pot, but I didn't correct him when he made that assumption.

"My mother has tricked out our barn with grow lights to start our crops."

"Righteous," he'd said. "My mom won't even let me vape on the property."

"It's our baby nursery." I smiled, for this was another truth. As infants, Susanna, Amy, Annie, Sprout, and I spent weeks beneath those lamps, developing our human features. I don't remember my transformation, but I witnessed my little sisters'. How, rather than green leaves, their cotyledons opened, revealing embryonic heads whose green-tinted cells became flesh once their eyes opened. Their stem buds burst forth as arms and legs, and when they were fully formed,

Mother severed their roots from their bodies like umbilical cords. "I'll bring you to see it, but you have to promise not to spill my family's secret to anyone."

He crossed his heart. "I promise."

"Then, I'll show you."

The drive from campus took seventeen minutes. Seventeen, just like me. Kismet. He sat beside me with his hand resting on my thigh as I pulled into our driveway.

I turned off the truck's engine and said, "The property's been in my family for five generations."

He whistled. "Rad."

I didn't show the boy inside the house, but that was never my intention. Mother said no males were allowed. My three sisters watched us through the window, like I'd watched when Susanna brought her boy home. They moved from one window to the next as I took him on a full garden tour, pointing out Grandmother Oak, my Aunt Lilac. And, of course, Great-Great Hedge, who embraced the entire property in a protective hug.

He gazed in my direction and said, "I've never seen anything so beautiful."

I wasn't sure whether he meant me or the garden, but it didn't matter. We were one in the same thing.

That was when Mother made her grand entrance, stepping from her shed, hedge clippers in one hand, garden shears in the other.

"Generations at work," Mother said.

"Mother, this is the boy I told you about."

"Nice to meet you, ma'am," he said, extending his hand, which Mother ignored.

I blushed as she furrowed her brow and looked him up and down. Up and down. He lowered his arm and shifted his gaze away from her, back to me.

"Ah, yes," she finally said. "He will do nicely."

She handed me the shears and pointed to the end of the rose path, where she'd made me dig a deep hole in preparation. I slipped the shears into my back pocket.

"Follow me," I said to the boy.

The closest bush we neared was the oldest. First generation. Its petals fluttered as I led the boy closer.

"This rose is named Mabel," I told him.

INCEPTION, PART ONE

No one knows how Mabel has survived for five generations, but then no one can explain anything about the process that created Mabel. Not really.

SEDUCTION

I touched Mabel's petals, and they shuddered.

"The plant hails from my Great-Great-Great-Great-Great Grandmother's time" I'd counted out the greats using my fingers. "We all just called her Great-Great."

"Like the Hedge?"

I nodded. "You catch on quick."

"A rose that old. Wow," the boy said. "That's crazy."

I smiled. "Truer words..."

I interlaced my fingers through his.

INCEPTION, CONTINUED

Great-Great's family sold her to the property's original landowner when she was sixteen. Her parents were poor, she was lovely, and the landowner paid a handsome sum to marry her. Unfortunately, his generosity ended there. He regularly beat and forced himself on her, saying her responsibility was to bear him a son. Great-Great took the abuse for almost an entire year.

SEDUCTION, CONTINUED

As the boy and I stepped deeper along the path dividing the roses, their branches closed around us so we could no longer see or be seen beyond their foliage. At that moment, every flower bud on all the plants opened simultaneously, releasing their heady perfume. The smell was intoxicating.

The boy's lips were salty when I leaned in for a kiss, and I wasn't surprised when he kissed me back. But it was my first time, and I was surprised by how I felt something good stir inside me. Something like the sun on my skin or fire in my veins. Or...magic. I didn't know, but I liked it, whatever it was. I was happy when he kept kissing me, happier still when his hands slipped beneath my shirt to touch my waist. When they crept like ivy up my belly until they cupped my breasts.

Mother's preparation talk was all about duty. She hadn't told me the process would be pleasurable.

I followed the boy's lead. I was used to following, and he seemed a natural leader, just like Mother.

INCEPTION, CONCLUSION

It was Great-Great's birthday, her seventeenth. She and her husband were outside (the land hadn't been cultivated yet and was little more than dirt and cactus), splitting firewood for the coming winter. Berating her for cutting the pieces too small, he threw Great-Great down. Her head struck the ground hard enough for her to lose consciousness. When she came to, her dress was up over her knees, and he was zipping up his pants. Her hair clumped together, sticky with blood from where she'd knocked her head.

"Get up," he'd ordered. "There's a cord of wood to chop."

Yes, there is, she'd thought. And taking hold of the axe, she used both arms the way he'd shown her, and she drove the blade squarely through his head, dividing it perfectly in half. He crumbled to the ground, and where he fell, his blood mixed with hers.

Of course, Great-Great panicked. She chopped up the body as best she could and buried it on the spot. Imagine her surprise when a week later, she heard crying and tip-toed over to find a tiny naked sprout weeping in the dirt. A blood-red rose bush stood in full, spectacular bloom near the infant, shading her from the midday sun.

Or so the family lore claims.

MAJESTY FOLLOWS

The boy gagged first. The cloying smell of the roses began sweetly enough, but as we finished our act, the fragrance thickened, became suffocating and coppery, like blood.

The boy fell off of me onto his side. My vision blurred, and I felt lightheaded. As the first thorns flayed me, I remember thinking, "I wonder where this nasty wind came from."

PREPARATION

Mother took me aside the night before I brought the boy home.

"Roses are full of deceptions," she'd said. "Pretty and fragrant, but it's all a disguise to sip your blood. Grandmother called them little demons. Aunt Madge said they were vampires."

"And you?" I asked because I knew she wanted to tell me.

"Naughty boys bruising for a fight."

I'd seen what happened to Susanna. She'd shown me

scratches that ran down her thighs. Gouges along her forearms. When I'd begged her to tell me how it happened, she said, "The thorny ones. Remember, Zoe, it's hard to be a nonviolent predator."

Those were the last words she said to me.

"May I wear gloves?" I asked Mother. I had a pair that went up to my elbows.

She set a hand against my cheek, and as she shook her head, her loose shirt sleeve fell to her elbow, revealing an intricate web of ropey scars along her forearm. I knew her legs and torso bore similar marks.

NO PREPARATION IS ENOUGH

I'd seen Susanna's wounds, seen the blemishes on Mother's body, but still, I wasn't prepared for the assault.

When the first thorns whipped against me, I wished I were dead.

And the poor boy I'd chosen, the one whose name I won't recall, took multiple hits for every one of mine. I bled. He bled. Our blood commingled and drained onto the roots of our assailants. The roses drank greedily, evident as the red of their petals immediately deepened.

I passed out, a coward's escape. I awakened from that altered state to the boy's screams as Mother pruned with abandon.

"The job is time sensitive," she said, and with a snip of her shears, she lopped off another useless limb.

Planted knee-deep in the hole I'd prepared, the boy looked nothing like the beautiful creature I'd brought home. Mother had whittled him down to his core, his bare minimum. But by the time my child came into the world, he would become another angry rosebush in our yard, yearning for its revenge, waiting for its taste of blood. Should I ever decide to have another child, he would get his licks at me. If I didn't, then Jewel, or my daughter, or so on and on... for generations to come. A never-ending cycle of life, death, and rebirth.

But, at that moment, the boy was mutilated, awaiting the rose to root and bloom.

I cried in red rivulets.

"Wipe your face," Mother said. "This is a time for celebration."

HOLLOW

My injuries healed, but no child came. Our blood had watered the earth but failed to germinate anything. I checked the ground where we'd laid daily. Nothing sprouted.

Mother said to keep my spirits high.

"Procreation isn't always successful. I had three passages before my first child came."

The thought nauseated me. More boys, more thorns, so much violence, and blood. My bare-rooted boy shrivelled and died. Which is what happened if their seed failed. We mulched his remains. Auntie Lilac loved the extra iron and calcium.

Memories of the boy's screams kept me up at night and haunted my dreams. Susanna was right. It was hard to be a non-violent predator.

DUTY, FEAR, GUILT

Months passed. Following breakfast one morning, Mother told me to remain seated, then sent the little sisters off to water the tomatoes.

"You've had enough time," she said. "Your term at school is about to end. Bring home another male. Passage is a duty and honour."

I grabbed her left hand and stared at her pinky finger.

"What if I—"

She yanked it away from me.

"No. Your Aunt Lilac tried over and over. She took three fingers from each hand until she could no longer hold a pair of shears. Nothing rooted, and she died soon after. Amy and Annie are the oddities. The only ones in five generations."

"But—"

Mother glared. Her face lost any softness and, instead, resembled tree bark. I knew that expression. It came with slaps and angry words. She clenched her fists and took a deep, slow breath.

"You will do as I say."

A silent moment passed before I responded.

"Yes, Mother."

Her face relaxed, as did her hands. She gave me one curt nod, took the truck's key from her pocket, and handed it to me. "I'll clean the dishes. You go along now to school."

I did her bidding like a good little daughter. At least the first part. I was sick of duty and terrified of another passage. Risking another boy's life would drive me insane.

I cut my classes and went to the college library, where I knew I could access a computer. I filled in the address I'd memorized, hoping it still worked. In the subject line, I wrote, "Help!!!" Then I typed, "Dearest Susanna. I need your help. Your Zoe."

I planned to check back at the end of the day to see if she'd responded, but she wrote back immediately.

"Zoe. OMG. I thought I'd lost you forever. Can we talk?"

At the student store, I used the allowance Mother gave

me for gas and academic extras to buy a prepaid cell phone. I sat on a bench under a willow tree and made the call. She picked up after the first ring.

"Hello?"

I burst into tears when I heard her voice. My big sister. The one who stood in age between me and Mother. Me and duty. Me and the roses.

"Susanna," I said.

"There's time for tears later. Tell me what happened."

I told her about the boy, the thorny ones, and Mother's insistence I try again.

I finished by saying, "I can't do it."

"Then you won't," she said.

Susanna lived a state away. We planned for how and when she'd return home to get me, though she refused to call it home. Then, in the background, I heard giggles and a happy shriek. She apologized for the noises her child was making.

"A child? How? Does Mother know?"

"Oh, she knows," Susanna said.

The night she'd found the tiny shoot pushing out from the soil, Susanna dug her up. She knew it was risky, moving the sprout from the homestead before she'd fully developed, but Susanna refused to stay another moment in what she called "Our blood-tied family." Using a shovel, Susanna scooped around the tiny stem. She took a bucket from the shed and filled it close to the top with the amnio soil. Her sprout cried a little as she patted the soil gently around its stem, but its lungs were too small to create a ruckus. We'd all slept through their escape.

"It gives me such pleasure to imagine the moment our mother realized not only was I gone, but I'd taken her first grandchild with me," Susanna said. "Mother leaves the house as the sky changes from the black of night to the dove-grey of dawn. She wanders to the roses, the same as every morning. There, she finds the hole I've left. Next to it, the thriving rosebush, a tell-tale sign our pairing resulted in a child. She screams and falls to her knees, yanking fists full of hair from her head. You see, I'm a bit vengeful. I hope her agony was crippling."

"She raged," I said. "For a day. Then said we were never to speak of you again."

Susanna gave a short, bitter laugh. "Sounds like our mother."

We were quiet for a moment before I found the courage to ask her the question I'd wanted an answer to for four years.

"Why did you leave us?"

"I didn't leave you. I left Mother. I left the smothering world she nurtures and insists we belong to. I needed better for my child, and I loved their father. After she killed him, I had to go."

"You loved him?"

"Yes."

Susanna said they fell in love at summer camp. I remembered Mother sent her away for the entire summer, though at the time, I didn't know why. Susanna spent twelve glorious weeks away from home. Three months with Daniel. And, yes, she knew and spoke his name.

"I'll show you a picture of him when I see you. We took it in a photo booth on the promenade. It's a strip with four tiny pictures. We made silly faces in three, but in the last one, we looked straight into the camera and smiled. All innocent and beautiful. We didn't know the horror awaiting us."

Susanna sighed and continued. "Thanks to Mother, all that remains of my child's father is a nameless, anemic stump."

"But..." I paused.

"What?"

"Mother says the blood alchemy is what allows our two species to procreate."

"How do we know that's true, Zoe? Since the Inception, no one has ever tried. Whatever happened to Great-Great, whatever it was that changed her, be it fear, anger, blood, or the land, whatever it was, it became a yoke around all of our necks."

"Mommy!" her child said, followed by an ear-piercing shriek.

I said, "Is she okay?"

"Not she, he. Though they waver back and forth between the two genders. Fluid like the blood that helped create them."

"Why?"

The child cried.

"I'm coming, sweetheart," Susanna said to them. Then she spoke to me. "He's hungry, and I don't know why Knoll is the way they are. But they're beautiful and live without the burdens of our childhoods. I'll see you as soon."

We hung up. A few minutes remained on my phone, so I hid it in my bag and headed home.

FALLOW

Susanna arrived a week later at the new moon as we'd planned. I met her outside our home. Knoll slept in a pack strapped against her back. I opened my mouth to say something, but she stopped me with the finger she brought to her lips.

I nodded. She was right. There would be time for words and hugs later, after we left. We slipped inside the house and tip-toed silently to the large bedroom where all the children slept. Susanna still knew where the creaky floorboards lay. We used to make a game of sneaking out at night to raid the cookie jar. We'd learned how to move like shadows through the old house.

Our younger sisters slept as we entered the room. Susanna wiped away her tears as we stood beside their beds.

"They've grown so big," she said softly.

I nodded. "I'll wake Amy and Annie first."

Susanna grabbed my arm and held me back.

She whispered in my ear. "No. Don't you see? They are not of the roses. They are of our mother. Let them stay."

I grimaced. "But—"

"They will always be hers. Always like her."

Annie's fists were clenched in her sleep, and the way Amy's hair fell about her face made her look identical to Mother. Susanna was right. They were of Mother, and besides, they'd never endure what Susanna and I had. What lay ahead for Jewel. Mother swore the in-between sisters would never prune the roses.

I knelt and gently kissed their cheeks. Each groaned and turned away from me.

Moving to Jewel's bed, I sat and rubbed her back until she opened her eyes.

"Hey, Sprout. We're going on an adventure. Sound fun?"

She blinked and nodded. Two little dips of her chin.

"Hurry," Susanna said.

I bundled Jewel in her blanket and picked her up.

Outside, I made a beeline toward the driveway, which intersected the middle of Great-Great Hedge. Once we made it off our property and onto the city streets, Mother wouldn't see us if she looked outside. We'd be safe. Susanna whistled softly to get my attention.

"What?" I said.

She headed toward the shed. "It's not enough to run away."

"Susanna. We have to hurry." I glanced back at the house.

Mother's bedroom window remained dark and empty, but she could wake up any moment. I wanted to be gone before that happened. Susanna disappeared into the shed and returned carrying two gallons of the gasoline we kept for our tractor.

She set the cans down and slipped the pack holding Knoll from her back.

"Stay here with Jewel and Knoll."

"What are you going to do?" I asked.

"Someone needs to end this. First down, the thorny ones."

I squatted, pressing the two sleeping children against me while Susanna doused the bushes with a gallon of gasoline. The plants writhed when the caustic fuel touched their leaves. They lashed out with their thorns, but Susanna anticipated that, and standing beyond their reach, she dropped a single, lit match into their midst. Their screams would have woken the dead, and I knew they'd wake Mother. Both children opened their eyes, crying. I leaped to my feet, slung Knoll in his pack onto my back, hoisted Jewel onto a hip, and hurried toward the driveway.

No!!" Mother's voice was thunderous.

I saw her looking out her window for a second before disappearing.

"Susanna! Hurry!" I shouted.

Susanna ran in our direction, carrying the second gallon. But she wasn't done. Instead of taking her crying Knoll into her arms, she kissed his cheek and turned to Great-Great Hedge. As she threw the gas onto the first of our kind, droplets splashed my arms. Susanna's arms were soaked with the liquid.

"Murder!" Mother shouted.

I turned and saw her barrel from the house, running toward the roses. The thorny ones' leaves crackled. They continued to shriek in as many voices as there'd been plants... or men. Mother keened.

Susanna smiled.

"Enough," I said.

Susanna shook her head, but she didn't look at me. Her eyes had turned toward Mother. Even from a hundred feet away, I could see the fury on Mother's face as she marched into the shed.

And Susanna laughed and skipped to Grandmother Oak, where she poured the last fuel and set the tree ablaze.

The trees cried out as Mother marched from the shed.

Grandmother Oak's branches contorted as they burned.

"You!" Mother shouted. "I should have killed you when you were little."

"As you sow, so shall you reap."

"Truer words were never spoken."

I don't think Susanna saw the axe until it was too late. I know I didn't because Mother hid it behind her until she was within striking distance. The metal glinted orange in the firelight as Mother brought it over her head.

"Look out!" I screamed.

I saw Susanna's startled expression. Then, as the axe fell, Susanna tossed the box of matches to me. I watched its trajectory as it landed at my feet and am forever grateful because I missed the moment the blade hit Susanna. I set the children down, picked up the box, and removed one wooden match.

Mother wiped the gore-covered axe against her floral dressing gown and advanced in our direction.

I pushed the children behind me and struck the match

against the box. The tip broke. My hands shook as I pulled out another. I tried again. Once twice, three times, I pulled the head across the striker until I held a tiny, fragile flame cupped in my hand. I stepped closer to Great-Great Hedge. The smoke choked me, and my eyes stung. I turned my palm and showed the flickering match to Mother.

"Stand back."

Mother laughed. "You lack the courage of your sister. What is lesson number one?"

"Protect our ancestors at all cost."

"At all cost," Mother said.

Behind me, four tiny hands grabbed my pants, clinging like burrs, and I thought, *protect the children.*

I dropped the match.

Great-Great burst into flames.

"No!" Mother ran to Great-Great.

I stepped away, almost knocking the children down. Turning, I knelt, swept them back into my arms, and hurried toward safety.

Mother attacked the burning hedge with the axe, hacking chunks away as fast as she could. But it was too late. As the fire licked her leaves, Great-Great's entire organism turned brown as if whatever magic kept her with us vanished at that moment. Within seconds, the arms that had embraced the homestead for over three hundred years surrounded us in a raging inferno.

Great-Great's ancient branches exploded, sending shrapnel fireballs everywhere. I'd misjudged how far to go. Some landed on Jewel's blanketed body and Knoll's pyjamas. *Protect the children.* Again, I set them down to beat the embers back using my bare hands.

Mother howled.

When the children were safe, I turned and saw Mother's

floral nightdress consumed in flames. I pulled the children close, pressing their faces into my body as Mother fell, writhing to the ground.

After I was certain she'd died, I used the remaining time on my phone to call for help.

REGENERATION

The in-betweens survived the fires but died days after. I have no way to prove my theory, hell, there's no way to prove anything about my family—but I think Mother died without passing along something they needed to survive. Maybe a piece more of her? Some blood? They grew smaller with every passing hour. By the time they died, they were the size of Mother's two pinky joints, the ones she'd used to make them in the first place.

I buried them alongside what remained of Mother.

Susanna never rose from where she'd been struck down. Her blood soaked into the earth, and a baby's breath grew on the spot the next day. I understood Susanna's message; I actually think it may have been her inside my head saying, "Protect the children." She needn't have bothered. I'd already decided to leave with Jewel and Knoll. I pulled the baby's breath, roots and all, and mulched it. It was what Susanna would've wanted.

News of the fire and deaths spread like invasive weeds. Once the police investigation found me blameless, I hired a broker to sell the property. She said we'd get a fair price despite my mother killing Susanna and torching the place.

"Prime property always sells," he'd said.

We'd make enough for Knoll, Jewel, and I to live on for quite some time.

I walked the property one last time. Knoll in the pack on

my back, Jewel by my side holding my hand. All that remained were ruins and ash.

I buckled the children into their seats in the Chevy. The truck had a full tank of gas, and we had Mother's hidden petty cash to get us started.

The cousins had already grown close, and they giggled and sang a song about ashes that Knoll taught Jewel. As we drove down the driveway, I thought about one of the proverbs I'd memorized:

"Death comes in intervals. We receive it as such, returning first to the earth from whence we came." - Great-Great, the First of Our Kind.

I almost said it out loud but decided not to.

Our tires hit the city asphalt, and I smiled, focusing on the road ahead.

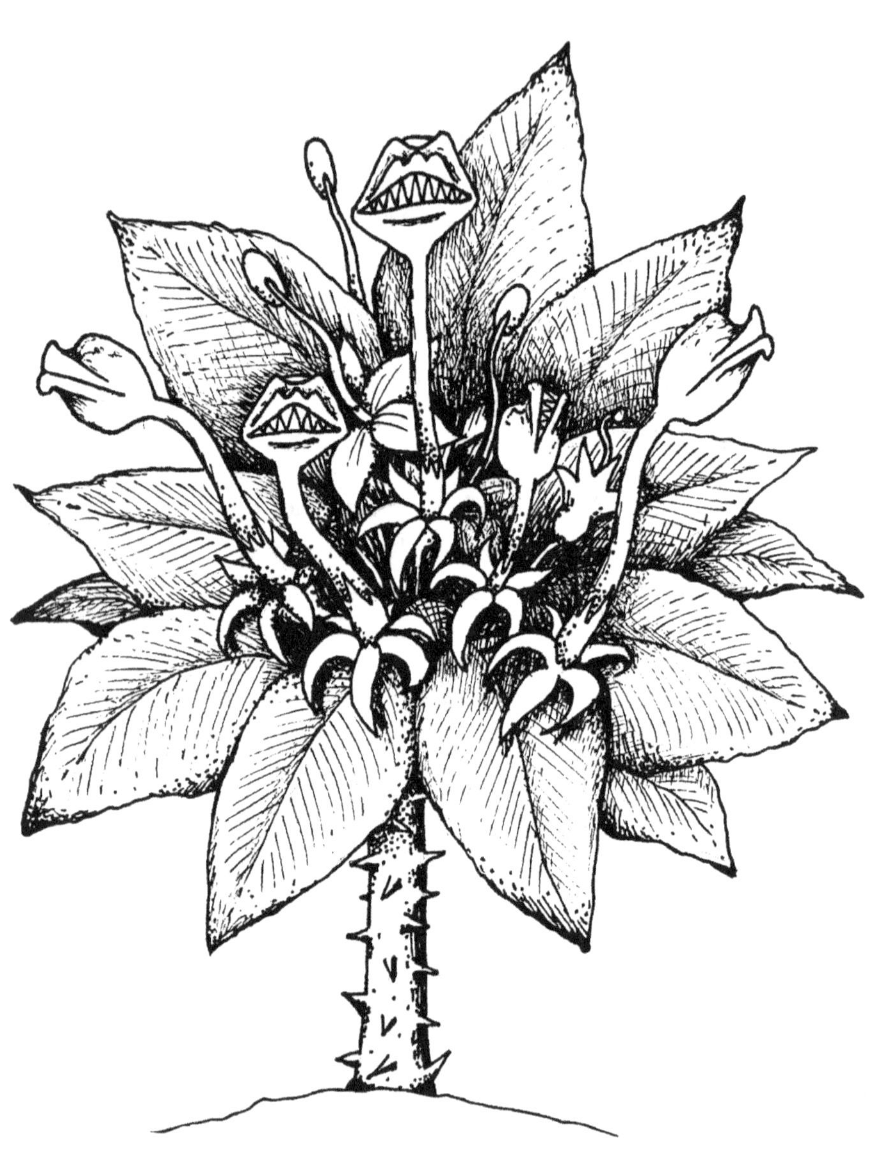

Tears Of Green*

Alex Grehy

40 YEARS AGO, KENT, UK

"Girls, slow down, and don't go too far into the woods!" Janey yelled as her daughters leapt from the car and ran up the overgrown path toward their grandfather's house. They whooped and giggled excitedly as a flock of goldfinches rose from the abundant flower seed heads.

"Let them run," laughed Greg, stepping out of the car and stretching. "I sure need to unkink after that drive. We should have stopped along the way."

"We just can't risk stopping in motorway service stations these days; things have gotten too weird. We came to my dad's farm to be safe, remember?" Janey's voice had a bitter edge.

Greg stepped around the car and hugged her tight. "Look at them, they're thriving. It's you I worry about. I hope you can relax a bit here, let go of..."

Janey pulled herself from his embrace and stomped up the

garden path. Her voice trailed behind her. "Let go of what, Greg? That I lost men under my command in Afghanistan? That the world's going to hell in a handcart? That people are stupid?" She stopped abruptly and turned to face her husband. "Or that you're such a dreamer you can't even see the danger we're in?"

Janey turned her back on him and ran along the path, shouting for the girls.

BREAKING NEWS: *Environmentalists have called for a ban on the sale of non-native Sandbox trees in the UK following the tragic deaths of two young girls in Kent. It's believed that Abigail, aged ten, and her sister, Laura, aged thirteen, were playing in their grandfather's orchard when a mis-thrown ball dislodged a fruit that exploded with unexpected force on contact with the ground. The girls died of their injuries an hour later. The Sandbox tree is a relatively new addition to UK gardens following the development of new hybrids, which allow it to grow in a wider range of conditions. Although first marketed as exotic ornamentals, in the current climate of unrest, the new hybrids, which are also exceptionally toxic, have been dubbed "Guard Trees". Environmentalists are now challenging the very human cost of this new security measure.*

50 YEARS AGO, CABINET OFFICE BRIEFING ROOMS (COBRA), LONDON

"I don't like working with the likes of him; it's all profit, not patriotism!" the Foreign Secretary said.

"Nothing wrong with profits. They drive our economy—that's virtually government policy," said the Home Secretary.

"But the ethics of genetic modification? The general

public doesn't want GM foods. They don't trust the technology," the Foreign Secretary pressed.

"Our public can afford ethics because they're well-fed, but Dr Quercus' GM crops have saved whole populations from starvation in third-world countries. Surely you saw that on your recent, ahem, grand tour?" the Home Secretary sniped.

"Indeed! And when the choice is starvation or GM crops, well, then there is no choice," the Foreign Secretary replied.

The Prime Minister thumped his fist on the mahogany meeting table. "No choice! We are out of choices! That is what brings us here today. Gentlemen, we are losing the war against terrorism using conventional weapons. We need Dr Quercus' particular skill set."

"I don't trust patriotism that has to be paid for," said the Chancellor. "It's little more than blackmail."

"Says the man whose father-in-law owns a munitions company," said the Home Secretary.

"Look, we commissioned this research," said the Chief of Defence. "The least we can do is listen to his results before we draw any conclusions."

The Prime Minister pressed the intercom. "Please send Dr Quercus in."

A tall, heavily-built man walked into the room. He was silent as he placed a briefcase on the meeting table and took out a laptop and a monitor, which he mounted flat in the centre of the table, screen pointing to the ceiling. He placed a blotter and a fountain pen by the side of his laptop, then finally sat down and addressed the room.

"Good morning, gentlemen. Thank you for agreeing to meet in person. Let's get straight to the point. I do not believe that traditional weapons serve you well when your enemies are gathered in small, scattered, but powerful cadres with a superior understanding of their local terrain. You—we

—need a way to suppress disparate hostile ideologies as they emerge, or, better still, before they emerge."

"And you think you have the answer?" sneered the Foreign Secretary.

"I believe that I have an elegant solution, which, unlike nuclear, will not destroy the planet we're standing on. And unlike chemical and microbiological weapons, our bio-engineered multi-celled weapons are not banned by the Geneva Convention."

The Chief of Defence looked bewildered. "If it's not nuclear, chemical, or microbiological, what IS it?"

"Gentlemen, please observe. I have prepared a brief holographic presentation of our new range of weaponized plants."

The monitor at the centre of the table lit up. Holographic plants seemed to spring into the air.

"I have genetically engineered a range of plants that we may use as offensive weapons," said Dr Quercus.

"Ha, what are they—man-eating plants? Giant Venus Flytraps? This is nonsense!" The Home Secretary scoffed.

"Oh no, nothing so lurid or ineffective. But if you do not want to know, I am sure there will be other parties who will wish to listen." Dr Quercus tapped his keyboard, and the bright holographic display winked out.

The men blinked and shifted uncomfortably as a sudden darkness crowded the room.

"No, please. I'm sure my colleague is just trying to inject a little levity into the meeting. Please continue," the Prime Minister urged.

"Very droll," Dr Quercus said with a thin smile. He tapped his laptop, and the holo-display lit the room again. "We have taken far more prosaic plants, ones that will cause no suspicion, and enhanced their natural defensive properties—thorns, toxins, and, of course, accelerated growth."

"So, your killer plants—how do they recognize the enemy?" asked the Foreign Secretary.

"Really, do you ask that of your bombs? You target the enemy by placing the weapons where they are and where you are not," Dr Quercus replied.

"And how do we clear the plants once they've done their job?"

"The same way as you clear minefields—you don't. However, unlike mines, these plants have genetic obsolescence—they tend to have a lifespan of no more than ten years, even the trees."

"They won't reproduce, set seeds?" the Home Secretary asked.

"The plants are not sterile, reproduction being a major motivator for growth, even among non-sentient plants. However, our patented hybridisation technology means that subsequent generations will breed back to the original genome."

"So they're safe?" said the Home Secretary.

The Chief of Defence snorted. "They're weapons—unsafe by definition!"

"Indeed," said Dr Quercus. "I had understood that your operational priority was to neutralize the enemy; had you informed me that control was more important, then I might have directed my research toward developing a genetic kill switch. Alas!"

"I'm sure we can handle the weaponized plants," said the Chief of Defence, glaring at the Home Secretary.

The Home Secretary appealed to the Prime Minister. "But we should commission research into the genetic kill switch; to keep the green movement happy."

"Very well," the Prime Minister said. "But that's for another time. Gentlemen, we have an election looming. We need to show the public that we're on top of the recent terrorist attacks. They've been baying for us to target the source." The Prime Minister held up his hand. "Yes, Chief of Defence, I know it's not that simple, but this is the public we're talking to. We need decisive action. Let's concentrate on what Dr Quercus has ready right now and at least be seen to be doing something."

"Yes!" said the Chief of Defence. "Dr Quercus, have you given any thought to deployment?"

"The weapons may be deployed in stages depending on the terrain. Observe." Dr Quercus tapped his laptop, and a holographic model of a mountainous terrain appeared, barren and grey.

"In this scenario, the first wave attack is brambles, growing at an accelerated rate of 30 centimetres an hour." As Dr Quercus spoke, a creeping fog of green spread across the terrain almost imperceptibly. "This variety has six-inch thorns which make movement difficult, though the finer thorns are more deadly. They are easily shed from the plant, becoming embedded in the skin, where commensal bacteria rapidly initiate necrotizing fasciitis. Now please note the fertile lowlands."

A dark green fog shimmered across the landscape, which then rapidly turned brown.

"The lucrative opium poppy crops, along with essential food crops, are being destroyed by bracken, whose toxins inhibit the growth of competing plants and also neutralize pollinating insects."

Around the border of the hologram, tall trees seem to spring toward the ceiling.

"Sandbox trees—modified, of course. The spiny bark has a fast-acting and deadly neurotoxin. The fruit explodes on contact with the ground, scattering seeds at high speed with an impressive blast radius greater than that of a hand grenade. The fruit is also neurotoxic—if, ah, shrapnel breaks the skin, victims are incapacitated almost immediately; death occurs within an hour. The trees act as an impenetrable boundary, imprisoning the enemy until starvation forces their surrender."

"And how do we access the territories once they've surrendered?" asked the Foreign Secretary.

"That is an operational matter for you to discuss. Again, do you ask the companies building your bombs to tell you how to clear up the debris afterwards?"

The Home Secretary laughed as the Foreign Secretary squirmed under Dr Quercus' supercilious gaze.

"Moving on..." the Chief of Defence said. "What about arid climates? Many enemies of our state have desert strongholds."

"Where there are humans, there is moisture. We are a perfect growing medium," Dr Quercus replied.

"Nonsense! A dead body maybe, but you don't see plants growing on living humans," the Prime Minister said.

"Until now. I prepared a small demonstration." Dr Quercus put on a pair of goggles, carefully checking the seal. He invited the politicians to do the same. Then he opened the conference room door and invited the two security guards who had been standing outside the room to enter. He quickly closed the door behind them.

"Please stand by the door for five minutes," the doctor instructed. The guards looked over to the Prime Minister, who nodded to confirm the order. The men did not question why members of the cabinet were wearing goggles. They stood at ease while Dr Quercus opened his fountain pen and let one drop of green ink fall onto the blotter. Then he sat down. Five awkwardly silent minutes later, Dr Quercus got up and invited the guards to approach the meeting table. He took a small camera from his briefcase and attached it to the holographic screen; As he pointed the lens at the men, the holographic display showed an enlarged model of their faces —the whites of their eyes were completely green.

The politicians leapt to their feet, shouting.

"Sit down, gentlemen. You are not in any danger." Dr Quercus removed his goggles. "The dosage was very small, and the delivery system is quite specific. The moisture inherent in the human cornea is enough to allow rapid cellular reproduction of my modified algae. To be specific, blanket weed, which forms a mat over the eyes causing debilitating irritation and blindness; established algae will then migrate to the tear ducts and swiftly reproduce in the mucous membranes, where they will eventually cause suffocation."

He gestured at the guards, who were now on the floor, rubbing their eyes. Dr Quercus tapped his laptop keyboard. "My specialist team will be in to care for them shortly."

The Prime Minister sat down and gestured to the guards, who had begun gasping for breath. "Will they be okay?"

"No, they will not be okay. Anyone who owns a pond understands how intractable blanket weed can be. But do not worry; my people are discreet, and there will be no repercussions on you. Presumably, they signed the Official Secrets Act?"

The Prime Minister nodded.

"Then you may record them as 'killed in the line of duty' without giving further explanation."

"But they're not dead!" the Home Secretary sputtered.

"Not yet," Dr Quercus agreed.

39 YEARS AGO, KENT, ENGLAND

"Son, you don't have to leave! It wasn't your fault."

"Yes, it was his fault, Dad. Who kicked the ball into that accursed tree?" Janey shouted, her face pale.

"It was an accident!" Janey's father remonstrated.

"Don't make excuses for him," Janey said. "It was an accident waiting to happen. He was always telling them to get outside and have some fun."

"Well, I agree with him. Children need fresh air; you can't grow up right cooped up in a cage. You were a wild child yourself, lost count of how many times you went climbing in the orchards and how many times you fell—it's a wonder you've got any collarbones left," her father said.

"More fool you for thinking that was okay! Besides, that was when trees didn't have exploding fruit. Why in the hell did you plant that thing anyway? It's as much your fault as his!" Janey yelled.

"I planted it for security—to protect the crops in the orchard. I fenced it and put up warning signs, but it grew a lot faster than I expected," her father replied.

"And your grandchildren paid the price!"

"Yes, they did, and now I'm paying for it in grief," her father said.

"Really? Yet you still think he"—Janey pointed at Greg—"was right to let them scamper around like squirrels!"

"Enough!" roared Greg, stepping away from the car. "Janey, you don't have to shovel your pain onto our heads. Don't you think we're hurting too? Don't you think we wish we could turn the clock back?"

Janey looked into his eyes, cornflower blue, just like Abigail's. She scowled, then turned away from the two men and walked back toward the house.

"I'd better go," said Greg, defeated. "Goodbye, Pops."

"Those girls were happy, as happy as weeds, growing wild and free, Greg." The old man put a hand on his son-in-law's shoulder. "It was a terrible accident, no one's fault. Try to remember that. Try to remember them happy."

Greg got into the car and rolled down a window. "I loved those girls, and I love Janey, but maybe if I get out of her sight, she'll have a chance to heal."

"We can only hope," said Janey's father, turning away and walking toward the house. He saw Janey standing by the barn nearby, holding a heavy chainsaw.

"Well, Dad, let's really see how sorry you are. Let's get that tree chopped down and burned."

"Can't let you do that, Janey. It's too dangerous. I shouldn't have to tell you. We can't get close enough. Just leave it be."

Janey threw the chainsaw through the open barn door and ran into the house, sobbing.

50 YEARS AGO, LONDON, ENGLAND

Memorandum (Classified):

To: Prime Minister; Chancellor of the Exchequer
Ref: Cost/inventory Plant-based Arsenal
Total Cost: £150 Billion

Key Components:

Rubus spp (Brambles) modification: accelerated growth (30 cm/hour); extended thorn length (6 cm); commensal bacteria - MRSA - necrotizing fasciitis. Purpose: infiltration; anti-personnel.

Pteridium spp. (Bracken): modifications: accelerated growth; enhanced natural defences: growth-inhibiting toxins (target native flora); enhanced leaf-borne toxins (inhibit pollinator lifecycle). Purpose: Limiting production of food crops (especially grains & cereals).

Hura spp. (Sandbox Trees): modifications: accelerated growth (30m/18 months); adapted to cold climates; drought resistant; enhanced neurotoxicity (spiny bark and fruit); high-explosive seed capsules (150 m/s, blast radius 300m).

Purpose: containment; anti-personnel.
Cladphora spp. (Filamentous algae - blanket weed): modified for accelerated growth; optimized for growth in human tears. Purpose: anti-personnel.

<u>Note:</u> Dr Quercus has offered an option on Filamentous algae adapted to marine environments (anti-piracy weapon).

Additional cost: £10 billion. *Cost does not include the genetic 'Kill Switch' (under development).

Signed: Chiefs of Defence.

Memorandum (Classified):

To: Chiefs of Defence
Ref: Acquisition of plant-based armaments

Budget approved subject to Dr Quercus relocating to allied country with the necessary manufacturing capability.

Signed: Chancellor of the Exchequer
Counter-signed: Prime Minister

Memorandum (Classified):

To: Prime Minister
Ref: Deployment of Plant-based Weapons

Successful deployment confirmed. Large seeds sowed by auto-mated drones. High-altitude helium balloons destroyed by the enemy, effectively self-inoculating their terrain with algal spores.

Signed: Chiefs of Defence

35 YEARS AGO, KENT, ENGLAND

"We have to leave, NOW!" shouted Janey from inside the car.

"We can't. We have nowhere to go. We have to defend our home," her father said stubbornly.

"You can see the flames; they're coming closer." Janey looked through the windshield— the farm road rolled away into a far horizon smudged with grey smoke, hemmed with a bright orange fringe as the fire devoured low-lying vegetation. As she watched, a sudden column of flame flared above the haze. A resinous pine tree, she assumed—a beacon heralding the approaching devastation.

"They're miles away. But if you can see the flames, it's already too late to run. That's what my sister said about the bushfires when she moved to Australia."

"This is not Australia!"

"No, this is England, green and pleasant. I'm not wasting any more time arguing, Janey. I've got work to do."

"But you'll die!"

"Always looking on the bright side, Janey. I'll die anyway—I'm not immortal. But I can choose the place, if not the time." Her father hefted a chainsaw. "I'm going to cut a firebreak through the orchards. If you won't help, then at least don't hinder." He stomped off.

Janey revved the car engine, then turned the ignition off.

"Hold up, Dad. How can I help?"

"Get the irrigation system going, then use the pressure washer to hose the house down."

BREAKING NEWS: *A father and daughter have miraculously survived a wildfire that encircled their farm yesterday. Peter Cooper (70) and his daughter, Janey (32), survived by clearing a firebreak around their orchards, then 'damping down' the house and barns to prevent ignition by stray embers. A spokesperson for the Fire Brigade made the following statement: "While we are delighted that Mr. Cooper and his daughter are alive and unhurt, the best way to avoid injury from wildfires is to follow your local evacuation plan and assemble at coastal rescue centres."*

The current spate of wildfires has been sparked by attempts to use controlled burns to eradicate the so-called super-bracken currently spreading across food-producing areas of England. The bracken is fast-growing and resistant to pesticides. The efficacy of burning is being challenged, however, as the mature bracken burns at a ferocious rate. The resulting wildfires have overwhelmed a number of farms and villages in rural areas. New growth of super-bracken has also been observed in burnt areas in as little as twelve hours post-burn, prompted, it seems, by the combination of warm soil and the water used to extinguish the fires.

Memorandum (Classified):

To: Dr Quercus
Ref: Illegal trade in restricted plants

The cyber security force is reporting increased advertising of restricted bramble hybrids on the dark web. The Chief of Defence assures me that military supplies are secure. I seek assurances that your biosecurity is adequate. I will be sending a team to examine your facilities tomorrow. Please make yourself available to them.

Signed: Prime Minister

Memorandum (Classified):

To: Prime Minister
Ref: Illegal trade in restricted plants

I can assure you that our biosecurity is inviolable, as your inspectors will discover when they attempt to access our facility tomorrow. We are running our own investigations into the potential theft of patented genomes. However, early conclusions suggest the following:

- YOUR military personnel are collecting seeds from weaponized hybrids and selling them on the black market.
- YOU are failing to follow protocol, allowing spores (bracken) and pollen (brambles) to travel around the globe embedded on uniforms and footwear.
- YOUR cybersecurity team is, and always has been, ineffective in controlling cybercrime, allowing unrestricted trade of illegal items.

Ironically, most sales appear to be to members of the ruling elite seeking effective 'hedging' to protect their estates from looters. I recommend that you have a discussion with them when you next visit your private members' club.

Nonetheless, I appreciate your concern and will undertake an audit of our procedures forthwith.

Signed: Dr Quercus

20 YEARS AGO, SECRET LOCATION, ENGLAND

"How did this happen?" the Prime Minister asked, looking over the smoking ruin that had been Dr Quercus' research and manufacturing facility.

"We're waiting on forensics, but eyewitnesses suggest—"

"Eyewitnesses? There were survivors?"

"No, Sir, but a rather lucky delivery driver was a couple of miles away on that rise when the explosion happened." The agent gestured along the broad driveway that led away from the facility. "He thinks it was a drone attack—he saw a blue glow, then his engine stalled. He was going to call it in when he noticed his phone was dead too. That's when the incendiaries landed."

"And your conclusions?" asked the Prime Minister.

"An EMP pulse to wipe the electronics, then a missile to kill the personnel."

"And Dr Quercus?"

"Dead, Sir. Confirmed by DNA."

The Prime Minister frowned. He'd always been concerned that the enemy might attempt to compromise their weapons capability at the source. "Any idea who did this?"

The agent handed the Prime Minister a singed leaflet. "We have a what but not a who. This is from a radical group in the UK which promotes natural methods."

"Natural methods?"

"Natural methods of everything—organic farming, no genetic modification, no technology."

"That doesn't make sense. They used a drone and sophisticated armaments."

"They seem to have made an exception for Dr Quercus—he was a vocal opponent of their movement." The agent smiled bitterly, shaking his head.

"I didn't like the man," said the Prime Minister. "But he was the leading expert in plant-based weapons. Do you really mean to tell me that we've defeated international terrorism just to be scuppered by a bunch of pitchfork-wielding luddites?"

"It would seem that way," the agent replied.

BREAKING NEWS: *The Department of Health has issued a press release regarding a worrying increase in the incidence of a novel disease the tabloids are calling 'Green Eye'. They are advising people*

to check their eyes in a mirror every day. If you notice a tinge of green, stay at home and ring the helpline number below. DO NOT go to your doctor or local hospital. A government official will contact you at home and direct you to the appropriate facility. Eye-colour charts will also be issued to every household within the next few days.

Government representatives are dismissing reports that "Green Eye" is being caused by toxic agents released in last month's explosion and Quercus Corp's manufacturing facility.

Memorandum (Classified):

To: Prime Minister
Ref: Terrorist Attack - Dr Quercus' Facilities

Mode of attack confirmed: Two-component bomb—electromagnetic pulse followed by exothermic explosion.

All data lost. Recovery teams searching for information on the genetic kill switch. Unsuccessful to date.

Signed: Chiefs of Defence

7 YEARS AGO, BRIGHTON, ENGLAND

"Greg, she's kicking. Come and feel."

Greg walked over to the sofa where Megan, his wife, was lounging with a pack of chocolate digestive biscuits. He put a hand on her stomach and felt the jerk of his unborn daughter's foot.

"She'll be a soccer player for sure," Megan said, laughing. Then she put her hand over her mouth. "I'm sorry, Greg. I didn't mean..."

"It's okay—we can always find a safe place for her to play," Greg said, though his face was creased into a frown.

"Don't worry so. We'll make a new world for her," Megan said. "We need to look for the beauty and joy in life."

"Hey, Feddan!" Greg shouted at his son, who was sitting at the kitchen table, flicking the pages of an old picture book. "Feddan, come and feel your sister kicking—better get used to it sooner rather than later."

"Eeeuw!" replied Feddan, walking over to his parents. "Dad, can I go outside to play?"

Greg looked over at Megan.

"Yes," she said. "You can go play in the garden. Remind me of the golden rules."

"Wear my goggles, leave my play clothes outside, and flick the air scrubbers on when I come back in," Feddan chorused.

"That's right. Just a few simple rules, and we can have all the freedom we need." Megan smiled.

"I'll come with you," Greg said. "I could do with some fresh air."

Megan reached for Greg's hand. "You go ahead, Feddan. Daddy'll be out soon."

She turned to Greg. "You have to let go; he's a sensible boy, too sensible. He needs to run around, skin his knees, and have a bit of fun without his dad breathing down his neck."

Greg nodded abstractedly, his memory drifting back to Janey and her pathological anxiety.

Memorandum (Classified):

To: Prime Minister
Ref: Plant-based Weapons

Plant incursions confirmed in all global areas. Reports of survivors in some desert cities. Rapid and uncontrolled hybridisation has been identified between modified and natural plants.

Plants are not sentient, but they have a powerful imperative to grow and dominate their environment. All human life is now at risk.

Signed: Chiefs of Defence

2 YEARS AGO, MIGRATION CENTRE, FOLKESTONE, ENGLAND

Janey clambered onto the trestle table that served as a stage and looked over the group of 500 people who had been selected for her migration group.

"Right, everyone, you have your briefing packs, but let me make some introductions and go over the basics. My name is Janey Cooper, and I am part of an initiative set up in the years before the incursion of weaponized plants took away our government, our infrastructure, and our way of life. I, and a hundred others, are equipped with the vehicles, fuel, and equipment that we need to migrate to the Middle East. Our target is Oasis, a desert city built forty years ago in the centre of Saudi Arabia, well away from the coastline. Our mission is to establish a colony in the high-rise 'Jewel' building, which once housed a shopping mall, offices, and private accommodation. Intelligence reports suggest that Oasis has been abandoned since international oil pipelines were fractured by invading vegetation. However, the city has solar power capacity as well as freshwater distillation technology. All we have to do is get there. Any questions?"

"Janey, is that really you?"

Janey looked across the crowded room. Greg was standing up and waving frantically. She ignored him.

"Right, let's break up into small groups. I hope you completed your inventories. My colleagues will need to understand what resources and liabilities you're bringing to our new community." She stepped off the table and was immediately swept off her feet.

"Janey, it IS you! I can't believe it—you look wonderful."

"Put me down, Greg," she instructed coldly.

"Sorry, I'm so excited to see you. It's fate, our being allocated to your group." He gestured to his children, who'd been standing behind him. "Hey kids, this is Janey, my..." He looked at Janey's stern face. "My old friend. Now I know that it'll all be okay."

"Hello, nice to meet you. My name's Feddan. How should I address you?"

Janey shook Feddan's hand. "Hello, Feddan. We're going to be travelling together, so I think you'd better call me Janey."

"Janey, this is my sister, Telyn. She's only five, but she's brave, like our mummy."

"And what's your mummy's name?" asked Janey, looking around the room at the people now sitting in clusters, discussing inventory.

Telyn piped up. "My mummy was called Megan; she was pretty and laughed all the time."

"Was called?" Janey asked.

"Feddan, why don't you take Telyn and our inventory list over to our sub-group; I'll be with you in a second," Greg said. Once the children left, he turned to Janey. "Megan died, but I don't like to talk about it in front of them. They've been so brave." Greg's voice caught in his throat.

"I'm sorry," said Janey. "What happened?"

"She was on a ship, on her way to see her mother in the Outer Hebrides. She should have been safe, the sea's deep and cold there, but they got mired in blanket weed between the islands. Well, you know the policy, no more sea rescues—they're too risky. She called me with the last of the power on her phone. They were starving and had Green Eye on board. She was intending to jump into the sea, end it on her terms..."

"I'm sorry," Janey repeated as Greg's voice faltered. She lifted her hand, intending to pat his shoulder, but he grasped it tightly. She was surprised at the electric charge of attraction she felt at his touch, as if he'd been holding a taser. She looked into his cornflower blue eyes, and memories of Abigail came flooding back. She pulled her hand away roughly and coughed.

"Okay," she said. "Let's see what we can do to keep her kids—your kids—alive. At least we can avoid the coastal algae. We'll drive through the channel tunnel, then it's overland to the Middle East."

"Do you think we can make it?" asked Greg quietly.

"I don't know whether we can make it. All that I know is that we have to."

48 HOURS AGO. SAFWAN, IRAQ/KUWAIT BORDER

"That's the last of the fuel," Greg said, shaking the can.

"How many miles will that take us?" Janey asked.

"Two-hundred, two-fifty if we're careful."

Janey checked her map, then bashed her fist onto the side of the truck. "We won't make it to Oasis."

Greg put his hand over hers. "What are our options?"

"Let me think." She looked up at the sun. "It's almost

midday. Get them to set up camp for a few hours. We'll set out again at dusk when it's cooler."

Janey spread the map across the truck bonnet and checked her GPS. It was ironic that the satellites were happily going about their business, out of reach of the plants, while she had to use a handheld, clockwork compass to pick up their signal. She ground her teeth and took a reading on their position. *Damn.* They were five hundred miles from Oasis. *Why did we even bother to leave home,* she reflected, recalling the thousands of miles they'd already travelled and the losses they'd suffered on the way.

"It's not looking good, huh?" said Greg, reading her mood correctly. "Here, have some food."

Janey munched on an energy bar and pointed at the map. "We can't get to Oasis. But I think we can reach... Kuwait City. Damn!"

"That's okay. We can rest up in Kuwait City, maybe find some gas, then get to Oasis later."

"Wouldn't that be peachy?" Janey said, resting her head in her hands. "Look, Kuwait City's close to the coast. If we're lucky, we'll find a skyscraper and set up home before the plants arrive; but I don't think we'll be leaving."

Janey lifted her field binoculars. She scanned the road ahead. In the far distance, she saw dust plumes rising. She hoped it was one of the other groups from England—maybe they would make it to Oasis. She swung around; behind her, the landscape shimmered in the heat, but the sandy haze was tinged with green.

PRESENT DAY. KUWAIT CITY

"MOVE!" Janey shouted as her rag-tag band of survivors faltered on the landing.

"We can't go any faster!" said Greg.

"We have to get to the 51st floor," she hissed.

"Not today!" Greg replied, supported by the nods of the adults and children slumped on the concrete floor.

"Let's at least get to Floor 32, the food hall." Janey looked at a worn 'Welcome' leaflet she'd picked up on the building's ground floor.

"Where are we now?" asked Greg.

"Fifteen," Janey replied.

"Okay." Greg nodded. "Just give us five minutes to have some water."

An unnatural silence wrapped around them. The cacophony of the cities had stilled over a year ago.

Janey opened her backpack and bit her lip; they had just enough clean water left. But she didn't want to risk running out before they settled in their new home and set up evaporator stills. "A sip each, no more," she cautioned the children.

A dozen heads nodded quietly.

Greg stood close to Janey and whispered, "They should be whining. They should be wanting more, should be running amok outside, playing ball games. They should be..."

Janey turned on him. "Isn't that what got us into this mess?"

Greg's shoulders tensed, and she heard him muttering as if counting under his breath.

"Blame the terrorists, blame the government, but don't you ever blame the innocent!" he said, his voice quiet and intense. "This stupid conflict has robbed us of so many freedoms, but the freedom of children to be *children* is the hardest to bear. Not that I expect you to ever understand that."

Janey ignored him, though she now clenched her own fists in anger. She looked around, seeing a few of the kids fidgeting with their swimming goggles. "DO NOT remove your eye protection!"

"Right, that's enough time," growled Janey, shouldering her pack. "The sooner we move, the sooner we can set up camp."

"Floor thirty-two. Good effort, everyone," said Janey. "I reckon we have two hours of daylight left. Have a quick rest, and then Unit One, look for bottled water and canned food; Unit Two—textiles and soft furnishings. Unit Three, check the perimeter and set up camp. Get the children settled. Remember—"

"Keep your goggles on and check that all windows are secure," Greg said. "We know our stuff, Janey, even if we aren't military personnel."

"Keep your eye on the prize. One more day of this"—Janey touched her goggles—"and then we can relax. We can't afford the materials to filter the air in this temporary camp." Janey dismissed Greg, moving to the food hall's glass walls. *Intact, double-glazed, sealed, good,* she thought, before helping the foraging parties to move their finds from deserted fast-food catering units into the centre of the hall.

She shook her head with disbelief at the supplies the fleeing citizens had left behind. *What a great haul.* They hadn't appreciated their treasure.

"Bingo!" shouted one of the foraging parties. The scent of ground coffee wafted across the room. Janey breathed in deeply, barely remembering the last time they'd had hot water for brewing. That would change soon.

"Careful, don't spill that ambrosia," she said. "That can be our treat when we set up home." Janey turned away. The scent of coffee had awoken memories of home, of Greg, before the kids, when life had seemed simple and carefree. She snorted; she'd never been carefree. She'd picked up a sackful of grief on her first tour of Afghanistan, and that sack had just got heavier with every year. But maybe, when the colony was established and they had a semblance of safety, she could lay that burden down for a little while.

Greg shook Janey's shoulder. She woke up with a start, alert and looking for the emergency. But instead, Greg handed her a bottle of water.

"Good morning, sleepy head." He grinned.

"What?" she replied, taking a sip.

"It's an hour past sunrise, but the settlers have been up since dawn. This is IT, Janey," he said, lifting her to her feet. "One last push, and we're home."

Janey returned his smile. This wasn't the Oasis she was aiming for. She could only hope that the other groups from England had made it—that they were busy forming individual colonies in their chosen desert skyscrapers, safe until the day they might be able to leave their strongholds and live together again.

"Report!" she demanded.

"Units One and Two are hauling supplies to the top floor. Unit Three is almost ready to move—we just need to wake the children," Greg replied.

"Good work." Janey allowed him a little praise. "You take Unit Three, and I'll follow behind and seal the doorways." She checked the building's leaflet, pointing at the plan. "Assemble here. The foyer area should hold us all. We can do an eye inspection there after we've run the air scrubbers."

Greg moved away, bouncing with excitement. Janey looked around, doing a last check for usable materials. She wouldn't allow them to revisit the lower floors once their colony was established upstairs. Her gaze swept through the windows. The early morning haze was tinged with green. She lifted her binoculars—the suburbs they'd traversed just days ago were already being overwhelmed by creeping greenery.

"Okay, everyone, here's our new home. If we're careful, we should be able to make a life here." Janey held up her hand. "Don't ask me how long that will be—you know the deal. Just make every day count, and don't look too far into the future." She looked over the group fidgeting impatiently in the top floor foyer and checked her watch. The air scrubbers had been running for an hour, and it would soon be safe to remove their goggles.

She addressed the group. "You know the drill. Remove your goggles one by one at 10-minute intervals; perform an eye inspection on your predecessor before you remove your own goggles."

"At last, I get to fully admire those baby blues," Greg teased, hugging her.

Janey frowned; this was no time for flirting.

Greg turned to the group. "Here we go! Let's count down."

"Three, two, one... Goggles Off!" Greg winked, then he and the other settlers swept their eye coverings off and threw them in the air.

Janey pushed Greg aside furiously. "Okay, you've had your fun. You'd better hope that the air scrubbers worked, or you'll all be in trouble." Janey grumbled, "Come up here for your eye inspections."

The group shuffled into line, presenting their faces to the clockwork flashlight that Janey held. Her expression was stony. They'd lost so many people to Green Eye, or more accurately, to carelessness. The algae was mindless; it didn't attack. But give it a place to grow by taking off your goggles to rub tired eyes, or be late putting your goggles on, or...whatever. Janey was tired. The deaths were always grieved as accidents, but she had no patience for excuses.

"Here, rest for a minute," Greg said, patting the empty chair next to his. "I saved you a little treat." Greg handed Janey a glass jar with a tiny dusting of fine pink powder inside.

"What is it?" she asked suspiciously.

"Dehydrated raspberry powder. It was in the restaurant."

Janey lifted the jar and licked the powder. She hummed approvingly as the intense sweetness hit her taste buds. "Ooh, that's good," she said. "Was there enough to share?"

"That was the last, but the kids had some for breakfast," said Greg. "I wish we could have a final forage for berries outside." He looked longingly at the desert blue sky.

"We can't risk it." Janey shook her head. "But the hydroponics are looking good." She waved to the troughs lining the skyscraper's glass walls. They'd only been in place a fortnight, but there was already a shimmer of green across the liquid-growing medium. She shuddered, but this was healthy growth from seeds harvested before the plant war.

"Did we bring any raspberry seeds?" she asked, licking the last of the powder.

"No, just strawberries."

"They'll do nicely." Janey sighed. "How long before our first crop?"

"It'll be a month for the fruit, but we should have some salad greens in a couple of weeks," Greg replied.

"And the root crops?"

"They can't be rushed."

Greg scowled as he looked across the city. The green invasion was advancing rapidly. Brambles had already climbed to the first-floor level of nearby tower blocks. In the distance, only the height of the amorphous green humps hinted that there had ever been buildings there.

"Cheer up!" Janey told Greg. "I've got a surprise for everyone." She then stood up and shouted, "At 13:00 hours, coffee and hot chocolate in the mess hall!"

"You got hot water?" Greg asked, picking her up and spinning her around.

"Well, I will if you stop clowning around." Janey grinned briefly, allowing herself to be swept up by his charm for a moment. Then she pushed herself out of his grasp. She saw his face light up with hope as he reached out for her hand, but she turned away. Her thoughts flashed back to being with him in their first apartment, delirious with love and joy. She shook her head. She couldn't turn the clock back, and she wasn't ready to think about the future, not just yet. "The heat exchanger's up and running," she said, "so the midday sun should bring the water to the boil. It needs tweaking, but it does the job."

Janey walked along the line of hydroponics troughs, admiring the blushing strawberries nodding among the trailing vines.

She smiled, imagining the tart freshness of the berries when they were picked in a few days' time.

Greg interrupted her reverie as he grasped her elbow.

"Keep smiling," he said. "We have a situation, but we can't afford a panic. Just walk with me to the conference room."

Janey struggled to casually acknowledge the settlers' greetings as she walked across the floor. When she arrived at the conference room, Feddan and Telyn were sitting at the table. "What are you doing here?"

"I'm sorry. We were playing chase, and Telyn fell against the emergency door. The bar tipped and..." Feddan faltered and looked down at his feet.

"They've been outside," Greg said.

Janey sat down abruptly, her breath whooshing out of her lungs. Then she sprang up and rummaged through her pockets frantically until she found her goggles and fitted them over her eyes. She sat down again, aware that Greg and the kids were staring at her.

"It was my fault. Telyn's only six, and she was laughing this morning like she hasn't laughed, ever, so I thought it would be okay to play tag," said Feddan.

"It was an accident," said Greg, "We should have told you to be careful."

"We did tell them, Greg," snapped Janey. She turned to Feddan, hitting the table with her fist. "All this time, I wanted you kids to have a chance of a childhood, and your *playtime* has finished us."

Telyn sat with her face in her hands, her words barely discernible between heaving sobs.

"You're mean! I was...having fun...outside was so pretty... gold and orange and pink clouds...not horrible like you said." The little girl lifted her head. Thready green tears leaked from her eyes as Janey punched the table again.

"You, stay here!" Janey barked as she moved toward the door. "You too! Check Feddan's eyes—and yours!" she said to Greg as he moved to join her. She strode out of the room. She leaned on the door as it closed behind her and took a deep breath before shouting, "Eye inspection, NOW! And run the air scrubbing cycle, stat!"

As the startled settlers gathered, one held her hand up.

"What?" Janey barked.

"We don't have enough clean filters for a full air scrubbing cycle."

"Then just use what we have," replied Janey. "But let me check your eyes first."

Janey shone her flashlight in the woman's eyes. Her hazel irises were a thin ring around her fear-dilated pupils. But Janey was only interested in the white of her eyes.

The green-tinged whites.

Janey checked the rest. The outer door could only have been open for a minute, but already the algal spores had invaded their eyes. In a matter of hours, they would be blinded by a mat of blanket weed growing across their mois-ture-rich corneas, and then it would invade their mucous membranes and slowly smother them.

She became aware of Greg standing beside her.

"Check my eyes," Janey ordered, lifting her goggles.

Greg shone the flashlight in her face. "You're in the clear. The boy is too."

Janey sighed, then sobbed. Of the fifty settlers, only she and Feddan were unaffected.

Greg's words cut through her thoughts. "I think you should stay here. You need to look after my son. Maybe he's immune; maybe you're immune. What if you're the key?"

Feddan was wearing his goggles again and holding onto

Telyn's hands, trying to stop her from scratching the stringy blanket weed from her eyes.

"I'll take the others. You can run the scrubbers. Maybe the air will come clean enough for the two of you. Someone should get to enjoy the strawberries." Greg smiled weakly and reached for her, but Janey stepped back.

"You still haven't forgiven me, huh?" he whispered bitterly. "I'd hoped we..." His voice trailed off.

"It's no use starting what we can't finish. You know what's coming," said Janey, leaning her head forward and allowing her hair to fall over her face, hiding her sadness.

Green tears streaked down Greg's face as he leaned over and kissed the top of her head. "I know what's coming. Will you at least look after Feddan as a mother would? I know you know how to love a child. Love him, for my sake. For his sake."

Feddan looked up when he heard his name.

"I'll take her now," Greg said, scooping Telyn into his arms. "I need you to be brave, Feddan, to live and find a way to mend this crazy world you've inherited."

"Dad, it was my fault. I should pay. Let me come with you," Feddan sobbed.

"You're not to blame for this mess." Greg shifted Telyn into the crook of one arm and kissed her cheek. He reached out with his free arm and hugged Feddan tightly.

Janey stepped back, wishing they were her kids, longing to be part of a family again. Greg looked up and gently pushed Feddan toward her. Janey gathered the boy into her arms and held him tight.

Greg turned to the settlers. "Come on. You know what we have to do. Let's go."

The adults crowded around him, sending the same old arguments whirling around his head—maybe they could wait, maybe this time would be different. There was a loud hubbub of shouting and wailing, then Greg shouted, "ENOUGH!" The crowd fell silent.

Greg lifted Telyn onto his shoulders. Her eyes were matted with blanket weed, her cheeks striped with blood where she had tried to scratch the plants away.

"Would you have her suffer anymore? Would you have them suffer?" Greg gestured at the children, already rubbing at their eyes. His voice was low and intense. "Would you drain resources better left for the few that might have natural immunity?"

Greg didn't wait for their answer but strode toward the door. Janey held Feddan back as the settlers streamed past her, eerily silent as they streamed onto the balcony. Far below, the brambles had already reached the pavement. Greg slammed the door shut behind him.

Feddan ran to the window, pressing his hand against the glass. Greg turned, putting Telyn down for a moment. The little girl's eyes were completely obscured, but Greg could obviously still see his son as he pressed his palm hard against the window, as if willing the glass to melt and allow them one last touch. Janey saw Greg shake his head, then he turned away and got the settlers lined up, facing the parapet. The adults hugged the children tightly. Through the thick glass, she heard his voice.

"Right, kids. We're going to learn how to fly. We grown-ups are heavier than you, so you'll need to show us how it's done. Let's go!"

Janey set the air scrubbers going and returned to Feddan. She peeled him from the window. The snot and tears that had glued his cheek to the glass were mercifully clear.

"Come away now," she said. "You don't want to remember them like this."

But Feddan refused to move. Janey sat on the floor next to him and watched. Half the settlers had already jumped, but a few hesitated, and some, already blinded by the choking weed, were stumbling, unable to find the edge. She saw Greg help and encourage them to take the leap. Minutes later, only he and Telyn were left. Greg turned and blew her a kiss, then he picked Telyn up in his arms, and they were gone.

Janey put her arms around Feddan's shoulders as he slumped, silent now, his sobs all spent. She breathed past the lump of sorrow lodged in her throat. Then she stood up and grasped his hand.

"Don't be sad," she said. "Maybe the strawberries will be sweet."

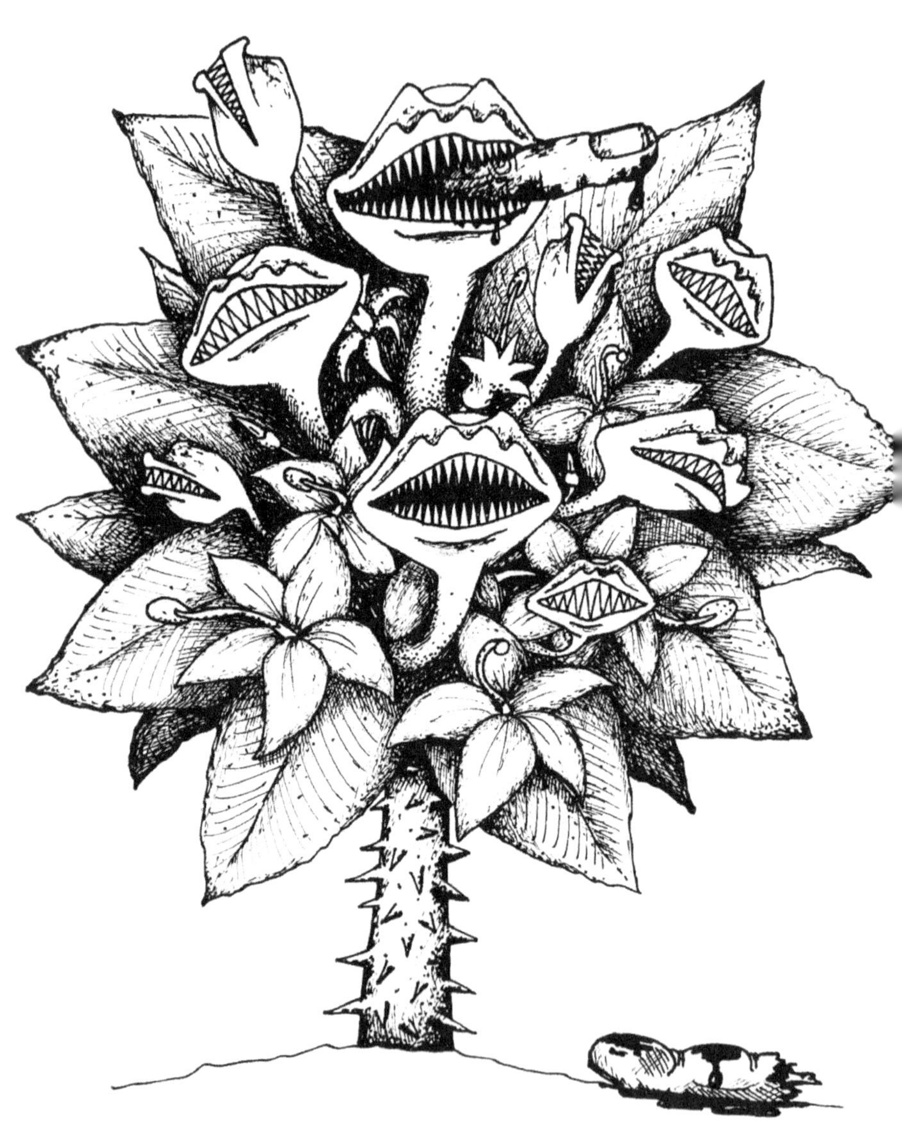

THE BUBBLE

R.A. CLARKE

370 days had passed since the meteor came down and life as we knew it ceased to exist. An entire year's worth of waiting. Watching. Fretting. Fearing.

I covered my buzz-cut with the moulded camouflage helmet I'd been issued for this mission and secured the chin strap. After popping on my backup mouth breather and energizing my facial shield, I conducted a quick mic test. "Berk76 to Control, checking in. Over?"

"Hear you loud and clear, Berk76," Megs, our mission dispatcher, sounded tinny through the comms. "Check-in confirmed."

My teammates' steady roll call faded into the background. I leaned against the corrugated metal wall of the base's holding hangar, reluctantly waiting for the green light for my team to approach the Bubble. Staring across the hundred-yard gap that stood between me and our infiltration target, I couldn't help but gawk at the sprawling dome erected around the meteor crater. It was a hasty patchwork mess of metal, wood, flexi-glass, and fine-webbed laser

209

shielding on the top half—the kind that trapped air. No other kind would do. The initial plan had been to asphyxiate the contaminated flora that grew and spread from the epicentre. But when that failed, and the plants persisted, they dug a chasm around it and switched the dome's purpose to containment.

Closing my eyes, I took a deep breath, the usual smell of vehicle exhaust, arid earth, gunmetal, and sweaty bodies now filtered from the air. Soldiers and techs walked to and from various hangars and science labs. Somewhere a horn honked, followed by the unintelligible barking of orders.

All I wanted was to rewind a year and go back to before it happened. *The before* was what everyone called pre-meteor life now—pre-bubble life. When people went about their business, making plans, laughing, and having babies without fear of their child never having a future. The day it crashed down to Earth still remained so vivid in my mind.

I sat outside with my wife Bianca and some friends on one of my few days off, soaking up the summer sun. I'd just cracked a cold beer, which my dog Sookey, a chubby shepherd mix, had impressed everyone by fetching when the sky overhead flashed white like lightning.

A brilliant fireball of golden light blazed across the sky, a whoosh echoing in its wake.

"What the hell is that?" My buddy Wes mumbled, rising from his deck chair.

Everyone automatically looked to me because I'd recently been accepted into the Extra-Terrestrial Intelligence Unit or ETIU. But it wasn't like I knew any more than the average soldier. I only took the post because it offered stability, something I desired for Bianca after being gone so long overseas.

As the flaming ball rocketed toward the ground not far from where we stood, perhaps only miles, I wrapped an arm around Bianca. "A meteor, maybe? It's hard to know for sure."

My wife clutched my side. "So, what, is this the end of the world or something?"

I squeezed her tighter. "No, no, I'm sure it's not that. It doesn't look big enough to do that kind of damage. But we should all get inside to be safe. And I'm gonna go make a quick call."

We all rushed into the house, but when I tried to split off from the group, my wife shook her head, refusing to let me go. Tiffany, Wes's wife, grasped Bianca's hand with a reassuring smile. I nodded, then ducked into our bedroom, but instead of dialing someone on the visiphone there, I grabbed my work radio. I needed to hear the chatter. And, boy, was there chatter.

"Alright, everyone, wake up!" A familiar voice sliced through my memory.

I straightened from the wall, spotting my square-jawed, silver-haired team leader bellowing from the hangar entrance.

"We're a go for Mission Recon. So, prep your shit, 'cause we're heading out in five!" Captain Meloon was gone from view a second later, likely to have a last-minute briefing with his superiors. Today's mission had been sanctioned by the government's top dogs, so without a doubt, they'd be clamoring for every last detail. This was a big deal. The first real attempt to enter the dome beyond sending in probes and planting cameras inside the entrance. That made it top priority, highly classified, and—unfortunately for me—dangerous.

It hadn't taken long for things to go to hell after the meteor struck, and irradiated ooze began flowing out of it, tainting everything it touched. It took even less time for me to regret my fresh transfer to ETIU.

Beanie leaned over from his spot beside me on the wall. "Hey, Berk. You ready to kick some alien ass? I hear you got an ace shot. I'm counting on that." The twenty-something-year-old was easily 6'5" and lanky—hence his nickname, short for beanpole—and was a lab geek through and through. He'd be the one taking care of all the sciencey stuff on this mission, collecting samples and taking readings.

I rolled my head to the side, cocking an eyebrow. "There are no 'asses' to kick in there, man. Just a bunch of sludge and contaminated plant life." *I sure hoped that was true.* "We're only going inside to test these fancy suits they got us wearing and collect some evidence."

Beanie chuckled and butted out the smoke he'd been pulling drags from. "Bro, they've seen *animals* on the cameras, and they don't look right. Who knows what's lurking deeper in. If you seriously don't think there'll be something to fight in there after all this time, you got rocks for brains."

"So about as smart as you then!" I shot back and laughed when he punched me in the arm. But the truth was, on the inside, I didn't like hearing his take. In no way did I want to fight any metastasized sludge aliens—or mutated animals. All I wanted was to be home with Bianca and be there for the birth of my daughter, due any day now. Instead, I had to be here.

Thankfully, the evidence we'd been tasked to gather was supposed to help the ETIU's science labs find a way to neutralize the spread—maybe even kill the invasive flora entirely. Nobody ever said it out loud, but everyone knew we were all living one step away from fucked. It was only a matter of time before the ooze's roots broke through the Bubble's perimeter.

So, while I didn't want to die inside some fucked up dome, I wanted my family to survive way more. I'd do whatever I could to ensure this mission yielded results and that no spore-infested plant life ever got anywhere near my loved ones.

Captain Meloon, a loyal military man only a handful of years older than me at forty, strode back into the hangar and stopped in front of us with a resounding heel click. "Alright, assholes, let's get a move on. I want to be in and out of that Bubble well before sundown." He tapped on the control hub circling his wrist, then brandished the time readout on the compact screen. "That gives us six hours—should be plenty of time as long as nothing goes sideways." With a crisp flick of his fingers, he led the way to the door.

Beanie walked behind the captain, joined by Garcia—a steady shot with a wicked ability to multitask under pressure. If you ever needed a vital task completed in the heat of battle, he was your man. Like me, he'd been recruited to provide coverage and firepower. I brought up the rear with a rifle slung across my back while Saints, our last-but-not-least team member, walked grumpily beside me. She was even less enthusiastic about going on this mission than I was if that were possible.

Saints—nicknamed for her ability to be an angel one minute and a nightmare the next—had to postpone her wedding because of this mission. I didn't blame her for being pissed. We'd all wondered why it *had* to be her that came. She specialized in topography and navigation and was placed in charge of the charting during our trek. But couldn't someone else with similar training have done that? If Saints knew the answer, she wasn't telling.

We stopped in front of the six-foot tall outer airlock door, which was affixed to a fully enclosed bridge about ten feet wide and thirty feet long that would take us across the chasm and right up to the Bubble's main access. The curved dome loomed beyond it—reaching a height of nearly one hundred feet, I was told—its sectioned walls angling away from us. From where we stood, it stretched triple that distance on either side, and its total diameter spanned two full miles.

Meloon knocked on the door and reported the required clearance via his Hub. His jaw flexed as he tapped his foot.

I glanced below the tunnel to where the government had ordered a chasm dug. It was as wide as it was deep at approximately twenty feet and circled the entire Bubble like a moat, minus the water. Shrivelled and cauterized roots protruded and hung lifelessly from sheared dirt on the opposite side. A patrol meandered by, giving us nods. They had heavy sear-guns slung across their camouflage backs, each chunky oblong barrel singed black from regular use. Those guns fired a concentrated laser that burned whatever it touched and were the only thing keeping the thicker below-ground roots from stretching across the chasm.

I wished I'd been issued one to carry inside, but the captain said they were too heavy. Said we needed to be agile, so regular old lead bullets would have to do.

A decorated military officer in a gold-brimmed cap and a government bigwig in a pantsuit met us outside the door, each exchanging businesslike nods with Meloon, then us, as they, too, waited.

The metal doors finally slid open, and the captain grumbled, "About damn time."

We strode inside the dimly lit tunnel, and I couldn't help but glance back as the doors shut behind me. A strange sense of finality set in. Like I'd just passed the point of no return. At the very end of the corridor lay the entry point manned by two ETIU soldiers. One sat behind a desk monitoring several screens while the other guarded the inner airlock. My jaw clenched. *Why couldn't I have been assigned there?*

Both soldiers stood at attention and saluted Admiral Zahn, then greeted the rest of us.

"Are we all set?" the tall, white-haired Admiral asked, his voice brusque. "All of your equipment is functioning—suits sealed up tight? There's no room for error on this."

I nodded, as did the others. We'd gone through rigorous

checks, and the suits themselves were tested thoroughly long before we ever donned them. It was the filtration system that took the longest to develop, as it had to be tailored for toxic components that the ooze-infused plants excreted. A full tox lab had been assigned for that purpose alone, holding tanks of toxic air inside for testing.

Sadly, several technicians became infected before they got it right.

They were never seen again.

Nobody in the lower ranks knew for sure what became of those brave souls, but it wasn't hard to guess. More casualties of war—forever heroes of the resistance.

Meloon waved us over to the inner airlock, and we stepped over a curved metallic threshold forming a goalie's crease around the doorway. He looked at his superior with raised brows, impatience written all over his face. "If there's nothing else, we'll head in."

The man was nothing if not task driven.

The Admiral's lips twitched. "I admire a soldier who gets straight to it. You know your orders. Get your asses back in one piece." He shook each of our hands, then nodded to the soldier behind the desk.

A barely visible golden shimmer erected from floor to ceiling, cordoning us within the semi-circle surrounding the airlock. The forcefield used the same airtight technology created to seal the top of the dome. I took deep, even breaths as the familiar sensation of claustrophobia took hold—as though my lungs were being squeezed. Saints gave me a thin smile, her weight shifting from foot to foot.

We turned to face the doors. My fingers tightened around the grips of my rifle.

The airlock opened with a *whoosh*, and a cloud of white sanitizing steam blasted down from a vent in the ceiling.

"Go, go, go," Meloon called as he led the way through the door. This was it. There was absolutely no going back now. Like Alice tumbling down the rabbit hole, I, too, stepped into an unknown world. Though this place was part of Earth, it wasn't the one I knew. It was something else now.

Something alien.

As the doors hissed shut behind us, thin sneaker roots matted inside the wall of the dome twitched and stretched their sinewy fibres in an attempt to breach the brief opening. Garcia swiftly chopped them away while I watched our front. The now blunted tendrils recoiled into the foliage.

Everything was quiet. No sounds. No sign of animals, though as Beanie said earlier, small game did get seen on camera from time to time. That fact remained a concerning detail in my head. They were not only different looking than they should be, their coats taking on patches of colour similar to the trees, but they were also still very much alive. If the government's quarantine (aka asphyxiation) plan had been successful, everything should've been dead, wilted, and rotten right now.

Meloon pointed to the readout on his Hub. "Filtration check."

"Ninety-eight percent," I reported.

"Same," Beanie and Saints replied in tandem.

Garcia gave a thumbs up. "Ninety-seven."

"And I'm ninety-nine," Meloon said. "Keep an eye on your levels. If they dip below ninety, report it asap. Understood?"

We all nodded.

The airlock we'd just passed through rested on a gravel road that cut forward through the forest. It headed deep into the Bubble and straight toward the ill-fated village of Flat River, which rested very close to where the meteor landed. The road had filled in with knee-high flora and tree sprouts over time—all of it multi-coloured. The once normal brown trunks and green leaves were now liberally spliced with pale greens, blues, and fuchsia tones.

We proceeded down the overgrown road. Beanie pulled out a handheld instrument and took continuous readings of the polluted air as we walked. Now and then, his arm snaked out to steal a twig off a tainted bush or a leaf off a tree, tucking them into sample containers. And every time he did so, the plant would shiver.

The atmosphere appeared thick and hazy, taking on a slight lime hue. Finite particles floated about in all directions, shining like disturbed dust catching sunlight.

Scientists had determined early on that the infected plants no longer turned carbon dioxide into oxygen. When it became clear the meteor's ooze spurred tainted flora to spread and release toxins at incredible rates, the government fast-tracked the dome. In the Prime Minister's nationwide broadcast, he'd referred to it as terraforming, saying, "This is a biological invasion. If it spreads beyond containment, we'll face an extinction-level event."

"Don't go to work," Bianca had begged me soon after that broadcast ended. "I don't want you anywhere near the crash site."

I took her in my arms, hugged her tight. "I know what you're feeling, and if it were up to me, I wouldn't. But it's my duty. I swore to protect this country, and by doing that, I'm protecting *you* from *whatever* this is."

Tears slipped down her cheeks.

I wiped them away. "Don't worry. I won't be near the crash site. They're stationing me at the base beyond the edge of the dome."

She cupped my face in her hands then. "You promise me

you'll stay there. Don't let them force you to do anything reckless."

I shook my head, kissed her. "I won't."

The sound of scampering on my right broke my mind free of the memory.

Gun up, I activated my visor's infrared mode and saw what looked like a squirrel running about within the cover of the forest. "All clear. Just a squirrel."

Saints relaxed her alert posture and resumed scanning. She'd been charting the area while we trekked, comparing everything from the time of the meteor strike to what we were seeing now.

I heard more pitter-patter sounds and activated infrared again. Two squirrels were visible in the bush line now, and they watched us—seemed to be keeping up with us. *Hmm. That's odd.* Since when did squirrels purposefully follow people?

I gave my best squirrel call—a stuttered chattering sound. They both stood on their hind legs, looking at me. When I called again, they instantly ran toward us.

"Hold up, everyone."

The group stopped as I scoured the kaleidoscopic weeds and grasses, trying to lay eyes on them. They'd moved so fast. A blink later, I spotted one perched on the trunk of a young tree. The second peeked out from behind a pink shrub a few feet away. I disengaged infrared, seeing the blue and green on their fur, the patterns haphazard yet reminiscent of an inkblot test. They were twice the size of a normal squirrel, and their ears were elongated with tufts at the top like a lynx. Both of the critters had two bushy tails instead of one.

Garcia and the Captain stepped up beside me while the others hung back.

"What do you see?" Captain Meloon asked, peering in the direction I looked.

"I got nothing but a couple of squirrels on infrared," Garcia glanced my way with raised brows.

"Yeah, it's the squirrels I'm looking at. They're acting funny—ballsy. I called to them, and they came running toward us like they were on a mission." I countered his confused gaze with a head shake. "Squirrels don't do that."

Captain Meloon lowered his rifle. "We're wasting time because of a couple of damn squirrels?" The barest growl escaped his throat, then he flicked his fingers forward. "Let's keep moving."

The squirrels responded like they'd been called to action, leaping forward and emitting cries that sounded like a mix of angry squirrel and screaming goat.

The closest one hurled itself onto my left leg and crawled up, biting as it went. I winced, feeling the pinches, but thankfully the thick material of my suit saved me from its small yet sharp teeth. I got a fist on the thing, punched it down to the ground, and fired a round into it.

The other squirrel didn't flinch from the gunshot. It targeted Garcia, its cry turning to a screech. He took it out with a couple of rounds well before it reached him.

I double-checked if my suit had been compromised, relieved to find it intact.

As we all stared in shock at their lifeless little bodies, the patchy colours staining their fur sloughed off and floated up into the air as if carried by a soft breeze.

A breeze that didn't exist in the Bubble.

"They must be releasing another kind of spore," Beanie said excitedly. "A last-ditch effort to propagate—an action independent of the host. Fascinating." Beanie quickly scooped up one of the squirrels and sealed it in a container before all of its colour wafted away.

I watched him examine the specimen within the collection tube, then secure it in his backpack. The man seemed to be in his element. A true scientist.

"Aggressive little bastards," Captain Meloon spat, then again, in his trademark no-nonsense way, he flicked his fingers. "Alright, let's go. Daylight's wasting."

Saints pointed up ahead. "There should be a stream not far from here. The bridge was blown out during the quarantine event, but charting images from *before* show a natural crossing—likely a beaver dam. Here's hoping it's still there. Otherwise, we'll have to chop a tree or two."

Beanie snagged a hairy-looking blossom off of a tall stand of wildflowers, pausing in awe as a tiny shriek emitted from the stem. Then he spotted a hissing beetle and collected it, too, before hurrying after us.

He winked at me. "Told you there'd be stuff to fight in here."

I responded with a dry smile.

Colour patches had been the first signs of infection. Anything presenting it had been instantly quarantined, no exceptions. Then came the spores. The dome got closed up before other symptoms presented—like mutations and clearly aggression.

As we walked on, I found myself wondering what other animals might be like? Or what if the people who got quarantined in Flat River actually did survive? An image of a zombie flashed through my mind, but I pushed it away. *No. Humans have never been seen on the cameras. Besides, even if they could breathe this air, they couldn't have managed being cut off from the outside world... Could they?*

The trees thinned and opened up to reveal a stream about

as wide as three pickup trucks. It didn't look too deep, but we were still leery of stepping into it. The water itself was murky, irradiated with the same shade of lime that tainted the air.

"It's likely ooze that leached in from the soil," Beanie said. "I definitely don't think we should be wading into that."

Saints slanted a look his way. "No shit."

I restrained a chuckle.

We cautiously approached the water's edge, and Saints spotted the secondary crossing she'd been after. It was a beaver dam, a big one that stretched all the way across. She smiled and glanced up to the dome ceiling, tilting her head enough that I noticed a partial neck tattoo just above the collar of her suit. A fire-breathing dragon.

I'd seen a tattoo just like that somewhere before... I was certain it meant something but couldn't recall what.

"Looks substantial enough to get us across. Let's go," Saints said.

"Wait." Beanie took a knee. He pointed to a patch of mushrooms growing out from the damp soil between the water and the tree line. "Look at these. I've never seen anything like them. I think it's an entirely new species." His eyes were wide, his voice impassioned while he scanned it.

"New or just changed like the squirrels?" Captain Meloon said.

"I'd say new. Look how they have these puckering lines across the top." The mushrooms had bulbous teal caps set atop charcoal stems. Three lines stretched across each of the heads, hairline slits that were framed by swollen lip-like ridges. Beanie's scanner beeped, and a message appeared on the readout. "Ah ha. There's no such fungi on Earth's records. So, yep, a new species." He pumped his fist.

One side of Saints' face scrunched. "Not too sure it's something to fist pump about."

I bent to get a closer look at the Agaric entity. "The colour alone might be a tip-off, hey? It isn't blotchy like everything else the sludge has infected—the colour is solid."

"Exactly! Not hybrids. These are pure." Beanie pulled out a collection tube and a knife to sever the mushroom. "I'll just snag one of these babies and—eeaaahhh!" His words morphed into a shout. He recoiled, jumping back from the mushroom patch, which now writhed and stretched their rounded tops toward him. The three puckered lines across each of the heads had split open to reveal comb-like teeth that snapped over and over.

The flora surrounding us shivered.

"What the—?" Saints muttered, stealing the words from my lips.

"Holy shit." Beanie held one nearly dead mushroom in his hand. "I cut this one out, and the rest just came alive!" He dropped his sample in the container and closed the lid, quickly inspecting the fingers of his suit. The shroom continued twitching and made tiny mewling noises as its mouths curled in the corners.

"You good?" Garcia and I asked at the same time.

Beanie nodded, flexing his hand. "No punctures. I pulled back just in time." He held the collection tube up to his eyes, looking at it with awe. "They must be interconnected, reacting to what they perceive as an attack. Perhaps the ooze links organisms together. Fascinating."

A ragged howl echoed from somewhere in the distance.

"Yeah, everything's fascinating. We got it." Captain Meloon grabbed the container from Beanie's hands and scrutinized it. "If these damn plants are operating with a hive mind, that's trouble."

Beanie looked down at his knife, his brows knitting together.

"Well, don't get all sensitive about it." Meloon passed the container back to Beanie and activated the comms on his Hub. "Control. Update for Admiral Zahn. We've reached the stream on approach to Flat River. Be advised the ooze has now spawned its own alien organisms—not hybrids. I repeat, *not* hybrids. They appear to be interconnected and aggressive. Awaiting orders."

"Copy, Captain," our mission dispatcher Megs replied. *"Stand by one."*

Meloon led the team closer to the dam and waved a hand. "Take a water break."

While everyone sipped, me and Garcia kept watch of our surroundings, lest any other miffed creatures come a calling. We did a filtration check. All levels were normal—the suits holding up.

Meloon's Hub finally chimed.

"Captain Meloon from Control. Be advised, the Admiral approves force if needed."

Meloon gave a half smile, muttering, "Just needed to hear the words." He then spoke into his Hub. "Copy Control. Thanks."

"Isn't that what we've been doing, boss?" Garcia asked. "They've already attacked, and we squashed it."

Placing his hands on his hips, the captain replied, "It's just good to get an official okay on the matter. A formality, you know, so the bigwigs think they're important." He played his barb off with a laugh.

Garcia scoffed. "Feed the egos."

"Exactly." Meloon turned to exchange a look with Saints. It was brief and oddly knowing—like they shared an inside joke. If I hadn't glanced his way at that exact moment, I'd have missed it.

What does she know that we don't? Something about the so-called formality didn't sit right. Such tactical options should've been settled before we left.

We continued over the dam, then veered to connect back with the road, following it past an old farmyard. More solid colour plant life in various pastel tones appeared interspersed with the mutated ones. The trees' upper trunks bent toward us, their leaves rustling violently. The hybrids flanking them trembled in response. My eyes continually scanned the kaleidoscope forest, searching for something, anything to explain the undeniable sense we were being watched. Cold prickles of unease crept their way up my spine.

Beanie and Garcia exchanged wary glances. Saints continued scanning, an intense frown etched on her face.

"We're getting close to town now," Meloon said. "Keep your eyes and ears open. We're not just dealing with spore-infested plants anymore. Be prepared for anything."

As we passed the farmyard, I noticed the stable door was open, and the grass in the paddock was short—not overgrown. A whinny reached my ears, and a horse stepped out of the stable. Its head raised as it watched us walk by, nostrils flaring as it sniffed for danger. It had an extra set of eyes, and pale violet splatters marred its dappled grey coat.

"Can I?" Beanie asked the captain, bright with interest as he motioned toward the horse.

Meloon shook his head, maintaining a trajectory that led us away. "Not now. We're too close to the crater. That's the priority. If there's time on the way back, you can try to get a sample then."

Beanie's head dipped, but he didn't argue. "Yes, Captain."

The horse huffed and reared behind the fence, stomping its front hooves down.

Saints cocked an eyebrow. "You might not want to get that

sample. If he's as mean as those mushrooms, you'll be hurting."

Beanie eyed the animal, which, as if on cue, pulled its fleshy lips back to reveal a gnarled set of teeth. "Yeah... maybe not."

Alien flora intensified the closer we got to the crater. Solid fuchsia flowers that looked like tiger lilies with nettled teeth loomed in the ditch. They swayed toward us, moisture dripping from their petals like a dog salivating for a treat, and we gave them a wide berth. Overgrown mushroom stands that reminded me of Medusa's hair snapped at us, and we had to shoot two more animals that came charging out of the bush—a two-headed bull moose and a piranha-toothed fox. Terrifyingly, the former nearly reached us, its hide so thick it took a barrage of bullets before it keeled.

After each death, the trees shook into an uproar, and more haunting howls echoed.

They sounded closer than before.

You'd think the animal attacks would've explained the unsettling feeling of being watched, but they didn't.

Soon, the road all but disappeared, and we had to pick and choose our way through the unwelcoming flora. The captain —ever prepared—brandished a neon paint marker and swiped markings across trembling tree trunks as we went.

Saints checked her map. "Nearly there."

After cresting a rise, our group looked down upon the sprawling crater. A lake of neon lime ooze surrounded the melting meteor resting at its heart. Thick sinewy swaths of pulsating roots climbed out of the sludge on all sides, disappearing into the forest floor beyond.

The epicentre.

"Holy shit," Beanie exclaimed.

Garcia mumbled, "My thoughts exactly."

As I stared down at it, equally disturbed and awed, a memory surged.

Bianca threw her dish rag in the sink, splashing dishwater on the shirt covering her pregnant belly. "You're walking into an alien minefield! Why, Berk?" She flung her arms to the side. "You have a baby on the way any day now. This child needs you here. I need you." Tears cascaded down her cheeks. "You promised me."

I sighed. "I know, but this mission could mean the difference between living or dying. We're collecting samples that the scientists need to neutralize the ooze. If we don't act soon, there might not be a world for our baby to live in." I pointed to her stomach. "That little one deserves a shot at real life."

Her hard edges softened ever so slightly. Bianca tilted her head. "But why you? There are plenty of other marksmen. Let it be someone else."

I met her questioning gaze. "They recruited me—and it's my job..." I braved Bianca's wrath and circled my arms around her. Surprisingly, she let me cradle her against my chest. "Listen, I wouldn't do this if I wasn't confident I'd be coming home to you. Meloon assures me it's an in-and-out mission. We have special suits. And I'll have a big ass gun."

She turned in my arms and hugged me, releasing a heavy breath. "I don't like this at all... but we'll be waiting here for you." Her lips drew in a hard line. "Don't you dare die on me, Berk Griffin."

I leaned my head against hers. "I won't."

Another grating howl ripped through the air, dangerously close.

I jerked in reaction, jolted from the daze I'd been in. I turned from the crater to scan the trees, blinking back the moisture that had gathered in my eyes. As I internally chided myself for being stupid and getting emotional, I noticed the captain watching me. I cleared my throat.

He stepped closer, his gaze never leaving the trees. "Get

your head in the game, Berk." His whisper was firm, unyielding.

I nodded.

Without another word, he strode away, barking, "Beanie, get down there and take samples of the ooze. *Do it safely.* Garcia, go with him for cover. I want to leave as soon as possible. Saints, chart this bitch."

The captain gave her another one of those knowing looks, and I nearly asked what that was all about. But I held my tongue. *Know your place in the pack.*

As the team descended fifteen feet or so to the edge of the ooze, Meloon's eyes rested on the meteor. "Looks different than I remember. This rock was solid when it first hit—until it started releasing ooze."

I glanced back at the meteor. "It's definitely not solid now. What's that inside of it?"

What looked like an octagon of metal panels poked out of the remaining stone shell, each smooth surface reflecting the ooze's glow. One pulsated with orange lights that formed a misshapen eye.

The captain sighed. "Whatever it is, it's definitely not human-made."

I swallowed hard, watching Beanie collect vials of ooze and carvings of shuddering roots while Saints set up scanners —ones I'd never seen before, with round bulges on top. But I didn't care about whatever prototype she was testing out. My jaw clenched as I glared into the forest. "Did the government know something was inside the meteor all along?"

The captain's mouth set into a thin line.

His lack of response spoke volumes.

The already heavy feeling in my guts doubled. My grip tightened on my gun. *How much more do they know that they're not telling?* My thoughts returned to Bianca, who was due any day. "Do you really think we can stop it?" The question slipped out before I could claw it back.

Perhaps the captain sensed the turmoil churning inside of me, or maybe deep down, he was an optimist. Regardless, his reply was assuring. "Yeah, Berk, we can."

A twig snapped somewhere across the crater, accompanied by rustling noises.

"Get back up here!" Meloon barked. "Guns up. Time to head back." The others rushed back, and we returned the way we came, following the marked tree trunks. More noises followed us, flanking us, but the foliage was too thick and strangely hot to get a good view of anything via infrared.

Just as we stepped back onto the gravel roadway, a human face emerged from the thicket behind us. It was a man with blue ink blots covering his exposed skin and a ragged beard. A military hat covered his dishevelled hair. He wore a camo flak vest with stained civilian clothes beneath, and his eyes—both irises glowed lime.

"Boggs. Is that you?" Captain Meloon said, clearly recognizing the man. "Damn, I was sorry to hear you were among the soldiers quarantined inside the Bubble."

"*Abandoned,*" Boggs countered. "We were left to die."

We stuck close to Meloon, who continued stepping backwards down the road while speaking to the disgruntled man.

"The town was too close to the crash site, Boggs. You know how things work. When the plants started releasing spores, everything contaminated had to be contained." Despite Meloon's businesslike tone, a note of compassion shone in his eyes. "It was a real shit situation."

"Abandoned. Left to die," Boggs repeated—his glower molten. He released a howl, and two others wearing grimy lab coats stepped from the trees. Fading bruises and irradiated cuts marked their faces, sewn with haphazard stitches.

"Nice suits," one of them hissed.

The other rasped, "We designed them."

The contaminated scientists...

Meloon raised a hand. "Look, we didn't do this to you. Maybe we can help you now—we're trying to find a cure."

"Of course, you did this to us! Everyone on the outside has done this to us!" Boggs snapped. "But we've been made better."

Two more Flat River citizens exited the trees, then a group of five—all splotched and haggard-looking. One man had what looked like moss covering his left cheek and neck. Leaf-like veins covered one woman's arms. They pressed forward, making us retreat faster to keep a safe distance between them and us.

"This isn't you talking. I know you, Boggs. You've been infected. Let us help you." Meloon gave Saints a sharp nod. She reached her hand into a vest pocket.

Boggs glared. "We don't need a cure." His lips pulled back from his teeth, and he let loose a feral growl, a stream of spores flying from his mouth. Then he burst into a run with his companions right behind him.

We spun on our heels and broke into a sprint. Quick glances over my shoulder revealed more hybrids appearing from the trees. "Do we fire, Captain?" I shouted, remembering the Admiral's order.

"Hold fire unless it's exigent!"

Our arms and legs pumped as we raced back down the road, avoiding flora that snaked out to grasp or snap. From behind, our pursuers hurled rudimentary weapons fashioned with repurposed wood and metal. An old farm scythe sunk into the ground mere inches from my foot.

Several more citizens dashed from the trees on either side, and I slammed one with the butt of my rifle and drop-kicked another who swung a knife at me. Garcia mirrored my actions on the other side, and Saints bashed a shrieking woman.

"Keep moving!" Meloon roared. "We'll lose them at the dam. Saints, ready a charge!"

"On it!" She called back.

"Why do you have explosives?" I spit words at her between heavy breaths.

Saints pulled out two strips of what looked like putty, a device attached to each. "We all have our parts to play. You just do *you*."

Hauling ass required all my focus, leaving no time to ponder her cryptic words. A few minutes later, we reached the stream and raced across the dam. Saints brought up the rear, deftly planting the explosives.

Once clear, she brandished a remote and triggered the bombs. The dam blew apart, and wooden shrapnel flew in all directions.

We dove for any cover we could find, but something slammed into the back of my shoulder before I slid behind a clump of boulders. A painful glance revealed the splintered end of a knife-sized projectile embedded there. It had sunk deep. Stunned, I stared at the ground. *I'm hit. I'm fucking hit.* I winced, reaching for the gun that had skittered from my hand. *My suit...* Each breath came faster. My throat tightened. Shouts swirled around me, all muffled like screams underwater.

"Beck, get your ass up. We gotta go!" Meloon's command emerged from the depths, popping into clarity like a bubble on the surface. My vision refocused on him—his steely eyes wide with urgency. I'd landed with my back shielded from view. *It'll be fine. Just move.* The torrent had settled, and the dam was a mere remnant now, but a din of rageful roars from across the stream reached my awareness. Meloon rushed toward me, but I warded him off. I climbed to my feet and forced myself into a run, ignoring the splashing behind us. My shoulder throbbed, and claws of fear strangled my throat, but I pushed it all aside, save for a dedicated thought.

Get home to Bianca and the baby.

We charged down the road, weaving and jumping over flora impeding our path. Up front, Garcia hammered five-foot tall flower traps that had inexplicably sprouted since we first came through, as cunning and opportunistic as the sneaker roots lying in wait around the airlock. I covered our rear, relieved our pursuers weren't gaining ground. If we kept up this pace, we could outrun them. But that was easier said than done. Fatigue had set in. Our sluggish feet faltered while our chorus of chugging breaths nearly drowned the stampede of footsteps. With every move, my shoulder panged. Lactic acid burned my leg muscles. My lungs were on fire.

Most of the Bubble folk dropped from view, but a fit handful still followed at a distance.

I could see the outline of the airlock now.

Saints stumbled, face-planting onto the roadway with a grunt. The team stopped, and I rushed to her side, hauling her up by the arm. I ran with her, but she sagged down again, crashing to her knees.

"Come on, Saints. Get up." I lifted her again, but her legs wobbled like Jell-O. I tried to thrust her arm over my shoulder, but she wouldn't let me. "Are you okay?"

She pointed to a bloody gash in her suit beneath her armpit and waved. "Just go."

"No, I won't leave you." Dizziness washed over me, and I swayed on my feet, leaning on her shoulder to steady myself. I panted while simultaneously trying *not* to breathe. Even as I told myself I was just in shock, I couldn't shake the reality that every single inhale might be contaminated by spores.

I glanced at my filtration readout and fought the urge to vomit. Eighty percent.

The others joined us, and I angled away from them, hiding my wound.

"Get up," Beanie urged.

"They're getting closer," Garcia warned.

The captain took a knee, checked Saints' suit, and stared into her eyes. She nodded, and so did he. With an anguished look on his face, Meloon squeezed her shoulder, then stood. "Leave her. Let's move out."

Saints pulled out her remote detonator.

"Wait—what's happening? What else are we blowing up?" Beanie blurted.

Then it hit me. I knew where I'd seen her dragon tattoo before. While overseas, I'd met a guy who had one. That mark signified an elite crew of bomb techs—maniacs who took on the riskiest of missions.

My vision swam around the edges, and a crawling sensation spread from the site of my injury. The burn in my lungs persisted even though I'd stopped running. Tears pearled in my eyes. *Bianca...*

"Captain..." Garcia said ominously.

"We're leaving. *Now!*" He pushed Beanie onward, and Garcia followed.

I hesitated, glancing back at Saints, imagining the wedding she'd never see.

She shifted uncomfortably, her eyes swollen with emotion. "I knew the risks, Berk." She waggled the remote in her hand. "I'll make sure they'll all burn."

The odd-shaped scanners she'd planted around the crater flashed through my mind. Her and Meloon's knowing looks. My jaw clenched. *That's why it had to be her that came. Saints was the main mission all along.*

But I wouldn't let her die for it.

"You can burn it from the outside." As the enemy closed in, I hoisted her off the ground, groaning from the pain it caused. She argued, and I ignored her, pushing myself into a laboured run.

"I told you to leave her!" Meloon bellowed from up ahead, but I ignored that too. She was getting home. I was getting home.

Her head lolled against my bouncing shoulder, a moan escaping her lips.

"Let us in!" Captain Meloon commanded as he reached the entrance. The doors slid open, and he waved everyone through. But when I tried to pass, his arm shot out to block me. "Shut the doors."

They closed, and my mouth went dry. My pulse hammered, echoing in my ears.

Meloon took Saints from my arms, laying her down gently. "She can't go back, and you know why." He glimpsed the blood trickling down the back of my arm, and his expression twisted. "Shit, Berk—why didn't you say something?"

I cleared my throat. "It happened so fast, and it's not even bad. I feel good. Fine, I swear." I locked eyes with the captain, imploring him to believe my lies.

"You're lucky it missed your lungs." The captain pulled the wooden chunk from my shoulder, then yanked out his med kit. "Cover us."

I fired warning shots in front of the approaching citizens, and they scattered. Meloon poured fast healing powder over my wound, then, with impressive speed, closed it with stitch tape. He did the same for Saints, whispering something to her.

When he stood, he glanced at my filtration readout—now well below seventy percent.

After more warning shots, our pursuers lingered inside the

tree line surrounding the entrance, watching with glowing eyes.

"Berk, I got word that your wife gave birth to a little girl named Zoey. Both mama and baby are healthy." He smiled. "Congrats. I was waiting to tell you after the mission."

My lip quivered. A smile stretched my sweaty cheeks. "Zoey..." I sniffed. "I need to see my daughter. Just take me to your lab—test on me—whatever—but let me see them, even if it's through glass."

"Sorry, it doesn't work that way. We can't risk what's inside of you getting out into the populus." The captain took a deep breath, and before I could react, he ripped the gun from my hands and turned it on me. "You and Saints have both worked hard for your country—we thank you for your service."

"You can't do this!" My pleading eyes bored into Meloon's unyielding ones.

"Open the doors," the captain commanded, then unceremoniously fired two rounds in front of my feet to keep me at bay. He backed into the airlock as Garcia dutifully chopped sneaker roots with averted eyes.

"Meloon!" I roared. A surge of rage unlike anything I'd ever felt filled my mind, then fragmented, devolving into a sob. "Will you at least tell my family I love them?"

"I'll tell them," Meloon promised with a curt nod before the doors slid shut.

I lunged forward as the airlock closed, a guttural cry shredding from my throat. Slamming my fists against the flexi-glass, I screamed myself hoarse to be let back in.

Saints patted her vest for the remote, then looked back the way we came. "Dammit!"

Rustling sounded behind us, and I turned slowly, remembering we weren't alone. I helped Saints to her feet, primed to bolt.

But where to? We were outnumbered.

Boggs' strode in front of his ooze-infused posse, his bulging veins and iridescent eyes on full display. He held a familiar, slender device aloft. "Looking for this?"

"He's got my remote," Saints hissed.

They charged. Boggs and another mutant barrelled into us while two others blocked the airlock windows, daring the soldiers inside to open the doors. The remainder fanned out, dropping stones beside the wall. But as I traded blows with Boggs, I realized they weren't rocks at all. *No...*

Exhausted and momentarily distracted, a violent punch wilted my resistance. I hit my knees as Saint cried out, then fell silent.

"What the hell is going on in there?" The captain's voice crackled over the comms. "Saints—do it already. Do it!"

But she was already unconscious—or dead, I couldn't tell —and was currently being slung over her assailant's back.

"Retreat to a safe distance," Boggs ordered, then turned back to me.

I swung my feeble arms, but Boggs wound up and hammered me with a dizzying blow. I lost control of my limbs and fell forward, limp. He ripped off my face covering before hoisting me over his shoulders and breaking into a run.

Spores sucked into my nostrils.

My baby girl... my promise... I'm so sorry...

I got dropped into a heap beside Saints. Prying my eyes open, the airlock was barely visible in the distance. A looming lily spread its toothy petals at me, paused, then returned to its dormant state.

I wasn't a threat anymore.

The hybrids released a slew of crooning howls as Boggs thrust the detonator into the air and activated it.

A mass explosion obliterated the dome's entrance, loosing

fireballs and churning plumes of black smoke. My captors cheered as flaming debris rained down and a searing concussion wave swept over us. Boggs thrust his hands up, letting loose a victorious roar.

All at once the ground came alive with snaking vines and unfurling roots that materialized from unseen places. They surged forward, a botanical army charging for the Bubble's molten hole.

Boggs dropped his hands and looked over at me. His lips curled into a euphoric smile. "Welcome to New Earth—*brother.*"

About the Authors

Alyssa Beatty has been previously published in Corner Bar Magazine, Suddenly, and Without Warning, Wishing Well Anthology, and 72 Hours of Insanity, An Anthology of the Writers Games. She holds an MFA from UT Austin. She lives in Brooklyn, NY.

Katie Ess lives in Colorado with her husband, two sons, a bulldog, and two ferrets. When she's not writing, you can generally find her cleaning up a mess. Aside from someday becoming a world-famous author, her most important life's goal is to teach the six of them to clean up their own messes. Twitter @KatieEss3.

Jen Mierisch's dream job is to write Twilight Zone episodes, but until then, she's a website administrator by day and a writer of odd stories by night. Jen's work can be found in the Arcanist, NoSleep Podcast, Scare Street, and numerous anthologies. Jen can be found haunting her local library near Chicago, USA. Read more at www.jenmierisch.com and connect on Twitter @JenMierisch.

Josephine Queen grew up in England and now writes fiction from her home in the northeast corner of the US. As well as writing short stories and numerous drafts of unfinished novels, she drinks too much tea and gets lost on hikes.

You can read her work in Devil's Party Press Halloween Party 2019, The Siren's Call, 72 Hours of Insanity Volumes 8 and 11, Fudoki Magazine, Little Old Lady Comedy, and Potato Soup Journal. She has a story upcoming in Spirits and Ghouls Anthology by Flame Tree Publishing. Visit: Instagram @writejosephinewrite, Twitter @Josephine1Queen, or Facebook @writejosephinewrite.

Lisa Fox is a pharmaceutical market researcher by day and fiction writer by night. She thrives in the chaos of suburbia, residing in New Jersey (USA) with her husband, two sons, and Double-Doodle puppy. Her collection of speculative short stories, *Core Truths*, was published in early 2023. Lisa's work has been featured in Uncharted, Dark Matter, Bards and Sages Quarterly, Metaphorosis, and New Myths, among other journals and anthologies. She has been nominated for the Pushcart Prize and for Best Small Fictions and is a previous winner of the NYC Midnight Short Screenplay competition. Contact: lisafoxiswriting.com or @iamlisafox10800 (Twitter).

Katie Jordan lives in the Pacific Northwest with her bonsai enthusiast husband, Brad, two daughters, and the world's most elegant guinea pig, Mademoiselle. Her work has been featured in *Enchanted Conversation*, *Marrow Magazine*, and *101 Words,* among others. Find her online at authorkatiejordan.com.

Melissa R. Mendelson is the author of the Sci-Fi Novella, *Waken* and the poetry collection, *This Will Remain With Us.* She has written numerous short stories in the Horror, Science-Fiction and Dystopian genres, and her short stories have been published both online and in print by Sirens Call Publications, Dark Helix Press, Altered Reality Magazine,

Transmundane Press, Owl Canyon Press, Wild Ink Publishing, The Yard: Crime Blog and The Horror Zine Magazine. She is in the process of working on numerous writing projects including completing and editing two Horror novels, *Lizardian* and *Ghost in the Porcelain*.

https://www.linkedin.com/in/melissa-mendelson-a98848ia5

Andrea Goyan (she/her) is an award-winning author. Recent stories are available in Dark Matter Presents: Monstrous Futures, All Worlds Wayfarer, Flash Fiction Magazine, and The Molotov Cocktail. She's also the co-host of Metastellar Magazine's "Long Lost Friends." Episodes are on YouTube. In her spare time, she loves to paint, especially animal portraits. You can find more of her words on her website, www.andreagoyan.com or follow her on Twitter @AndreaGoyan.

Alex Grehy (she/her) has a sweet life in the UK, filled with narrowboating, rescue greyhounds, singing and chocolate. She is a regular contributor to *Sirens Call* and the *Ladies of Horror Flash Project*, and her work has featured in a wide range of zines and anthologies, including *Aphotic Realm, Water Dragon Press, Red Penguin Publishing* and *Gnashing Teeth Publishing*. Her essays on her experiences as a 'lady of horror' have featured in the Horror Writers Association Newsletter and The Horror Tree Blog. She is recognized for her original view of the world, expressed in vivid prose and thought-provoking poetry.

R.A. Clarke is a former police officer turned stay-at-home mom from Portage la Prairie, MB. She wrote *Let Your Lips Twitch*, a collection of humorous short stories, and has won international writing competitions such as The Writer's Workout "Writer's Games", the Writers Weekly 24 Hour

Short Story Contest, and Red Penguin Books' humour contest. She was also named a Hindi's Libraries Females of Fiction finalist and a Futurescapes Award finalist in 2021, a Dark Sire Award finalist in 2022, and her novella *Becoming Grace* won the Write Fighters 3-Day Novella Challenge in 2023. R.A.'s work can be found in a variety of publications and her debut sci-fi western novel *Race to Novus* is pending release in 2024.

Visit: www.rachaelclarkewrites.com or https://linktr.ee/raclarkewrites.

Thank You For Reading

Thank you for taking the time to read the stories within this anthology. Every one of them were unique and tackled the theme of deadly flora so wonderfully, providing a variety we absolutely adored. We hope you found some stories to love, too. If you did, we'd be honoured if you could take one more moment to leave a review on Amazon, Goodreads, or anywhere else book reviews are posted. Whether two words or fifty, all reviews are vital in expanding a book's visibility, and reaching more readers.

We are a small, but growing company, eager to pass unputdownable tales into the hands of fiction lovers. You can check out our other books and/or subscribe to our email list by visiting our website: https://www.pageturnpress.com.

More ways to get in touch, follow, and stay connected:
Twitter: https://www.twitter.com/pageturnpress/
Facebook: https://www.facebook.com/pageturnpress/
Instagram: https://www.instagram.com/pageturnpress/